To Catch a Treat

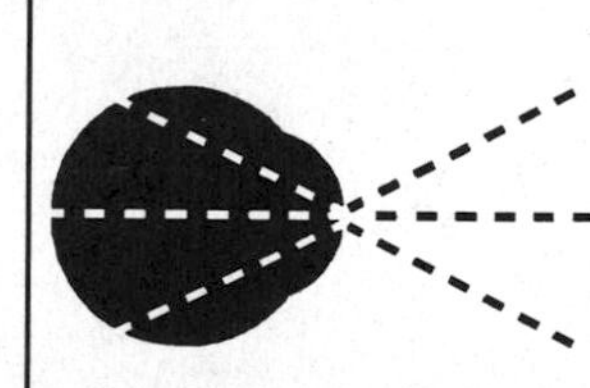

This Large Print Book carries the Seal of Approval of N.A.V.H.

A BARKERY & BISCUITS MYSTERY

TO CATCH A TREAT

LINDA O. JOHNSTON

WHEELER PUBLISHING
A part of Gale, Cengage Learning

Farmington Hills, Mich • San Francisco • New York • Waterville, Maine
Meriden, Conn • Mason, Ohio • Chicago

Wheeler Publishing, a part of Gale, Cengage Learning.

Wheeler Publishing Large Print Cozy Mystery.
The text of this Large Print edition is unabridged.
Other aspects of the book may vary from the original edition.
Set in 16 pt. Plantin.

LIBRARY OF CONGRESS CATALOGING-IN-PUBLICATION DATA

Names: Johnston, Linda O., author.
Title: To catch a treat : a Barkery & Biscuits mystery / by Linda O. Johnston.
Description: Large print edition. | Waterville, Maine : Wheeler Publishing, 2016. | Series: Wheeler Publishing large print cozy mystery
Identifiers: LCCN 2016030955| ISBN 9781410492333 (softcover) | ISBN 1410492338 (softcover)
Subjects: LCSH: Dog owners—Fiction. | Murder—Investigation—Fiction. | Large type books. | GSAFD: Mystery fiction.
Classification: LCC PS3610.O387 T63 2016b | DDC 813/.6—dc23
LC record available at https://lccn.loc.gov/2016030955

Published in 2016 by arrangement with Midnight Ink, an imprint of Llewellyn Publications, Woodbury, MN 55125-2989 USA

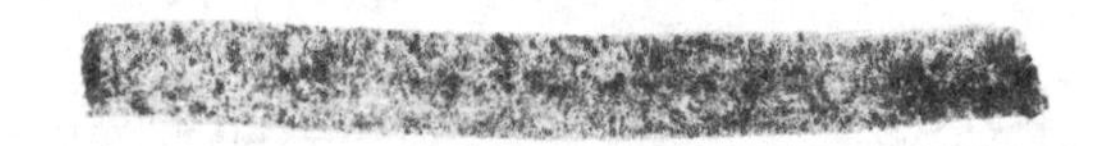

Printed in the United States of America
1 2 3 4 5 6 7 20 19 18 17 16

I dedicated *Bite the Biscuit,* the first book in the Barkery & Biscuits Mystery series, to people who love their dogs and want to feed them the best and healthiest treats, as well as to people with a sweet tooth — and mystery readers who enjoy stories involving pets and food. But I think the *entire* series should be dedicated to them!

In addition, I particularly want to dedicate *To Catch a Treat* to those who read and enjoyed *Bite the Biscuit,* especially readers who told me so!

Plus, as I always do, I dedicate this book to my dear husband Fred, in gratitude for his patience with my murdering people so often.

One

I ignored the cell phone vibration in my front pocket. That was the rule, both for myself, Carrie Kennersly, and my employees at my two adjoining bake shops, Icing on the Cake and Barkery and Biscuits. Customers came first.

I was currently serving a woman dressed in a fashionably casual outfit. She appeared to be in her early thirties, same as me, and had a leashed Great Dane mix sitting beside her on the portion of the shop's blue tile floor that was decorated as a large beige biscuit in the shape of a dog bone.

We were in the Barkery part of my shops. Dogs were more than welcome here, although not so much on the people side, Icing.

I glanced toward the corner where my own dog, Biscuit, a wonderful golden toy poodle–terrier mix, lay on her rug in her large open-topped crate. She watched the other dog with interest. As always, I stifled the urge to go hug her for being so well-behaved.

The customer kept telling me to add more dog cookies and biscuits to the box I'd been filling for her and her dog. No way would I interrupt that.

I kept on the move behind the glass-fronted refrigerated display case, pulling out the selected dog treats while inhaling and loving the combined scents of sweetness and meat that wafted from the kitchen behind me. Over on the Icing side, which I could see through the wide doorway that connected it to the Barkery, the aromas were always sweeter — since they were generated by human treats.

After more than two months, I still adored having turned the original Icing bakery into two stores, and baking and selling both dog and people products. I'd been told often by purchasers that both kinds of treats were wonderful, which always delighted me.

"That'll do it," my customer said, just as the phone in my pocket vibrated again. I totaled up the order on the electronic cash register and accepted the woman's credit card without peeking at who'd called.

"Thank you." I gave her dog a freebee farewell treat, a small carrot-flavored biscuit.

"No, thank *you,*" she responded. "We'll be back."

I grinned as she picked up the bag into which I'd slid her box of dog goodies, and she and her pup left. I reached into my pocket for my phone just as the door opened again and four customers, with one dog each, poured into the shop.

I backed toward the door to the kitchen and opened it. Dinah Greely stood by the long, waist-high counter of shelves that divided the Barkery side of the kitchen from the Icing cooking area. My young-looking, highly competent full-time assistant wasn't baking, fortunately, but sorting already prepared items. "Can you help me?" I asked.

"Sure thing. Icing is busy, but Frida has it under control." Frida Grainger was one of my new part-time assistants. "What do you need?"

Dinah took over waiting on customers at the Barkery while I hurried toward Biscuit, patted her softly frizzy head, and at last pulled my phone from my pocket.

The first call was from Dr. Reed Storme, one of the veterinarians at the Knobcone Veterinary Clinic where I still worked part-time as a vet tech. He was also a guy I'd been dating. I'd been expecting his call, so I returned it immediately, sitting down on a chair at one of the small tables located off to the side of the tile bone. I let the latest customers flow around me.

"It's a go, Carrie," Reed said. "Hugo and I will meet you at the resort. We're really looking forward to going with you on Neal's hike."

I was, too. Reed's presence with his dog would make my brother's tour that evening even more fun.

"See you in an hour." I hung up.

The second call had been from my brother. "Are you still planning on coming tonight?" Neal asked when I called him back.

"Absolutely. And Reed just confirmed he'll be joining us."

"Very good." As Neal paused, I watched Dinah do the same thing I'd done — give the dog of her latest customer a treat sample as the guy and his pit bull mix prepared to leave after paying. "Any chance of your coming a little early?" Neal finished.

"Maybe." The tour started at seven, and I closed my shops at six. "Should I?"

"Janelle said she'll be here any minute, so it wouldn't hurt if you got here early, too."

In other words, my bro hoped to introduce me to his latest love interest — whom he'd apparently met all of two days ago — before incurring the distraction of the tour he was hosting.

"Okay," I said. "See you soon."

It was six thirty, and Biscuit and I had just entered the lobby of the Knobcone Heights Resort.

My gaze panned the posh, vast lobby with its tall, slanted ceilings. Multiple seating areas in the middle surrounded tall stone fireplaces. Offices lined the wall nearest me, opposite the bar, restaurant, and spa overlooking the lake at the far side. The place was crowded, with the hum of multiple conversations filling the air. I've seldom seen it otherwise.

I quickly spotted Neal, standing near the spa by the rear doors that opened to the concrete walkway down to the beach. A young lady was with him, with wavy, light brown hair that reached below the shoulders of her gray hoodie.

"Come on, girl," I said to Biscuit. She was also looking around, probably for other dogs, who were welcome here at the resort. I pulled gently on her leash, and she easily kept up with me on the hardwood floor as we wended our way through the crowd toward Neal.

"Hey, Carrie." My brother smiled and

held out his arms for a brief hug, which told me the impression he wanted to impart to the lady with him. Neal and I were close, but we didn't always hug in public.

Neal is twenty-eight, four years my junior. He's six feet tall and, like me, has the Kennersly light blonde hair. We also share the Kennersly longish nose and blunt chin, as well as fairly sharp cheekbones. He keeps his hair a lot shorter than I do, though, and, fortunately, I don't have the shadow of a beard on my face that he generally does. In case you can't tell, I really love my bro, even if I don't always agree with him.

I was reserving judgment on his new romantic interest — particularly since they had apparently just met.

As we backed away from one another, Neal said, "Carrie, this is Janelle Blaystone. She's from LA. Janelle, meet Carrie. And that's her dog, Biscuit. Hey, Bug." That was his nickname for my pup. He petted her on the head.

A strange look of pain seemed to flit across Janelle's pretty features, quickly replaced by a large smile that revealed lovely white teeth between full lips. Had I been mistaken about the fleeting expression? "Hi, Carrie." She held out a slender hand with short manicured nails. Her eyes were large and blue and friendly, her brows well arched, her complexion perfect.

In short, she looked like a good possible match for my brother. But was she? Looks weren't everything.

As I shook her hand — her grip was firm and quick — I thought briefly of Neal's prior romantic interest, the resort waitress Gwen Orway. I didn't know Gwen well either, nor was I aware of what had happened between her and Neal. He'd seemed utterly smitten with her, despite being hurt that she apparently had another boyfriend somewhere off the mountains. If Gwen had truly been interested in Neal, she hadn't acted on it. Even so, that hadn't stopped Neal from going after her — before. I'd figured that if Gwen didn't start reciprocating more, he'd move on. My handsome, personable bro had never had any trouble attracting women.

So now there was Janelle.

"Good to meet you, Janelle," I said. "I assume this hike with Neal will be a first for you. For me, too. Neal's invited me a lot, but hiking isn't my thing."

"I like hikes," she said. "Neal's told me a little about you, and I figured from what he said that dogs, not hikes, are your passion." Once again, that strange expression rushed over her features, to be replaced by friendly blankness. What was going on here?

"Very true." I kneeled down to pick Biscuit up in my arms. My little dog looked at me and licked my cheek. "I'm sure, if Neal talked about me, he mentioned that I'm a veterinary technician as well as the new owner of a dual bakery. It has one side for dog treats and the other side for people. And, like Neal said, this is Biscuit."

"Hi, Biscuit." Janelle's voice sounded hoarse. Even stranger, her eyes filled and a couple of tears escaped down her cheeks. Again I wondered what she was thinking. Could I get her to explain?

"Are you a dog-lover, too?" I asked, not sure how to approach this.

"Yes, she is," Neal said. "In fact —"

But whatever he was about to say was interrupted as four people approached and greeted him. Fellow hikers, I presumed — those of the paying sort, unlike me. All were dressed in jeans, sweatshirts, and athletic shoes, which is what I'd changed into, too. Two had dogs — a golden retriever mix and a Rottweiler mix, it seemed.

This hike was one of the outings sponsored by the resort, though Neal also freelanced as often as he could, taking visitors out independently on walking tours or boat tours — and even skiing expeditions of the water or snow sort, depending on the time of year and weather conditions here in the San Bernardino Mountains. I was happy that he got paid not only to staff the resort's reception desk but also to do what he loved — work outdoors.

The timing of the arrival of these folks was not ideal for our conversation, though for Neal's pending expedition it was perfect. But I couldn't complain about the timing of the next person who joined us: Reed. Beside him was his gorgeous, smart Belgian Malinois, Hugo.

"Hi, Carrie," Reed said. He waved toward Neal, who remained with the others. That group was growing, including the number of dogs. I wondered how many people — and canines — would be with us on this scenic hike around Knobcone Lake.

Too bad I hadn't brought leftover treats to entice my fellow hikers to visit the Barkery tomorrow. But I still could do that verbally.

"Hi, Reed. Hi, Hugo." I bent to hug his dog, even as Hugo and Biscuit traded nose sniffs. As I straightened up, I realized Janelle had backed off. Despite the hint of a smile on her face, she looked lost.

Was Neal's interest in her because he was

a gallant gentleman, hoping to ease some pain from this lovely woman's life? He was a good guy, sure, but that would be something new for my devil-may-care brother. My curiosity was definitely stoked. Who was this woman, and what made her tick?

I grabbed Reed's free hand and pulled it slightly in Janelle's direction. "Reed, I'd like you to meet one of our fellow hikers, Janelle. Janelle, this is Dr. Reed Storme, a veterinarian at the clinic where I work. And this is his dog, Hugo."

I shuffled the fur on Hugo's head. Both dogs were starting to pull on their leashes — apparently they wanted to go meet nearby canines. I didn't loosen Biscuit's leash, though. She'd have plenty of time to meet the others on our hike. Plus, I wanted to get some sense from the owners about how friendly their dogs were before I let Biscuit get too close. I assumed Reed felt the same way about Hugo, although the Malinois was probably big enough to scare any aggressive canines off with a growl.

"Glad to meet you, Janelle," Reed said. "So's Hugo." By then, Hugo had gotten the message of Reed's gentle pull on his leash and had taken up sniffing Janelle's leg instead.

"Thanks." Was that moistness in her voice again?

Best I could tell, whatever brought on her emotionalism apparently had to do with dogs, since it had come out when she'd been introduced to Biscuit and Hugo. Clearly this group wasn't going to tiptoe around the subject of dogs, though — not with a small pack of them walking with us.

Consequently, I decided to just ask, although I'd start out with a touch of subtlety.

"So do you have a dog, Janelle?" I inquired. At the same time, I noticed that Neal had walked away from his group of hikers and was approaching us, behind Janelle. Was it time to leave? But instead of waving us forward, he was moving his hands in the air in front of him — in a gesture I read as an attempt to erase what I'd asked, and perhaps to make sure I knew to drop the subject.

If so, it was already too late. "Yes." Janelle's voice was soft and moist and unutterably sad. Her expression, as she stared down at Biscuit, also looked lost. I understood why immediately, though, when she added, "No. Not now. But I did. I should."

As she looked up at me, almost defiantly, Neal joined her. He put his arm around her shoulders. "Let's get ready to go, okay?"

But my curiosity wasn't going to dissipate unless I had answers. "What do you mean?" I asked Janelle. "You had a dog? Where is it?"

"Yes, I had — have — a dog. He's the most beautiful, smartest Labrador retriever you ever saw. But —"

She stopped and took a deep breath, looked again at Biscuit and then Hugo, and then back at me.

"But . . . ?" I prompted. Poor lady. Had her dog died? But the last thing she'd said indicated she still had the dog — didn't it?

"Go has been dognapped," she finally replied, in a soft voice that wailed with despair.

Two

It was seven o'clock. Neal had to get his hike started. I could sense his discomfort as he looked down discreetly at the watch on his wrist. "Sorry," he said. "It's a really hard story." He gave Janelle a warm hug. "We need to get going now, though." After another sympathetic glance at Janelle, he started herding us all toward the rear door beside the enclosed spa.

Reed and I remained with Janelle. "I want to hear what happened," I told her. I really did. A dognapping? How terrible.

"I guess we can talk as we walk," she said. I had a sense, though, that she felt relieved at the reprieve. I gathered that it might be hard for her to describe what had occurred, even if her dog's disappearance was always on her mind.

But I did want to hear about it.

Janelle hurried to join the others as Neal, at the top of the steps, waved the baton he always used to show his group where he was. He called it his staff, which was intended as a kind of pun, since he viewed the baton not only as a way to stay visible to his followers, but also as his assistant. He used it to lead his gang on trails, especially up and down hills, and it was his walking stick when the path was level. It was a bright, glossy red, about four feet long with a crook at the top.

I'd lied somewhat to Janelle when I'd said this was my first hike with Neal. I'd accompanied him on a couple when he first followed me to Knobcone Heights, California, and became a part-time tour guide here. I'd wanted, then, to help increase the size of his crowd. That had been three years ago or so. His crowds these days tended to be substantial, and had picked up again over the last couple of months after a lull, so I hadn't been a member of one lately. Until now.

I waited till the entire group had gone down the concrete steps to the lakeside beach, both people and dogs — except for Reed and Hugo, who stayed back with Biscuit and me. "What was that about?" Reed asked.

"I guess we'll find out together," I replied as Biscuit and I headed down the steps.

"Soon, I hope."

At the bottom, I waited on the back portion of the sand for Reed and Hugo to catch up, then held back a little as Neal again called out to his tour group, waving his staff.

"Neal's smitten with Janelle," I confided quietly to Reed. "I don't know anything about her except what I just learned: she's pretty, and she's sad, which I certainly can understand if her dog has been stolen." Shuddering at the very idea, I bent to hug Biscuit. Then, because Hugo was right beside her, I hugged him, too.

I knew I'd never be able to bear it if I lost a dog in any manner, dognapping or otherwise. It was bad enough that dogs didn't live as long as their human family members — a fact I was all too conscious of as a veterinary technician.

I noticed that Janelle had quickly caught up with Neal. As we started walking along the waterfront, she stayed with him. Apparently she didn't want to discuss her lost dog with me.

Or maybe she was as smitten with my bro as he seemed to be with her and wanted to get to know him better. After all, best as I could tell, they'd met only a couple of days ago.

The sand was dry and the air was cool

here along the lake. I was glad I'd worn a sweatshirt — one I'd had specially made. Like some T-shirts I'd acquired, it had a Barkery and Biscuits logo on the front. This one was blue. I'd obtained a variety of colors, and I gave them out to my shops' staff, as well as some particularly good customers now and then. Not to discriminate against my other store, I'd also had shirts made up for Icing on the Cake.

The craggy cliffs at our left side were tall, and the Knobcone Heights resort was not the only hotel, nor home, to grace their top. Fencing ran all along the upper areas in the interest of safety, which seemed a good idea to me.

On our right was the lake, wide and fairly calm, with a hint of waves caressing the shoreline. I believed the waves were caused not only by wind but also by the many boats that traveled back and forth. Although there were often swimmers and sometimes sunbathers along the shore, here on the side of the dock where boats were frequently moored, I didn't see any now — but of course the evening was getting late.

I did, however, see a flock of ducks splashing in the water. Overhead a large bird soared — a falcon, I believed. And beyond the far side of the lake, more mountaintops were visible.

I shrugged away my concerns about Janelle's dog, at least for now, and smiled as I lifted my chin and inhaled the fresh air. Reed and Hugo walked on my right side and Biscuit on my left.

Reed was a great-looking guy, with what I'd call "a ruggedly handsome face," as they say in romance novels. He had thick, wavy black hair, and a hint of five o'clock shadow that I'd come to realize he always got this late in the day.

The walk was utterly enjoyable. I was glad I'd accepted my brother's invitation this time.

"So how are things going at your shops?" Reed glanced down at me in the fading daylight with his dark brown eyes. He asked me this often, usually when we had a moment to talk when I was at the clinic on a shift. But Reed and I had coffee together fairly often. Dinner sometimes, too.

I liked the guy. A lot. But I didn't think I was ready to really dive into a relationship. Besides, there were a couple of other men who'd expressed interest in me lately, and I'd decided not to commit to anyone, just let things take their course.

"Things are going very well," I said. "As always, I could use some more help, but

Dinah's doing great as a full-time assistant. And my new part-timers are learning things just fine." I'd previously employed another part-time assistant, inherited from my friend Brenda when she'd sold me Icing on the Cake and moved away. But that assistant, Judy, was no longer with me.

"If you find someone else, can you schedule more time at the clinic?"

This was a long-standing issue. I'd been told that the veterinary hospital was looking for at least one more vet tech. I had even been warned — by Reed — that I'd better concentrate more on that part of my career if I wanted to have any time at all scheduled there. But that had been partly due to a terrible mix-up that had since been resolved. The head vet there, Dr. Arvus — Arvie — Kline, had always remained on my side, as Reed seemed to be now. And they had hired only one more vet tech, not a bunch.

That was another reason why I was somewhat reluctant to get closer to Reed. He had almost threatened me about my schedule at one time, and he hadn't, at first, given me the benefit of the doubt.

"We'll see," I said now, in response to his question. As much as I loved being a vet tech, my new ventures occupied a lot of my time, as they should. Though my choice was not to give up entirely on my former career, I was dead-set against doing anything to jeopardize my new one.

We were lagging a little, so I picked up my pace to catch up with the last of the hikers on Neal's outing. There were about fifteen of them, dressed, like the others, similarly to Reed and me — jeans, sweatshirts or hoodies, and athletic shoes. Some also wore knit hats, although the temperature seemed a bit too warm for that. At least I didn't see anyone wearing gloves.

There were, additionally, seven dogs besides our two, of different breed backgrounds and sizes, all the way from what appeared to be a Yorkie mix to an energetic pit bull. We all walked along the path at the edge of the beach, not on the empty road that paralleled it.

"Any interesting cases at the clinic that I'm not aware of?" I asked Reed. We were keeping things fairly neutral now, which seemed a shame. And since I thought that way, I realized that, no matter what I'd been telling myself, I liked it when he seemed romantically interested in me.

"None that I can think of," he said. "We have a senior cat with respiratory issues hospitalized with us, and a dog whose heart murmur we're monitoring overnight. Of concern, sure, but not unusual, either of them. And both seem to be responding well to treatment."

I smiled, glad to hear that. We soon reached the end of the nearly straight path, which, like the road, turned to circle the far side of the lake. The entire group had gone around the corner ahead of us.

That's when I noticed Janelle lagging back. In a minute, she was walking with Reed and me. She was a little taller than me, slim in her jeans and hoodie, and her shoes were bright purple, contrasting with the beigeness of the sand.

"Hi," she said. "Isn't this great? I'm so glad Neal invited me."

"Me too," I said, purposely vague about whether I was glad he'd invited her or invited me.

"Where do you come from?" Reed asked. I glanced at him. His expression was friendly, but I didn't think he was flirting — and I gave him a brownie point for that, since Janelle was attractive.

"Santa Monica," she said. "I've always enjoyed walking on the beach there, too."

"Now that's really a beach," I said. "I enjoyed it, too, when I worked in LA." That had been several years ago, after I'd studied to become a vet tech; a short while thereafter, I'd moved here. "But I'm delighted that Knobcone Heights has this one."

"Yes, this is really nice. I haven't seen everything here, of course, but I like this town a lot."

And do you also like my brother? I thought, but I didn't ask. That was between them.

But one thing wasn't — and I had to ask. "If you don't want to talk about it, that's fine," I began, "but if you do, I'd like to hear what happened to your dog."

She stopped so quickly that I thought she'd tripped. I reached out my free hand to steady her, but she just stood there for a second, not falling, not moving. Then she spoke hoarsely. "Like I said, I know from what your brother told me about you that you're a real animal lover, especially dogs." She looked toward Reed, who had also stopped with us. "If you're a veterinarian, I guess that's true of you, too."

He nodded. "You've got me pegged." He smiled, clearly trying to be friendly and encouraging. I added another plus to my feelings about him.

"Okay." Janelle kept her head down but started walking again, following Neal's crowd, which had gotten a ways in front of us. "Here's what happened. My dog is named Goliath. I call him Go. He's a purebred black Labrador retriever. I'm a photographer by profession — and you can guess how many photos I have of him."

Her grin seemed full of irony as she raised her head and looked from Reed to me. We continued walking briskly.

"I'd love to see them," I encouraged her.

"Sure. Maybe. Anyway, I take — took — Go nearly everywhere with me. One of the most fun things was going to dog parks all over Los Angeles. There are even a couple in Beverly Hills and West LA, and several in Santa Monica."

I'd never been to dog parks in LA's West Side, but figured those in affluent areas like that were probably quite nice, maybe even spectacular.

"Anyhow," Janelle continued, "I got to meet a lot of other dog lovers that way. Made a lot of friends for Go and me. Took a lot of fun pictures that I could sell to the owners, or even online or to media outlets. Then I started hearing really sad rumors of dognappings that were going on here and there. From what I gathered, it was mostly purebred dogs who disappeared, or designer dogs like cockapoos or labradoodles. I felt really sorry for the owners but . . ." She stopped walking again, seemed to need to catch her breath, then continued both walking and talking. "I never believed that could happen to me. I mean, I'm an ordinary person with a wonderful dog, sure, but I'm not wealthy. I couldn't really afford to pay a ransom — although from what I gathered, the people whose dogs were apparently stolen weren't often contacted for money, at least not at first, so some assumed their dogs were being kept as pets or even being resold."

In some ways, the latter made more sense to me. If the pets truly were stolen, it might be easier for the dognapper to get away with it if no one knew what really happened, rather than contacting owners who might be able to bring authorities down on them.

On the other hand, to resell purebreds and make money off them, wouldn't they have to be able to prove to buyers that the dogs had pedigrees?

"But it did happen to you," I prompted Janelle. "How?" I didn't see her as the kind of person who'd let her dog loose without supervision in dog parks or at home, or leave him in a hot car, or do anything else careless enough to make me shudder.

"It happened so fast. And unexpectedly. Some of the dog parks have off-leash fenced-in areas so your dogs can get more exercise, usually by playing in packs. Of course, people who have animals with aggression issues aren't supposed to let them loose in those areas. Go was anything but aggressive, and I always observed the dogs who were loose before letting him off his leash there. I'd done so that day, about a month ago, and as always I watched him carefully. But there was a dog altercation at one end of the fenced-in area, and it sounded pretty fierce. I wanted to make sure Go wouldn't be affected, so I moved toward that location, hoping to help. He was loose, but I kept watching him, but then someone called frantically for help and I turned away. It felt like just an instant. And by the time I stepped in, the fight was over. All the people in the area seemed to have congregated there also to try to help. And when I moved away from them to get Go . . . I couldn't find him."

She'd been doing so well with the story, just getting it out. But now Janelle sobbed. "No one saw what happened, but he was gone."

Three

As sorry as I felt for Janelle, the first thing to cross my mind was that Go could have gotten distracted, as dogs do, and run off. His disappearance didn't mean — necessarily — that a person had been involved. Having heard about possible dognappings, Janelle might have jumped to conclusions.

But as if she read my mind — or maybe because she'd told this story often before — she continued. "I looked everywhere around there for him. I called him, and so did other nice people who were around. I had flyers made later that day and posted them everyplace I could think of, even at the nearest veterinarians and doggy daycare facilities and pet stores. I posted all sorts of notifications on social media sites, too. But I never heard anything more."

We kept walking on the dirt path next to the beach. Low-cut weeds grew along the waterside, and more substantial bushes grew on the other shore, at the lake's end. The air smelled moist and earthy and wholly pleasant.

Janelle strode beside me, and so did Biscuit. Reed and Hugo had dropped a little behind us, and I doubted Reed had heard all that Janelle had said. We all walked a little more briskly now to catch up to the other hikers.

Or maybe I was just following Janelle's determined lead. When I glanced toward her, she was staring ahead as if she couldn't bear to look at me and risk seeing scorn at her losing her dog. But what she would actually see was pity. And concern. I didn't blame her. I felt sorry for her.

It crossed my mind that someone could have found Go and taken him in, then fallen for him and perhaps chosen not to turn him over to an owner whom they assumed was careless.

"In case you're wondering," she said, "Go had an ID tag on his collar, plus he was microchipped with my contact information. But no one ever contacted me, and although I notified the microchip company, they didn't hear anything either."

"I'm really sorry to hear of your loss," I said, knowing those were the same words people said to others who'd had beloved family members die. Pets are family members, and although Go might not be dead, perhaps he was dead to Janelle. In any event, he was lost to her, at least for now.

I felt awful as she stumbled beside me on the path, and I reached out to steady her. At the same time, Biscuit moved in front of me to check her out, nearly causing me to trip on the leash.

"Careful," Reed said from behind us and reached out to steady both of us, one hand on each of our backs.

"Thanks." Janelle's voice came out in a raspy croak. When I looked at her she had tears running down her face. Damn. I certainly hadn't meant to make her feel worse.

I decided to try to change the subject, at least a little. "So what brought you to Knobcone Heights?" I made my tone sound cheerful, as if I was a representative of the town encouraging tourists to visit. In some ways, all of us who lived here had that kind of aspiration, since our town was fairly small and thrived a lot on having outsiders come to our shops. Even the veterinary clinic's business was bolstered by people who came with pets, since they sometimes got ill or injured. Pets of those who lived here were the majority of our patients, though, and that was probably a good thing. It would certainly turn tourists off to think that visiting animals were in jeopardy in our town.

"Oh, I just needed to get away," Janelle said.

I glanced at her again as we continued walking, my breathing a bit faster than when we'd started out. There was something about her tone, too lighthearted all of a sudden, that made me sure her answer was a lie. But she still walked quickly, looking down toward her purple shoes as if to be sure she wasn't about to trip over anything. Her hair swept forward enough that I really couldn't see her expression.

Then she stood up straighter again, slowing her pace as she looked at me. Although she appeared sad, there was a kind of resolve I hadn't seen before on her pretty face. "Thanks so much for listening to me, Carrie. It's hard to talk about Go, but I feel better afterward when I do. I'm just hoping . . . well, I want to get him back someday, and if he was dognapped he's at least still alive. I'll do anything I can to find him."

"I understand," I said. "And if there's any way I can help, please let me know. I'm always around. When I'm at my shops, I may need a few minutes to get away — but I will."

I didn't know her well, and neither did Neal, at least not yet. And he might never. But I understood and appreciated animal lovers and could definitely read her pain. I meant it. If I could help, I would.

"Thanks." Janelle bent momentarily to give Biscuit a pat on the head without breaking stride. When she was fully upright again she said, "Right now . . . well, I want to catch up with Neal and maybe finish this hike with him."

"I get it." I smiled at her, which in moments resulted in smiling at her back as she sped forward.

Reed was immediately beside me. Biscuit and Hugo didn't slow their pace as they continued along the narrow dirt path, and neither did we humans.

"Tell me what that was all about," Reed said. "I heard part of it. She lost a dog?"

I briefly told him about Janelle's belief that her Goliath had been dognapped nearly right in front of her at a dog park while she'd been distracted.

"That's a shame," he said. "I assume she's tried the usual stuff like flyers to find him?"

I repeated what she'd said: everything from flyers to social media. "It all happened down the mountain, in Los Angeles," I said. "She said she was here to get away from it all. I gather she's not likely to stay very long, which could be a bad thing for Neal."

"Did she take a leave of absence from her job?"

"She said she's a photographer. Maybe she's freelance. I'm not sure."

"Okay."

When Reed grew silent, I observed him instead of the trail. There was an intense expression on his face as he looked ahead. I wanted to know what he was thinking, so I asked.

"I'm just trying to come up with some other avenues for Janelle to try to find her dog. From what you've said, sounds like she's done a good job of the usual stuff. But what if her dog really was stolen?"

"I'm wondering that, too," I agreed. "She didn't tell me if she'd contacted any authorities, but I'd guess she did, considering the rumors that a lot of other dogs had been stolen lately from around where she lives."

"Then you think she's a fairly smart woman?" Reed looked toward me. "Worthy of your brother's interest?" His grin only made me smile back.

"That remains to be seen." I wouldn't find out right now. "Hey, why don't we catch up with our fellow hikers? I think it's time for me to get to know them — especially the ones with dogs."

"Going to invite them to the Barkery?"

"How did you guess?"

We increased our speed so that soon we were in the middle of the group that followed in Neal's footsteps. There were nearly as many women as men, and some of the hikers appeared to be couples. I still wasn't pleased with myself for neglecting to bring samples from both the Barkery and Icing, but, practically speaking, I wouldn't have been able to carry a large amount anyway. I wasn't even wearing a backpack. And my lack of treats didn't prevent me from being friendly.

I introduced myself as Neal's sister — as well as bcing the owner of two premium bake shops in Knobcone Heights. I issued a lot of invitations to the smiling hikers — including promises to hand out samples to those who visited either or both of my shops tomorrow.

Because I'd thought our hike would only involve walking around Knobcone Lake, I was a bit surprised when Neal, still ahead of us, turned left onto Pine Lane, a road heading up the steep hillside near some small lakeside hotels. This was nearly opposite where the resort sat at the far side of the water.

In this area, some pretty sumptuous estates overlooking the lake lined the streets and the ridge. I'd never visited any of these homes, although one person who lived up here was my friend Wilhelmina — Billi — Matlock. I hung out with her often at Mountaintop Rescue, the animal shelter she ran in Knobcone Heights, or at my veterinary clinic whenever she brought some of the animals in for treatments or shots. She also owned the Robust Retreat, a posh day spa and fitness club. I got together with her for coffee or meals when we could both work it in — not always easy for either of us, especially since we both had multiple careers. She was particularly busy, considering that in addition to her two businesses, she was also on City Council.

Despite how we were becoming good friends, she hadn't been at my small home and I hadn't been at her large one, although I knew where it was.

I was buddies with Billi's fellow City Council member Les Ethman, and his home was up here, too. Not the rest of the Ethmans, though; although they were one of the town's most elite families, and Neal's bosses at the resort, their estate was in a different affluent area. But many of the town's wealthiest residents did maintain their vast homes here. And even though I knew that some of the hikes Neal conducted included the hillsides and remote views of the estates located there, I hadn't thought today's tour was one of them.

Without explaining why to Reed, I tugged Biscuit's leash lightly and hurried ahead to catch up with my brother. Janelle was beside him, unsurprisingly, on the sidewalk along the unexpectedly wide street. Or maybe it wasn't so unexpected, considering the people who lived here and the limos they might ride in to reach their homes.

Neal held his red staff in his left hand and was pointing at a large wrought-iron gate with his right one.

I was a bit out of breath as I caught up. "Hey," I said, "aren't we off our planned route?"

My bro looked at me with his blue eyes that resembled mine and smiled without slowing down. "Hey yourself, and the answer's yes. I imagine my paying guests will be glad there's no additional charge for this detour that'll show them some of the fanciest homes in the area."

"It's my fault," Janelle chimed in. She didn't look out of breath at all, which I was sure added more bonus points for her on my brother's scorecard. "I did my research on Knobcone Heights before I came and know that some families here are pretty well known and wealthy, and some of the ones I've heard of in LA also have vacation homes in this area. I asked Neal to show me where. I hope it's okay with you and the others."

"I'm fine with it," I said. "Don't know about the others, though." But when I turned around, I didn't see irritation on any faces, just a bit of awe as they looked past a fence toward the mansion beyond.

"Who lives here?" asked a young woman holding a leash with a Rottweiler mix on the other end.

"The Frenches," Neal replied without even hesitating. He'd obviously done his homework, possibly for prior hikes he'd led. It might not be particularly kosher to give out specific information, in case someone used it for some ill purpose like planning a theft, but it wasn't as if chatter about who lived where wasn't available online anyway.

"Whose place is that?" called a guy without a dog who stood with a group of other men. He pointed to across the street, to where a stone mansion was barely visible behind the trees lining its fence.

"The Morgans," Neal said, and he continued walking up the hill. Of course, we all followed.

The road was quite steep and I panted as we walked. We passed two more estates, on each side of the street, whose owners Neal named before we reached a road off to the right that lay flat along the mountaintop: Vistaview Place. I was glad to get there.

We headed right, toward where a tall wrought iron fence circled a green, well-landscaped yard with a huge house beyond it.

"And whose —" began the first woman who'd asked questions.

"The Arnists," Neal responded before she finished.

"Oh," Janelle said, and she stopped walking. At the other homes, she had barely seemed to glance beyond their circling fences, but she appeared interested in this one. In fact, she stood still, her hands around the metal of the fence, and peered through it.

The mansion was constructed of huge gray stones. It was a couple of stories high, and definitely nothing I'd ever be able to afford. It was a gorgeous place, possibly the epitome of a minor palace. I could see why it would attract attention.

Janelle's seemed glued to it, her frowning expression intense and unreadable. Fascination? Anger?

Neal waited with her for maybe a minute, then said, "We'd better get going. I know this area's pretty spectacular, but we really need to end this hike soon since it'll be getting dark, and coming up here added quite a bit of time."

"I understand." Janelle's voice was almost a whisper, and she had her head cocked just a bit, as if she was waiting for the mansion beyond the fence to call to her.

Okay, maybe that was an exaggeration on my part, but I still had some kind of sense that she was really enraptured by this place.

She didn't follow Neal when he first set off, and she seemed to aim a longing gaze at the mansion before joining him.

I really wondered what Janelle was thinking, but I suspected she wouldn't tell me the truth if I asked.

Surely she wasn't casing the place, prepared to come back and rob it later — was she? If so, why this house above the others?

Or was she thinking she could survive without her dog if she only had someplace like this to come home to?

FOUR

Back down the hill, we soon passed the town's impressive House of Celebration, which fronted the lake before the path started around the final curve. By the time we reached the resort, the daylight was nearly gone. But no one complained as we turned that last corner of the looped trail and walked back alongside the water, on the sand.

Reed and I and our dogs remained in the middle of the hikers, behind Neal and Janelle. Those two seemed to chat quite a bit, and I wished I could hear what they were saying. Or maybe not. Despite Janelle's sadness and her unreadable reaction outside the Arnists' mansion, they were now clearly flirting, and I didn't want to be a meddling older sister if theirs was a genuine romantic relationship in the making.

But I didn't know Janelle well enough to figure her out, and if she was somehow using Neal without potentially caring for him . . . now where had that come from?

Maybe just my usual suspicions of people — which had been stoked recently thanks to some events that occurred after I opened my shops — blended with my concern for my brother.

Neal turned, waving his staff and calling, "We're nearly done. And you're all still with me. You all rock!"

I didn't have a staff, but I waved my fist in the air. "So do you, Neal. This has been great, hasn't it, everyone?"

A cheer went up around me, and I couldn't help grinning. I glanced at Reed and saw that he, too, was cheering even as he looked back at me, as if he wanted to be sure I recognized his outspoken agreement.

I heard a cell phone ring then. It wasn't my tone, and it sounded as if it came from somewhere in front of me. Janelle reached into her pocket and drew out her phone. With a slight frown, Neal regarded her as she began talking.

I couldn't hear her, but he probably could. The call didn't last long, at least. Her phone was back in her pocket in less than a minute.

Was her ending the call so quickly worth adding a brownie point, or should one be subtracted because she'd answered her phone at all, plus even had her ringer on? That was up to Neal, but I supposed he could consider it a wash.

My brother soon led us up the stairway from the beach, and we stopped at the rear of the resort's main reception building, with its sloping slate roof over thick white walls and dark wood-framed windows. The similar-looking but smaller guest buildings framed it on either side.

Before we entered the back door, a woman came out. She seemed to scan our crowd until she saw Janelle, and then they both smiled at each other.

The woman was probably in her forties, with a short cap of black hair and a snub nose over a wide mouth. As if she, too, had gone on a hike, she was dressed in jeans, a black sweatshirt, and athletic shoes. She held a phone in her hand, and I guessed that she might have been the person who'd called Janelle. I felt even more certain of it when the two of them walked together toward the guest buildings off to the left. Neal glanced quizzically and not especially happily toward Janelle as he led his hikers inside, with Reed and me and our dogs bringing up the rear.

Neal said his goodbyes and thank-yous, and so did the other hikers, including me. I reminded people that they were invited to sample treats at my shops the next day. Then Reed and I were left there with our dogs as Neal walked toward the lobby door with some of his guests.

The lobby was crowded as always, including more people who'd brought dogs. I liked this place and was glad that Neal worked here, despite the fact that his prior boss had been murdered a few months ago — and I'd been all but accused of killing her. But that fortunately was behind me. The current manager was also a member of the Ethman family that owned the resort: Elise Ethman Hainner, who was married to Walt Hainner, an excellent and very nice local contractor.

While Neal continued his goodbyes, I started to say good night to Reed but saw Janelle and her friend enter the lobby. Rather than heading toward Neal, they stood near the door for a few seconds, then hurried through the crowd in the direction of the bar, which was toward the rear of the lobby beside the restaurant and also overlooked the lake.

I admit it. I was curious. Biscuit and I started walking that way, too.

"Are you interested in a drink?" Reed sounded a bit surprised as Hugo and he caught up with me.

"Maybe," I said. If that was what Janelle was after, I'd be glad to grab a drink — and possibly eavesdrop. Fortunately, although I knew dogs weren't welcome in the restaurant, it was okay to bring them into the bar.

I stopped at the doorway, since it was a lot darker in the bar than in the lobby. I soon spotted Janelle and her friend beyond all the full tables, standing beside the bar itself, which was lined with mostly occupied stools. The tables consisted of fairly small squares of wood veneer, with chairs on all sides and lots of drinks set on top of them — or else in the hands of the loud and boisterous patrons. The entire room was crowded, and a TV on the wall was tuned to a baseball game, although I'd no idea who was playing.

"Let's go over here," I said to Reed. "We can grab a drink with Janelle till Neal gets here." Maybe.

Reed looked at me as if he was as dubious as I felt. But I didn't want to explain anything to him right now. I just wanted to find out what this woman — a woman my brother was interested in — was doing in the bar without him.

I tightened my grip on Biscuit's leash so she had to walk right beside me, and saw

Reed do the same with Hugo. We had to maneuver through the crowd, and as I inhaled I thought I might get tipsy just from the aroma of liquor that permeated the air. But in a minute, I was able to sidle up beside where Janelle stood.

"Good to see you up here," I heard her say to another woman — not the one she'd entered with — who was sitting on one of the stools at her other side. "Are there any dog parks up here? If so, I hope you'll tell me where. And where's your dog?"

The woman looked barely old enough to be in here, but since she had a glass of wine in front of her, I assumed she'd been carded if the bartender had found it necessary. She had curly hair that was so blonde it was nearly white, and unlike the people I'd hung out with all day she was wearing a dress — a skimpy red one, with shoulder straps and no sleeves and a deep neckline.

"I'm not aware of dog parks here, although there may be some." The woman's voice was shrill . . . her normal tone, or just her attempt to be heard over the crowd noise here? "Jojo's at home in LA with my sister. I didn't bring her."

"I figured that," Janelle said. "I happened to hike by your family's house here this evening and didn't hear any barks. Are you staying there while you're here?"

"Well . . . yes. Some of the time." The woman had slid off the barstool and was now standing on the floor, her hands on her hips as she confronted Janelle. Was she an Arnist? We'd passed homes owned by a lot of other elite families in the area, yet Janelle had definitely appeared most interested in that one.

But why? And why was she asking this woman so many questions?

"Oh, really?" Janelle said. "Your family house looks so nice. Where else are you staying?"

Instead of answering, the woman asked, "Why are you here, Janelle?"

Before Janelle could answer, the woman with whom she'd conversed on the phone entered the conversation. "We're here on vacation, Ada. For fun. You know. You mentioned Knobcone Heights sometimes when we saw you at the dog parks, and it sounded so wonderful. You know that Janelle's dog Go is missing — she needed to get away for awhile, so I came with her up here."

"And you're —"

"I'm her friend Delma Corning. My dog's Shobie, the Boston terrier mix who was with Go a lot in the parks."

"Well, good to meet you, Delma, and good to see you, Janelle. I hope you have fun while you're here. My family and I have always enjoyed the area."

Was her family here too? I hadn't been able to tell whether the house was occupied at all when we'd walked by. But that was true of some of the other mansions as well.

"I definitely intend to have a good time," Janelle said. "And I'm sure I'll be seeing more of you here. Unless you're leaving now?"

"Not immediately, no," Ada said. "Maybe we could get together one of these days." She picked her purse up from beneath her stool and headed for the door, just as Neal came in.

He must have seen the look on Janelle's face that I did. Maybe Neal knew her well enough to interpret it, but I didn't. Not really. But it was clearly emotional.

"Are you okay, Janelle?" he asked quickly.

"Sure," she said, much too brightly. "But I've been waiting for you. I want to introduce you to Delma — and most of all, I want a drink."

We stayed only long enough for each of us to have one drink. I chose a glass of a Napa Valley Zinfandel. Janelle and Delma also chose wines, although I didn't hear exactly what they ordered, and Reed and Neal got beers.

The dogs received a bowl of water to share.

Maybe because Neal worked at the resort, although primarily at the reception desk, the bartenders managed to push two empty small tables together despite the continuous, noisy crowd. We all sat around them chatting, mostly about the hike and what we'd seen — although the houses on the far side of the lake were like the elephants in the crowded bar, sitting heavily on our minds, or at least mine, but not mentioned.

Neither was Ada, who was no longer here, but there'd been an undercurrent between her and Janelle that I hadn't understood.

My wine was excellent, and so was my immediate company. I had the sense that Reed knew what I was wondering about, and perhaps he was thinking about it, too, but he helped to keep the general conversation going. He cracked a couple of jokes about all the boats on the lake heading to bed at this hour, perhaps unlike their owners, and about how the dogs in the bar had to bark to go out soon, before the people with them got too sloshed to drive them home.

When we were done drinking, Janelle and

Delma said good night and left together. They apparently had a room in a hotel near the resort, but a lot less expensive. I got the impression that Janelle was paying for the room and that Delma had brought her dog and left him in his crate there. I wondered how long Janelle intended to stay in town.

Reed and Hugo left by themselves, too, although Biscuit and I walked out to the parking lot with them. Reed and I stole a quick kiss beside his black sedan, which felt good. No commitment in it, but it nevertheless hinted at the possibility of good things to come, as did our kisses on past dates.

Neal and I had come to the resort separately, so we each drove back to our home — which we shared and which I, primarily, paid for. Despite Neal having a job and leading local tours, his income was a lot lower than mine was as a veterinary technician, so we'd gotten into the habit of me supporting him.

Our financial arrangement hadn't changed when I'd opened my shops, since I'd put a lot of money into buying and opening the adjoining bakeries. I'd borrowed from Arvie, my boss at Knobcone Veterinary. I'd begun paying it back now, but not too quickly.

Neal knew this, and he'd started paying

me some rent — *some* being the operative word. But that was okay. I loved my brother, and since our divorced-and-remarried parents were much more into their second families than caring about us, we were all we had.

Neal arrived back at the house before Biscuit and me. I pulled into the driveway and let Biscuit sniff around for a minute.

I'd lived in my house for five years, having bought it shortly after moving to town. It was about twenty years old, in a nice, pleasant residential neighborhood that had streetlights on at this hour. It was a single-story home covered in attractive wood siding stained a cedar shade, with several small wings with sloped roofs. I had a fenced dog-run on the side for Biscuit, but I tended to walk her more often than just letting her out by herself.

When we went inside, Neal was sitting on my fluffy old beige couch in the living room, watching the news on the TV mounted on the wall.

He used the remote to mute the sound. "So what did you think of the hike?" he asked.

I took a seat at the other end of the sofa. "Fun!" I exclaimed. "I enjoyed it. And, before you ask, I'd be glad to do it again sometime, or try one of your other tours — just not in the dead of winter."

"Great. And . . . well, I'm curious what you thought about Janelle, too."

I'd need to be a little more careful how I answered that. "She seems nice," I said. "Interesting that she apparently came with a friend and they knew that other visitor here, that Ada. I gathered she's one of the Arnists who own one of those houses we saw. Did Janelle come here because they're friends, too? I gathered that Ada had suggested a visit here."

"Janelle told me she'd just run into Ada a few times in dog parks and that Ada had told her about how wonderful this area is. She might even have mentioned she was planning a trip here soon. That wasn't important to Janelle — finding someplace to go to try to get her mind off her lost dog was what she was after."

"And I gather that hasn't been successful," I said.

"No. I think maybe only the passage of time, or maybe getting another dog, will help her with that."

I wasn't sure if Biscuit understood the word "dog." Even if she did, she probably wasn't aware that she was anything different from a human — except maybe a little smarter. In any case, she stood up from where she lay by my feet and nuzzled my leg.

"I think she says it's bedtime," Neal said, watching her.

"I think she's right," I said, standing to head to my room.

Five

Despite the fact I'd gone to bed a little late last night, on Sunday morning I was in the kitchen of my two shops right on time: five o'clock a.m.

I wasn't alone. My new part-time assistants — especially Frida Grainger — really loved to bake. This morning, Frida had asked to work in the Icing part of the kitchen, which was fine with me. She would be the one to bake human cookies and cupcakes and scones and other people treats, while I got into lots of kinds of dog biscuits and cookies. As always, Biscuit would hang out in the Barkery in her large, open-topped enclosure, since no dogs were allowed in the kitchen. This was for sanitary reasons, as mandated by the local health department and our occupancy permit.

My longer-term assistant, Dinah, worked five days a week now, usually Tuesday through Saturday, although this week would be a bit different to accommodate some scheduling issues with our part-timers.

"So how was your hike yesterday?" Frida asked as she kneaded a large chunk of dough for cinnamon cookies.

"Fun," I said without giving details. "And what kind of culinary masterpiece did you create?"

"I'm working on a new gourmet Irish stew," she said with a huge grin on her pretty, round face.

She stood opposite me, across the center dividing shelves. On my side was the stainless steel utility counter for mixing and preparing dough for the Barkery, and huge ovens were behind me, against the wall. Frida's side was the mirror image of mine. But I'd made it clear that no one was to combine ingredients from the two sides, since some human stuff, like chocolate, was poisonous to dogs. On the other hand, similar-tasting carob was used on both sides. I'd had a special ventilation system installed so that the aroma of meaty animal treats wouldn't contaminate the people goodies containing sugar, chocolate, and more — and vice versa.

Frida had graduated from one of the Art Institute of California campuses a couple of years ago and had been working as a chef at some pretty high-class restaurants in San Bernardino County since then. It was fortunate for me that her fiancé had gotten a job in Knobcone Heights as the local manager of a supermarket. He apparently had aspirations of moving up in the company, but for now, at least, the couple was here, and Frida had needed a part-time job that used her skills at the same time I'd started looking for additional help. In her off hours, she created new people cuisine at home.

Although I would never tell her so, Frida looked as if she enjoyed her own creations a lot, as well as the goodies we cooked here. She was far from obese, but she definitely wasn't svelte. And one of the things I liked about her was that I almost never saw anything but a smile on her face.

"That stew sounds great," I said. "I hope you'll allow me to be one of your guinea pigs when you've perfected it."

"Of course. After all, Zorro has offered to be your guinea dog whenever you work on new dog treats." Her dog Zorro was a beagle mix.

"Biscuit will be glad for the company." I grinned and paused, then said, "Just so you know, I'll have a brief shift at the vet clinic today. Vicky is scheduled to come in at noon, so she'll be around to help you while I'm gone."

Vicky Valdez was another of my new part-timers. One of the things she was particularly good at was scheduling, so she helped me figure out who was coming in when. She had selected today as one of her days, once I gave her my vet tech schedule for this week.

"Perfect," Frida said, and smiled again.

"And by the way," I added. "I promised people on the hike that they could come in and get dog and people treats today, including samples."

"Got it."

My shift at the Knobcone Heights Veterinary Clinic was short that day, but I came in partly because Arvie had asked me, and partly because I'd be glad to see Reed again. Oh, and it didn't hurt that coming when asked was a way of ensuring that my part-time job there continued.

Which made me very happy. As much as I loved being my own boss at my bakeries, I also appreciated helping animals in other ways, too — including helping to heal them while they were injured or sick, and to keep them well via vaccines.

At the clinic, I got to carefully shave and

clean an area around an injury a French bulldog had received on his side. He'd squeezed himself between a couple of garbage cans in an attempt to get some meat scraps the owner said had fallen, unbeknownst to him, out of a neighbor's trash bag. Unfortunately, someone had also left a sharp-edged, unraveled wire hanger there to be disposed of. Fortunately, after Arvie further cleaned and stitched the wound and prescribed some antibiotics, he said the dog would be fine.

When my shift was over, I picked up Biscuit at the clinic's doggy daycare, where I always brought her when I was on vet tech duty. Then I headed toward Mountaintop Rescue, as I did after shifts whenever I had time. I generally had leftover Barkery treats with me. I usually made some available at the veterinary hospital, too, but figured that the rescue dogs at the wonderful local shelter could use even more TLC, including special doggy goodies.

Our walk along Hill Street, a block away from the Knobcone Heights town square, was short but fun. The veterinary clinic and the animal shelter were only a couple of blocks apart.

We soon reached Mountaintop Rescue. From the outside, it was hard to tell the function of the attractive, gold-colored stucco building. It was a couple of floors tall and well-decorated, with windows surrounded in attractive tile. But that was just the façade. Behind the main, compact building were other structures that housed the resident animals.

Biscuit and I walked up the short path into the building, where I opened the door and stepped inside. A familiar receptionist, Mimi, sat behind a large, chest-height wooden desk that kept visitors out until they were welcomed inside — which we were.

"Is Billi here?" I asked, but I needn't have. Billi walked into the waiting room from an inside door and stopped and smiled.

Wilhelmina Matlock wasn't merely a City Council member or the owner of a posh day spa and this wonderful animal shelter. She was also one lovely woman. She was slim, and I'd never seen her appear anything but perfect in whatever she happened to be wearing — which, today, was jeans and a T-shirt like me. Her shirt was bright red, with *Mountaintop Rescue* written on it along with a caricature of one happy, grinning dog. Mine was a blue Barkery and Biscuits shirt. Her hair was dark with golden highlights, and right now she wore it long and loose. Her deep brown eyes glanced happily down at Biscuit, then back up at me.

"Have any treats for us today, Madam Barkery?" she asked, her smile broad.

I held out the bag I'd carried under my arm. "What do you think?"

"I think we're going to have a bunch of happy residents today."

We smiled at each other. "I'll bet they're always happy here," I said.

We left Biscuit in Mimi's care as we headed toward the shelter area at the rear of the property: a group of long and attractive buildings and also some outdoor enclosures. The dog kennels were separated by metal fencing that was actually attractive, all adorned at the top with decorative circles.

Like the indoor kennels, the surfaces in the outdoor kennels were made of a smooth cement that could be cleaned easily. All of the enclosures had slightly raised platforms at the rear where beds and toys were placed. The cat areas were all indoor, but similarly designed. And each enclosure housed some delightful pets awaiting their forever homes. Each pen had a card attached outside that described what was known about the resident: where they'd come from, when they'd arrived at Mountaintop Rescue, and anything else pertinent, including health info.

"So, can I assume, like always, that I won't recognize any of the dogs I'm giving treats to?" I asked Billi.

"Maybe a few," she said. "You were last here only a few days ago."

Fortunately for the residents, the turnover at Mountaintop Rescue tended to be phenomenally fast. Homes were found for most of the animals really quickly, which was a very good thing. Billi and her family had contacts all over, including many good and mostly private no-kill shelters in other cities in the mountains and also down the hills. Each of these shelters shuttled adoptable pets around to where they were most likely to be adopted fast — especially if a potential adopter came into one of the shelters with a preconceived idea of the size or breed background they wanted.

As we walked along the corridor inside one of the buildings where some of the smaller dogs were housed, we were greeted loudly by pups. They were housed mostly two-by-two in their kennels. The Chihuahua mixes and terriers were loud and yappy, as usual, as if they wanted to outdo each other to get humans' attention.

Billi stopped walking and shouted toward me, "There's a newcomer I especially want you to meet. We picked her up yesterday from the Lake Arrowhead shelter. We traded a springer spaniel mix for her since someone who visited that shelter asked whether they had any medium-sized spaniels available. They didn't, we did. Sweetie's right down here." She gestured ahead with her left hand.

"Sweetie?"

"You'll see."

And I did, a few seconds later. There were two small dogs in the kennel Billi indicated. One was cute, too — an apparent Jack Russell mix. But the other . . . She looked a lot like Biscuit, gold in color with an apparent toy poodle background, and, perhaps, more terrier.

"Don't suppose you'd have room for another one in your life? A pack member for Biscuit?" Billi had been trying to talk me into a second pup since we'd met. She knew how much I loved dogs, and it was always hard to say no. But as a vet tech and new business owner, I simply couldn't give more than one the special attention they deserved.

That didn't mean I wasn't tempted, especially when Billi opened the kennel door, bent down sideways to keep the other dog inside, and took Sweetie out, placing her into my arms.

Sweetie snuggled with me and licked my face. Oh, yes, I was tempted. But the timing was all wrong. Still . . .

"I wish . . ." I began, shouting to be heard over barks and yips while glaring at Billi. "You know I can't. Not now. But what I will do is ask around, keep my eyes open for people searching for this kind of dog."

"The right people," Billi reminded me.

"Absolutely. And you know . . . maybe we should finally start those adoption events at my Barkery that we've been talking about now and then."

"This would be a good time," Billi agreed, her eyes moving from Sweetie to my face and back again. She smiled.

"Before winter starts," I said with a nod.

I snuggled with Sweetie a while longer, then moved her so I could hold her tightly to me with one arm. With the other, I reached down toward my purse where the bag of Barkery treats now protruded from the top. "Here you go," I told her after maneuvering her around her kennelmate to put her back behind the gate. I took a peanut butter biscuit out, broke it in two, and handed each of them a half through the mesh.

"You sure about leaving her here?" Billi asked as we started to walk away, the slightly declining barking behind us. I looked back to see little Sweetie watching me pleadingly.

Okay, I was reading that into her solemn look. She was getting to me. But I had to be realistic. And I had to think of Biscuit as well as my multiple careers. Sure, she might enjoy the company of a new pack member. But if she didn't, even just at first, I wouldn't have time to work with the two dogs the way that would be needed.

"Unfortunately, I'm sure," I told Billi.

I continued to break treats in half and pass them out to the small dogs. And I was glad when we finally left that building. I thought about Sweetie a lot.

I'd definitely have to help find her a home.

The larger dogs were in the next building, and I distributed treats there, too, without breaking them. Billi took some and hurried ahead of me, passing out treats to dogs I hadn't yet reached.

I stopped in front of one of the kennels. In it were two Labrador retrievers, one black and one gold. They appeared purebred, but I wasn't sure. Even so, an idea permeated my mind.

We finished up in that building with only a few treats left. In the meantime, some of the kennel staff came in and out, sometimes taking dogs out of the kennels to let them meet up personally with people who'd come to see if they could find their canine soulmates here.

Eventually we walked back to the main building, where Biscuit leaped into my arms after Mimi released her from the area where she'd been confined in my absence. As I bent to hug her and accept a myriad of doggy kisses, I thought again of Sweetie.

But there was something else more pressing to think about, I told myself. No, I *convinced* myself.

"Thanks for the tour," I told Billi.

"And thank you for all the treats, as usual," she responded, giving me a quick hug. I smiled. I liked her a lot as a person, and especially for what she did here. The fact that she ran a spa? That was fine, too. And her being a City Council member? Well, I was sure it didn't hurt to have friends in high places. And I had a couple of them, since Councilman Les Ethman was a buddy, too, thanks to his dog Sam — an English bulldog he sometimes brought to my vet clinic, and had also brought into the Barkery for treats.

Biscuit and I left soon afterwards to walk back to the shops. On the way, I made a quick phone call to Neal, who fortunately answered despite being on duty at the resort's reception desk.

I told him what I had on my mind, and I could hear the excitement in his voice as he said, "Sure. Why not. It won't hurt, at least."

We made plans to get together in a couple of hours.

We met back at Mountaintop Rescue. It was late, but I'd called Billi and told her what I had in mind. She was fine with it. In fact, she sounded as excited as I felt.

I got there before Neal. Billi and I were chatting in the reception area, since she'd let the rest of the staff except the overnight crew leave. As I held Biscuit in my lap, we talked over ideas for promoting my baking businesses more and holding those adoption events there.

When the outside door opened, we looked up from where we'd been leaning against the reception desk. "Hi, Neal," I said. "Hi, Janelle." I quickly introduced her to Billi.

"Nice to meet you," Janelle said, but her voice was soft and sounded confused. "But — I'm not sure why Neal brought me here." She turned to look up at my brother's face. They were holding hands and he was beaming with pride, as if their visit to the shelter had been his idea — and as if it were over already and had gone as well as I hoped it would.

"Carrie has something to show us," was his nebulous response.

SomeONE to show, I thought, but didn't contradict him. Sure, this could be a big mistake, considering Janelle's attitude about her missing dog.

I hoped not.

I put Biscuit into the enclosed reception area. "That's right," I said. "This way."

We walked through the small dog building, and it was as noisy as before. The pups had had some time to rest their vocal chords, I supposed. I smiled sadly as we passed Sweetie.

Then we entered the building where the larger dogs were housed. "Here we are." But before we continued, I decided it was time to give Janelle an explanation. "I hope I'm not entirely wrong about this."

But I was worried that I was. Her attractive face seemed pale, and I thought I saw as much pain as before in her large blue eyes.

Was this a big, bad blunder? Well, I had to follow through now, even if so. But I hoped that if she was a good match with my brother, she wouldn't hold this against him if she just ended up feeling more hurt.

"Come on." I gestured to her. "There's someone I want you to meet."

Rightly or wrongly, I was hoping that Janelle would fall for one of the Labs here and adopt him, to help her get over the loss of her own missing dog. As a dog lover myself, I knew that a new dog wouldn't be a replacement, but having one around might lessen the agony of loss.

I took the lead, with Janelle following and Neal and Billi at the end of our line. I stopped a few kennels down, where the two Labs, black and gold, were inside.

Janelle quickly stood beside me. The black Lab immediately started hurling himself toward the mesh gate, jumping and falling and jumping again. He made a crying sound from deep in his throat.

Janelle knelt on the concrete floor outside the kennel run and thrust her fingers inside. The dog started licking at them crazily, still making the frantic noises.

Janelle watched and crooned, too. And then she looked up toward where I still stood trying to figure this out — and thinking that, somehow, I already had.

"It's Go," Janelle whispered.

SIX

How was that possible? From what I'd understood, Janelle's dog had been stolen in LA. She had decided to come up here, to Knobcone Heights, to try to get away from her sorrow, although she'd seemed unsuccessful at staving off her depression . . . before.

But now, she'd found her missing dog. Or it certainly seemed that way.

Billi had opened the kennel door and blocked Go's roommate inside, then closed it again. Now Janelle sat on the room's cement floor, laughing and crying as the black Lab jumped all over her and licked her face. The dog, too, made whining noises. They were communicating so loudly that I easily heard the two of them over the usual kennel barks.

I looked at Neal, who was watching Janelle and the dog with a huge smile on his face. He turned to face me. "I knew you were one great sister," he said, "but how on earth did you do this?"

"I wish I could take credit for it," I said, "but I can't. Like I told you on the phone, my hope was to help Janelle heal by introducing her to another dog she might want to adopt."

"This is a whole lot more than that," my bro said, coming up to me and hugging me closely to his side.

The smile I aimed at him was far from smug. It was more wry than anything. I aimed it next toward Billi, who now stood beside us, also watching the emotional reunion. "Do you know how this dog got here?" I asked her. "Did he come from another shelter, or —"

"One of my staff said he was wandering in the alley behind the shelter just this morning. They brought him in and checked for an ID tag or microchip to try to reunite him with his owner. Apparently he was chipped, but our scanner couldn't capture the information. Then, as a matter of course, we had the dog checked out at your vet clinic before taking him in here. He got a clean bill of health, but their scanner couldn't grab the data, either."

I'd never heard of that happening before, but it suggested there was something wrong with the chip, not the two scanners.

"So there's no official way of confirming this is Janelle's Go?" I asked. What if this was all an act on Janelle's part?

Although I didn't know why she would do such a thing, or how she could have gotten the dog to mirror her excitement. She didn't appear to have any treats, and it sure looked to me as if the Lab was as thrilled to see her as she was to see him.

"Not really," Billi said, "although I'd suggest you look at the records at your clinic. Maybe there's something about scars, or other things we could ask Janelle about that would be unique to her dog."

"I'll do that," I said.

We all headed toward the reception area. Billi gave Janelle a leash to borrow. Clearly, Billi was going to allow Janelle to take this dog with her, whether or not he was actually Go.

But their mutual reactions were convincing me, more and more, that this was really Janelle's missing dog.

Since the receptionist had left for the day, Billi extracted the usual adoption paperwork from the office files. I didn't pay a lot of attention, since Biscuit dashed over to me, then headed in the direction of the other dog in the room to greet him, too. The dog who was probably Go had seemed just fine with the other Lab in their kennel, but I wanted to keep a close eye on him with my smaller, more energetic pup.

I clipped Biscuit's leash on her but let her stay close, at least for now, to the dog who was apparently Janelle's. Fortunately, after trading nose and butt sniffs, they both settled down. Go did not appear inclined to attack Biscuit, and of course my little girl wasn't about to hurt anyone either.

As we stood there, a few straggler daytime staff members entered the room to log out, and Billi told them that the Lab was leaving for a new home already that evening, which wouldn't have been permitted so quickly under other circumstances in case the dog's owner showed up. Since Janelle was apparently that owner, it worked this time. Everyone seemed delighted.

Billi then handed the paperwork to Janelle, along with a pen, and gestured toward a table and chair near the door. "I'd like you to fill this out. I understand that this appears to be your dog — we named him Boomer, by the way, but we always say adopters can change the pets' names, and this time it's clear what he responds to. In any event, since we started our own file on him, it'll be cleaner just to act as if he's another adoption. If it turns out you're mistaken and the real owner shows up, though, you'll be agreeing here to bring Go back."

"He's definitely my dog," Janelle said, "but I'll sign this so I can take him now."

That also meant Billi would collect information such as Janelle's home address and phone number. That might be handy to have.

Of course, if Janelle was just making things up for some unfathomable reason, she'd fake her data like everything else. I couldn't figure out why she'd be doing that, though. And Neal still seemed so interested in her that I could only hope that not only was she for real, but so was what had happened here with the dog she was calling Go.

A coincidence? If so, it was a huge one. I still couldn't figure out how a dog stolen in LA could wind up here, in a town his owner was randomly visiting.

My mind kept circling those questions as Neal knelt to play with Go. I stood off to the side with Biscuit and Billi while Janelle filled out the forms.

"What's really going on here?" Billi asked quietly.

I couldn't brainstorm with her now, with Janelle around, so I merely said, "I hope to figure that out." But since I in fact felt sure this couldn't be a coincidence, and I hoped it wasn't some kind of weird game Janelle was playing, I wasn't surprised when my thoughts came to rest on the two people Janelle knew from LA who'd shown up here around the same time as she had.

She seemed very friendly with Delma. That didn't mean Delma hadn't played a really nasty prank on her buddy Janelle.

But was the more likely candidate for stealing the dog and bringing him here Ada? Janelle had met her at dog parks. And something had seemed strange in their brief contact I'd observed.

Still, why would a member of the clearly wealthy Arnist family steal anything — unless there was something behind the theft that I simply couldn't see? And bring the dog here? Why? Was Janelle lying about everything? Or was my imagination just coming up with ideas that had no basis in any kind of reality?

And no matter who it was who'd brought Go to this town, why hadn't that person hung onto him? Even a really smart dog like a Lab wouldn't have known to come to the town's only animal shelter to be taken care of. Therefore, a person, maybe the dognapper, had to be involved.

"Here we are." Janelle sounded thrilled as she stood and handed the completed forms to Billi. "Can Go and I leave?"

Billi, now standing closer to Janelle, skimmed the paperwork. "It looks in order, I think. Is that your cell phone number?" She pointed to the page.

"Yes," Janelle said.

"Good. I'll be able to get in touch with you if I have any questions."

"Definitely." Janelle again knelt and hugged the dog — who was now, and possibly previously, known as Go. "Come on, boy. We're out of here." She looked toward Neal. "Can you drive us to my hotel?"

"Absolutely," he said. "Let's go."

At the door, with Go by her side leaning against her leg, Janelle turned back. "Carrie, I can't thank you enough. Or you either, Billi. Look — I just want to spend some alone-time with Go tonight, but why don't you all meet me at the resort's bar about this time tomorrow? I'll buy you all drinks. Maybe everyone in the bar — although I . . . well, never mind. I'm just so excited. Will you meet us there?"

I'd probably buy my own drink and some others', too, since I'd gathered that professional photographer Janelle wasn't exactly wealthy and was paying, at the least, a hotel bill to stay here. But I wanted to learn as much as I could about the situation. And so I said, "Sure. I'll see you tomorrow."

I actually saw her much sooner the next day than I'd anticipated. Go, too.

It was early in the morning, seven o'clock. I had just opened the Barkery, and Dinah was in Icing getting it ready to open, too. I was placing some of that day's newly baked dog treats in the glass-fronted display case when I saw the front door open and heard one of the door chimes ring. It was Janelle who entered, with Go on a leash.

Biscuit was already in her large, open-topped crate in a corner of the room. She stood up on her hind legs and woofed her greeting. At the same time, I maneuvered out from behind the display case to greet them, too.

"Hi," I said. "Welcome to Barkery and Biscuits. Is it okay to give Go a sample treat?"

"Definitely. I'm planning on buying him some treats. Spoiling him all over again." Janelle smiled hugely. She wore jeans and the same purple athletic shoes I'd seen her in before. Her T-shirt was also purple and said *Knobcone Heights,* clearly a souvenir of her visit here. But what really looked different about her was how real that smile on her pretty face appeared. It was wide and relaxed and suggested she was ready to break into laughter if anyone around her said something that even hinted of a joke.

Apparently, finding Go had been a really good thing for her. I could understand that.

Her light brown hair wafted about her face as if she'd been in a breeze. Or maybe Go and she had run here.

"I assume you'd like a treat, too," I told her after retrieving a carob and peanut butter biscuit for Go from inside the refrigerated case. "How about an apple scone next door?"

"I'd love that," she said.

I was glad to see her and wondered if I could get her talking. Last night, after driving Go and Janelle to their hotel, Neal had come back to our place rather dejected. He was delighted that Janelle had found her dog and was clearly feeling better, but he was also worried that now that she was no longer depressed, she might decide there was no reason to stay in Knobcone Heights.

No reason to get to know him better.

Could I help? I doubted it. I didn't fully trust Janelle or the situation, and yet I really liked how happy she was to be apparently reunited with her dog — and wanting to spoil him. Plus, I'd hated to see my brother's dismay when his prior relationship hadn't seemed to lead anywhere. Might this one?

Certainly only if they could see each other frequently. That meant staying in the same town. And if Janelle was here for a while, maybe I could figure out what had really happened with Go.

Now I moved back out from behind the counter and handed Go most of the biscuit. The large black Lab scarfed it down, then looked up at me with big, dark eyes that seemed to plead for more. I just laughed and patted his head, but then I walked over to give my Biscuit the rest of that biscuit so she wouldn't feel jealous.

"This place is every bit as charming as I thought it would be," Janelle said, her eyes moving from the glass-fronted case containing multiple kinds of fresh dog treats, to the wall shelves behind it where filled dog-cookie jars were stored, to Biscuit's enclosure area. Then she scanned the few tables and chairs on the decorative blue-tile floor.

I just smiled with pride. "Before we go into Icing on the Cake, we can hook Go's leash to Biscuit's enclosure. Dogs are more than welcome here in the Barkery, but not in the human bakery."

"Sounds great."

I took the end of Go's leash and looped it around the hook at the outside of Biscuit's crate, then led Janelle into Icing.

Dinah was there, scrubbing down the wall shelves that contained jars of human cookies. The layout of Icing was a mirror image of the Barkery. When Dinah turned around, I introduced her to Janelle.

"Dinah's been around here longer than I have," I said. "She worked here in Icing when it was the whole shop, and now she's my full-time helper."

"That sounds wonderful." Something in Janelle's tone grabbed my attention. She was looking around Icing the same way as she had the Barkery, appearing not only interested but wistful. Her next words confirmed what I'd been sensing. "I'd love to work someplace like this."

Really? I'd thought she was a photographer.

But did that pay enough to support her and a medium-sized dog? Plus, even though she'd apparently only been in town a short while, could she keep up with whatever photography commitments she had while vacationing here?

If I hired her in my shops, that meant she'd stay in town a bit longer, perhaps get to know Neal better. Was that a good thing?

And would I really get a better feel for what had gone on with Go?

Although I had Frida and Vicky on staff now, I actually had been thinking about trying to recruit another part-timer. But did I know Janelle well enough to offer her a job?

And how would Neal feel about it? I imagined he'd be delighted, since it would provide Janelle a tie to Knobcone Heights. Not that she couldn't unravel it immediately, should she so choose.

Even so, I impulsively decided to ask him about it. I didn't know if Janelle could cook, let alone bake, but we tended to use many of the recipes over and over so I figured she could learn.

"Dinah, would you please give Janelle one of our apple scones? I need to go in the back and make a quick call."

"Sure." As my assistant opened the back of the display case, I slipped around the counter and through the door into the kitchen. There, I hurried to my tiny office at the rear of the Icing end of the kitchen, closed the door, and called Neal.

"What's up, Carrie?" he asked almost immediately. His voice was low, so I figured he was on duty behind the resort's check-in desk.

I told him, asking whether he had any idea

if Janelle could handle a part-time job like this, once she was instructed on the basics.

And whether he wanted me to offer it to her.

"I knew there was a reason I love my big sis," he exclaimed before I was done.

Well, this, plus the fact I practically supported him. And I'd helped to raise him since our parents hadn't done much.

But I didn't mention that.

"I take that as a yes."

"Yes!"

I soon hung up and returned to Icing. The next thing was to smooth over Dinah's feelings in advance. I told her there was something I needed to discuss with her and invited her to join me in the kitchen.

"Meantime, you can just sit at one of the tables and eat your scone," I told Janelle. Although Icing was laid out exactly as the Barkery was, the floor was patterned in pale gold and brown, not blue. I'd hoped, when I chose the decor in here, that it would entice people to buy the similarly hued pastries.

When Janelle had taken a seat, I motioned for Dinah to follow me. I headed again to my tiny office and once more closed the door, this time behind my youthful, acne-faced and somewhat chubby — but absolutely wonderful — helper. I explained the situation to her, at least a bit, including that I didn't know if Janelle would accept an offer if I gave it, nor how well she'd do helping at the stores. "But if all goes well, it could help Neal." Or ruin any possible relationship for him if it flopped, I realized, but I didn't mention that — either to Dinah or to Neal.

"It might be an interesting thing for me to base a story on," Dinah mused. In addition to working for me, Dinah loved to write. I wasn't sure whether she'd ever gotten anything published, or even published anything on her own. She'd never told me anything other than how much she loved to create stories.

"Maybe," I said. It might even get more interesting if I could figure out the Go situation. "So I'll go ahead and make the offer to her?"

"Sure," Dinah agreed.

We both returned to Icing, and I invited Janelle to accompany me back into the Barkery, ostensibly so she could pick up Go and I could see my little Biscuit. I hadn't heard the bell on the door ring, so I didn't think we had any customers at the moment.

"Okay, here's the thing," I said to Janelle after we got both dogs loose and sat down at one of the Barkery tables. "I could use some more part-time help at my stores, and you indicated you might be interested in working here. If you'd like, you can stay around for the rest of today and I'll show you how we do things. Then, if we're both happy about the situation, I'll offer you a job and we can work out a schedule and salary for you. What do you think?"

Instead of saying anything, Janelle rose, and I was suddenly engulfed in a huge hug from a thin yet very strong woman.

"Thank you, thank you," she exclaimed.

"I take it that's a yes?" I said to her as I had to Neal.

"Yes!"

Seven

For the rest of the afternoon, I demonstrated how I liked clientele to be served, as well as how to count and pack up treats and use the electronic cash register. Dinah also stepped in and helped out. She seemed fine with the newcomer. But then, she was a great model for our part-timers to emulate.

I particularly liked Janelle's attitude. She watched what we did, then did it with our next customers. She asked a lot of questions, tasted both people and pet treats — something I encouraged everyone to do, since what we baked for dogs contained only the best, healthiest ingredients that humans could eat as well — and said she'd look forward to being taught how to bake this stuff.

Apparently always a photographer, Janelle also took photos of dogs and people eating treats. She always got their permission first, which was a good thing. And then, using her smart phone, she posted the shots on social media sites, mentioning how all the humans here in Knobcone Heights enjoyed sweets from Icing on the Cake and how the dogs always begged for more treats from Barkery and Biscuits.

I never quibbled with free publicity, as long as it was of the positive sort. And I really did like what she was doing.

At one point, when we were in the Barkery with confined Biscuit and leashed Go, I was about to ask Janelle what vet she took her dog to back in LA. But then some customers came in and I had to wait. It needed to be the right time, anyway, and sound casual.

But I intended to contact her regular vet and ask about any identifying characteristics Go had, like scars, to confirm whether "Boomer" and the black Lab now across the room from me shared those traits.

Sure, I wanted to like and to trust Janelle. So far, the former was definitely a possibility. I hoped things would work out for the latter as well, at least if she and Neal became an actual item. And for Go's sake — I was always happy when I saw a pet bond as a family member with its owner.

And what if Boomer wasn't Janelle's Go?

What difference would it really make, with the two of them clearly so close now?

It wouldn't matter, as long as Go didn't belong to someone else. But what mattered most to me was my brother, and whether he was getting involved with a liar or a very lucky pet owner.

I was also amused when Janelle notified nearly every customer she waited on that she was putting together a big party at the Knobcone Heights Resort bar that night. It would be "no host," after all, so she had decided not to pay for anyone else's food or drinks. But she was absolutely forthcoming about how thrilled she was that she had just found her lost dog Go and wanted everyone possible to join in the celebration.

I would certainly be there with Biscuit. I also called my clinic and spoke to Arvie and Reed. I invited them to come to the party and hoped they'd be there.

We had a lot of customers in both shops that day, including some of Neal's hikers from the other evening who said they hadn't come in yesterday but hoped they could still get samples.

Of course they could.

It was a fine time to be showing a new assistant both the good and bad things about busy bakeries, such as having to be patient with people who took forever to make up their minds despite how many other folks were in line behind them. Or those who changed their minds even after some of the treats were packed and ready to go. Or who couldn't make up their minds whether to pay by cash or credit card. Some of the best buyers, at least, were those we'd given samples to.

I told Janelle the history of the two shops — how the former owner of Icing on the Cake, my good friend Brenda Anesco, had had to move down the mountain to care for her ailing mother and had not only sold her business to me but also supported my dividing the store into two shops. Plus, I passed along Brenda's favorite instruction about Icing's products: "Make them sweet, and make them good."

Eventually the time neared six o'clock, our closing hour. "Here's what we do when we close up," I told Janelle, and Dinah and I showed her that, too: how we locked the doors, including the one at the rear of the kitchen, got some things ready for the next day, and made sure that all computer and accounting information was locked in the office.

"This place is amazing," Janelle gushed, and I again wondered if she was for real.

"Will I see both of you at my party tonight?"

My answer was an unqualified yes. Dinah's was more equivocal, but she said she'd try.

We exited the door at the front of the Barkery, a necessity since Janelle and I had our dogs with us and could not walk through the kitchen. I locked it behind us, then told Janelle to come around to the back of the stores, where my white Toyota was parked, as well as Dinah's car. There was one other parking space. "If it's vacant, you can use it when you're on duty," I told her. "We haven't really discussed it yet, but tomorrow afternoon I'll work with my assistant Vicky, our best scheduler, to put together a proposed schedule where you'll be able to work sometimes with Dinah and/or me, and also sometimes with our other part-timers." We had already discussed Janelle's hourly rate by then, and she was okay with it, for now — until she had more experience.

Fortunately, with the amount of business we'd been getting, I could actually afford having this many assistants, especially since the majority only worked for me part-time.

"I guess that means I'd better not get too blasted at my party tonight," Janelle said. "No matter how happy I am." She bent and hugged Go, who panted a little and wagged his long black tail.

Biscuit jumped on my leg as if to remind me that she needed some attention, too, and I obliged. Then I opened my car door and watched her jump in. "See you in a little while," I told Janelle. And wondered how the party would go.

I hurried home to feed Biscuit her regular dinner, not Barkery treats. Plus, I changed clothes and freshened up.

I wasn't sure why, but I really did want to party. Maybe because Reed had indicated that he, too, would be there. He had even offered to pick me up and drive me to the resort, but I'd demurred. This was far from being a date. But if he wanted to ask me out again another time, by ourselves, that would be a different story.

I'd received an email that day from Jack Loroco, a guy who'd expressed romantic interest in me as well as business interest in my Barkery treats. When I'd met him several months ago, he'd said that he hoped to buy some of my recipes if his employer, the national quality dog food manufacturer VimPets, gave him the go-ahead. He lived in LA. In his email, he said he was hoping to visit Knobcone Heights sometime during the next few weeks, but he didn't nail down a date. *Hopefully soon,* he wrote.

Just as well. I found the guy good-looking and otherwise attractive, but I was just as happy right now pursuing a possible relationship with Reed. I didn't need any distractions as long as things seemed to be progressing well.

I hadn't really gotten deeply involved with a man since I'd left a bad relationship behind in LA. I'd once believed that I'd found the love of my life — a handsome guy, a corporate executive named John who owned Rambo, one of the sweetest pit bulls I'd ever met. But to further his career, John decided to move to an upscale condo built by one of his company's affiliates. There were restrictions there about dogs — size and breed.

Without even discussing it with me, he'd decided to get rid of Rambo by dumping him at a public, high-kill shelter.

Fortunately, he admitted it to me in time for me to rescue Rambo. I helped to find the dog a new home through the vet clinic where I worked at the time. Then I dumped John the way he'd dumped Rambo, half wishing I could leave *him* in a high-kill shelter.

Since I wasn't sure how many people

would be at the party that night, let alone dogs, I'd decided to leave Biscuit at home so I wouldn't have to worry about making sure she stayed right beside me and wasn't the subject of any other dog's playfulness or wrath. I took her out for a quick walk in the waning daylight. When I shut her into the kitchen, she scowled at me and cocked her head, as if objecting to this heinous treatment.

"I won't stay late," I promised.

I arrived at the resort in my car a short while later, took a ticket from the machine at the entry, and tried not to think about how much parking in this lot would cost even with a validation for buying drinks and some snacks here. Neal, a peon on the resort's staff, could only help once in a while.

I found a spot fairly quickly, though not close to the door. Then I locked my car and headed in.

Good timing. On the way I saw Reed walking a row ahead of me and hurried to catch up with him. "Hi," I called. He hadn't brought Hugo, either, so we'd both be dogless for the evening.

He turned immediately. "Hi," he called back, stopping and grinning under one of the parking lot lights. When I reached him, I was pleased that he bent down and we kissed — not extremely sexily, but in a way that suggested more than remote friendship.

"So what are you anticipating for this evening?" he asked. "What's the situation with Janelle and her dog?"

Since I'd already explained to him over the phone all I knew, he was aware that I wanted to see the clinic file on the dog known as Boomer, for comparison once I'd gotten more information from Go's vet.

"Guess we'll just have to see how things evolve tonight," I told him.

He bowed slightly, waving me through the door first in a gentlemanly manner, and I nodded my thanks, grinning.

The large reception area at the resort was crowded, as it was so often. I decided to first see if Neal was behind the desk before I headed to the bar to find out whether Janelle's festivities had started.

I gestured to Reed to join me. "I want to check on my brother," I told him over the noise of the crowd.

We passed the offices along the outer wall. All were closed. As far as I knew from Neal's reports, the senior owners of the place, Trask and Susan Ethman, still weren't around much. They'd continued to leave management of the resort in the hands of their daughter Elise Ethman Hainner, ever since the death of the prior manager, their son Harris's wife, Myra.

When we reached the reception area, I saw my bro deep in conversation with slender, blonde Elise, who was dressed professionally, expensively, and well, with a perfectly made-up face. I'd known practically since my arrival at Knobcone Heights that the Ethmans had money, and this resort helped add to it. Elise's expression seemed amused, not irritated, so I figured Neal wasn't in trouble, even though he was currently occupied. "Let's head for the bar," I said to Reed.

"Great. I could use a drink."

Once more, we had to maneuver our way around groups of loudly chatting people. A few had dogs with them, and I half wished I'd brought along some treats for promotion. But that wasn't the reason I was here this evening, so it was just as well I'd come empty-handed.

Unsurprisingly, the bar was also busy. I'd looked around for Janelle on the way in but figured I was more likely to find her here, possibly with Go, celebrating their reunion. But I didn't see her here, either.

I started edging my way up to the bar,

Reed close behind me. While I maneuvered, I studied the crowd. When I spotted Ada Arnist sitting on a stool toward my right, I headed in that direction.

The young, thin, highly bleached blonde was chatting with a guy who sat beside her. Judging by the serious expression on her face, they weren't flirting, so maybe she hadn't just met him.

That didn't matter to me. What did matter was what Ada knew about Janelle's having found Go — and whether she happened to know how the dog had gotten to Knobcone Heights.

Yes, I was probably stretching things, but I wondered, seeing Ada in the bar, whether Janelle or her friend Delma had told Ada about finding Go and invited her to the party. If so, was it because they suspected Ada of being the dognapper?

As we approached, I was glad to see someone vacate a stool on the other side of the guy Ada was talking to. I edged over there, around another woman who'd possibly staked it out, and quickly sat down. Then I turned back toward Reed. "I'll order for us here, and maybe we can take our drinks into the lobby soon if we can't find another seat." But not immediately.

The bartenders were all busy. While waiting, I leaned forward over the bar and looked at Ada from behind the guy she appeared to be with. "Hi," I said brightly. "Good to see you here again." We'd originally met, after all, in this bar. "Are you here to celebrate with Janelle about finding her dog?"

"I sure am," Ada gushed in her shrill voice, tearing her gaze from the guy. "It's so cool."

The man who sat between us shifted on his stool. I didn't know who he was but figured it wouldn't hurt to find out. I tapped him on the shoulder. When he turned, I said, "Hi. Are you here with Ada to celebrate? I'd imagine everyone here tonight knows the story."

The look the guy leveled on me looked more irritated than celebratory. He appeared to be mid-twenties, older than Ada. His eyes were sunken in his long face, and he wore a dark mustache plus a lot of beard shadow. "Yeah, I know the story," he said. "Glad to hear the lady found her dog. That's it, right?"

"This is my friend Tim Smith," Ada called from over his shoulder. "He lives near here. Do you know when Janelle is coming?"

"No." But as I said it, I heard the crowd's noise ramp up. I turned and saw Janelle walk through the door. Because of the crowd, I couldn't tell for sure if Go was with her, but a lot of people were looking down and exclaiming and clapping, so I assumed he was.

Behind her, Delma also entered the room. She was carrying a Boston terrier. Delma didn't stay with Janelle; seeing me, she headed in my direction. "Can I borrow your stool for a minute?" she asked.

I wanted to say no but was curious what she was up to. It didn't sound as if she wanted to order a drink right away. In fact, I still hadn't gotten to order mine.

"All right." I got off and moved toward Reed, who was still nearby.

Instead of sitting down, Delma put her leashed dog on the floor, then edged up to the bar and grabbed a bottle of beer that was in front of Tim. She picked up a knife that happened to be on the counter, maybe because the people on the other side of me had been eating some appetizers, including hummus to be spread on pita bread. She started banging the knife loudly against the bottle, drawing a scowl from Tim. But instead of backing off, she started shouting.

"Welcome, everyone!" she called. Conversations immediately started to drop off, and she repeated, with less noisy interruption,

"Welcome, everyone! In case you don't know, we're here to celebrate tonight. My friend Janelle has been reunited with her stolen dog, Go. So if you don't already have a drink, it's time to get one so we can toast them both."

"Let's do it!" said a man who'd apparently followed Delma and her dog and was now edging his way around Reed. He wasn't carrying a drink, though, so I assumed he'd not been here much longer than me.

"Hey, can we get some drinks out here?" Delma demanded of one of the nearest bartenders.

"Absolutely." The guy waved the small notebook in which he apparently jotted orders. "If you want something quick, make it wine or beer."

"I think we were here first," I said, moving so that Delma was somewhat behind me.

"You certainly were," Delma acknowledged. "We'll hold the toast until after everyone's got something."

That took another five minutes, even as the other bartenders started focusing on serving the bar's new guests. I soon had a glass of imported Shiraz, and Reed had a locally brewed beer.

"This situation is really something, don't

you think?" asked the guy who'd followed Delma. He looked at me with laughing green eyes in a face that appeared mid-forties. His hairline must have rolled back a bit, since his wavy brown hair was combed slightly forward in front, and his facial features were well-defined. A nice-looking fellow. But was he flirting with me? I didn't want him to, even if Reed hadn't been here.

"It is," I replied to him. "And as a dog lover I'm really happy for Janelle." I paused. "Do you know her?"

"No, but I heard of the situation. My name's Garvy Grant, by the way. I'm a visitor here in Knobcone Heights. Great place — especially this kind of party."

Janelle had reached the bar, with Go leashed beside her. Rather than ordering anything, or waiting for Delma to get everyone joined in a toast, Janelle approached Ada and grabbed her shoulder.

"Did you do this? Did you steal Go, then leave him as a stray outside a shelter to protect yourself? He could have been hurt. He could have died, you miserable b—"

"You're wrong." Ada's face had gone ashen enough to be nearly as white as her hair. "I'd never hurt a dog. I swear."

"You go ahead and swear," Janelle said. My new assistant still wore the T-shirt, jeans, and athletic shoes she'd had on all day at my shops. What looked different was the rage on her otherwise attractive face. "I'll swear right back. Did you steal him to ransom him? I know your parents still support you, but I've heard you're spending more than they give you. If I ever find even the slightest shred of evidence that you did this to me, to Go, I'll make you sorry, no matter who your family is."

With that, and still not waiting for Delma to say anything more, Janelle knelt, hugged her black Lab, then stood again and strode back out of the bar.

No one got in her way.

For a few moments, everyone seemed stunned. At least there were no further conversations. But then the crowd started roaring as people regained their breaths and began to talk once more, even louder.

"Why did she do that?" Ada asked, her shrill voice audible even despite the increasing loudness.

"Let's get out of here," Tim said without answering.

I glanced at Reed.

"Let's just take our drinks out on the back patio," he said.

It sounded like a good idea to me. I'd hoped to order some snacks, but not now.

Neal joined us on the patio a short while later. "What happened?" he demanded. "Some of the guests were telling us at the reception desk about a really nasty time in the bar . . . with Janelle."

I told him how Janelle, instead of hosting her party, had come in and immediately confronted Ada. "She apparently feels sure Ada had something to do with Go's disappearance," I finished.

"Maybe so," Neal said. "But acting like that, especially when she's already found her dog . . ."

"Let's just hope that was the end of it," I said.

But I couldn't be sure that was the case.

And I knew it wasn't when I learned early the next day that Ada Arnist's body had been found around dawn, in the lake near the resort.

Rumor had it she'd been murdered.

EIGHT

When I first heard about Ada that morning, I'd already been at my shops for a couple of hours, baking. Dinah was with me, and Vicky was due later. I'd thought about inviting Janelle to come in for an early cooking lesson, but luckily I'd decided she should wait to start work until the next day.

It was nearly seven o'clock, opening time. Dinah had just pulled some of Brenda's wildly popular red velvet cupcakes out of Icing's oven, and I was about to put a tray of pumpkin and yam biscuits into the Barkery's oven, when my cell phone rang. I put the tray back down on the counter between the two halves of the kitchen and pulled my phone from my pocket. It was Neal.

"Open the back door, Carrie," he said without responding to my initial hello. "I'm right outside." Something in his tone told me I'd better do what he'd commanded, right away.

I quickly headed for the rear door and opened it. Neal burst in.

"What's going on?" I demanded. I knew something was wrong. First, Neal seldom got up this early, and even if he did, he almost never came to my shops then. Second, his complexion was strange. This time of year, mid-summer, he was almost always tan, and he'd looked handsomely tan as recently as last night. But now he appeared ashen, his skin nearly as light as his blond hair.

"You didn't hear, I guess." His voice was raspy and emotional.

"Hear what?"

"Ada Arnist? She was apparently murdered last night."

"What! No, wait. Let's go into the Barkery and sit down." I was concerned that if he didn't sit he'd fall over. He appeared that unsteady.

"I want to hear, too," Dinah said. "I'll still be able to keep an eye on what we're baking."

I didn't take time to object or tell her to open the shops on time or anything else. I just followed Neal through the door into the Barkery.

Since we weren't open yet, Biscuit was loose there. She immediately bounded over toward her Uncle Neal and perched herself against his leg. "Not now, Bug," Neal croaked, gently pushing her off as he lowered himself into a chair.

That was another sign of how upset Neal was. He always acted like the champion and good friend of his "Bug."

I kind of gathered where this was going. Of course it was horrible if there'd been a murder in Knobcone Heights, especially after the murder of Myra Ethman only a couple of months ago. But to see Neal this upset over someone I wasn't sure he knew very well didn't ring true.

Unless . . . the killer was Neal's new squeeze, Janelle.

It certainly couldn't involve Neal himself. Could it? My heart stopped its racing. In fact, it felt for a moment as if it had stopped altogether. I quickly lowered myself into a seat near my brother.

He surely wouldn't do such a thing, even to someone arguing with a woman he was attracted to.

Dinah joined us at the table. The expression on her young face was solemn and interested. "Do they know what happened?" she asked. I wanted to hug her for asking exactly what I wanted to know.

"No. At least I don't think so." Neal

rubbed his face with one of his large hands. "From what I heard, one of the guests at the resort went out early to see the sunrise off our beach, started walking, and . . . found her. She was face down in the water, and it was too late to save her. There was some bruising on her, around her throat, or at least that's the rumor so far. The cops are still there conducting their investigation."

"You didn't go to work this early, did you?" I asked, knowing that the answer had to be no.

"No, but if you want to know how I learned about it, Gwen called me. She's on breakfast shift at the restaurant today. She thought I'd want to know."

That was intriguing. I suspected that if Gwen still had some interest in Neal, or wanted him to think so, she might have been delighted to let him know that his current main squeeze may have gotten herself into trouble. Real trouble. Like murder?

Or was I just letting my imagination run wild after having helped to solve the town's other recent murder?

I needed more information. "Why would Gwen think that?" I leaned forward across the table, trying to settle Neal's wandering gaze on something — me. What was he really thinking?

"The police who're at the resort started asking people questions already. So far, apparently no one saw anything, at least nobody who's come forward yet, not even any boaters, so they think it happened pretty late." Neal briefly aimed his blue eyes at me. "Some of the people the cops are talking to were apparently at the bar last night and heard Janelle arguing with Ada. They started gossiping about it at breakfast in the restaurant, and some cop must have overheard."

Or the cops were informed by someone who could easily eavesdrop on those breakfast conversations. Someone like a nearly invisible server.

Someone like Gwen.

"Then the police are focusing on Janelle as a suspect?" I'd seen and heard that argument, too.

Neal shrugged. "I don't know. Maybe." He finally looked me straight in the eye. "Probably yes. That's what Gwen hinted at."

"And that's why she called you." I didn't make it a question. "Maybe we should discuss your non-relationship with Gwen one of these days." As my brother opened his mouth, clearly to protest, I lifted my hands to stave it off. "You can tell me in your own good time, but in any event, she might not have been thrilled that you found someone else to date recently. Could she be somehow trying to throw Janelle under the bus?"

Or you, I wondered. At least Neal hadn't suggested that he was a suspect, as I'd feared, but that didn't mean he wasn't one — or that Gwen wasn't trying to make him one, too, out of vindictiveness.

"I don't know the situation," Dinah said, "but who's Gwen?"

"Someone I was sort of dating before," Neal said.

"Then she could be making some of this up to get back at you?" Dinah's eyes gleamed. I recalled how much she liked to write fiction in her spare time. Was she hatching a plot in her own mind? Or was she being astute about what was really happening?

"Has Gwen suggested to the cops that you might have killed that woman to impress Janelle?" Dinah continued.

Had I even told Dinah that Janelle was Neal's new romantic interest? I didn't recall, but if not, she'd clearly guessed.

"What!" Neal looked and sounded shocked. He skyrocketed to his feet, scaring Biscuit enough that she rose from where she'd been lying on the tile floor, skidding on her paws before dashing toward me and leaping onto my lap.

Apparently that last possibility hadn't crossed my brother's mind before. Either that or he'd been taking acting lessons. I would never anticipate that he could feign such a reaction.

"Neal would never do such a thing," I told my employee firmly. Or so I hoped. And believed. "Anyway, aren't there some things in the oven that you need to tend to?" There actually were, plus I knew she'd get the unspoken message: not to make up things about my brother.

Even if I'd thought of them, too.

The look Dinah leveled on me said a lot, like she was reading my mind. When she'd left the room, I said to Neal, "You need to consider that the police might wonder the same kinds of things. I can vouch for your being home last night, so it all should be fine."

But what I could also vouch for was that he had come home a bit later than I had. And could I swear he'd been home all night?

At least Biscuit hadn't barked, as she sometimes did if she heard Neal moving around in the middle of the night. I could *almost* swear to it.

But I hoped I wouldn't have to. And that neither Neal nor Janelle would be actual suspects.

Despite how much I feared otherwise.

Vicky arrived in the early afternoon. I again felt relieved that Janelle wasn't at the shop today. No matter how much I wanted to talk to her, or at least get her assurance that she'd had nothing to do with what had happened to Ada, her absence was a whole lot better than her presence when, mid-morning, my shops received some visitors who weren't customers.

Not that Detective Wayne Crunoll couldn't have just needed some treats from the Barkery — he and his wife owned two dachshund mixes, Magnum and Blade. But he had used them as excuses a few times to drop in and quiz me about the last murder that had occurred in this town. He'd also come without his dogs several times. Cops didn't really need excuses, did they? Assuming it wasn't an official search or interrogation.

His superior officer, Detective Bridget Morana, certainly didn't worry about it. I knew she owned a cat named Butterball, whom she brought to the vet clinic now and then. She occasionally bought some human treats from Icing on the Cake.

But when they walked through the Icing door this time, I saw that neither had a pet with them. They both wore dark suits, which confirmed to me that they were on duty. Bridget was the older and more experienced one, a middle-aged woman with a professional-looking cap of light brown hair and bushy, somewhat darker eyebrows on a face that, at this moment at least, held no expression yet still managed to stab me with apprehension.

Wayne, who reported to her, looked even younger than Neal; he was in his mid-twenties, perhaps. His hair was dark and short, his face pudgy, his light brown eyes gleaming and smug — as if he'd known he'd wind up back at my shops to ask questions, no matter that the last situation he'd heckled me about had been resolved.

Still, I didn't know for sure why they had come. I assumed they were looking into Ada's murder, since they were detectives and had investigated the last murder in town. But even so, what would have brought them to my shops?

I tamped down my speculations about Neal and even about Janelle. Good thing I was the one currently staffing Icing, since I didn't want them confronting Dinah, and certainly not Vicky. My assistants were both in the Barkery now.

The bell that always rang when someone came in the door had given me the impression of a death knell — although the death it harbingered was more my peace of mind than anything else. From what I'd heard, Ada was already deceased.

Drawing my eyes away from the detectives for the moment, I finished waiting on the only customers in the shop: a woman with a toddler attempting to exit his stroller. "May I give your little guy a butter cookie?" I asked. "And would you like one, too?"

The woman agreed to both with a smile. She appeared happy as she paid and left Icing with a box of cupcakes.

Then I looked again at my visitors, who both took a few steps forward to face me across the counter. "Hi," I said, feigning cheerfulness. "What kinds of sweets are you looking for today?"

"Not sweets," Bridget corrected, crossing her arms as she regarded me. "We're looking for information."

"I can't guarantee I have any of that," I said. "Cupcakes are a better bet. I've just gotten some of our favorites, red velvet, out of the oven." I gestured toward them in the glass-fronted case as if I were a TV hostess on a game show. "Or would you prefer scones?"

"We'd prefer your telling us what you heard last night at the Knobcone Heights Resort bar." Wayne's voice was flat yet insistent. His arms were crossed, too.

They clearly wanted to be in control.

"Oh, the usual," I began. "There were a lot of people there. And a celebration was going on."

"Yes, tell us about that," Bridget said.

I leaned forward slightly against the counter, buying myself a little time. Without thinking about it, I'd boxed myself into a corner of sorts by mentioning the celebration — since it had gone woefully awry. And its existence had led, at least somewhat, to the verbal altercation between Ada and Janelle.

Well, heck. I had no intention of obstructing justice, whatever justice might be in this situation. Maybe by telling what little I knew I might even be able to protect Neal a bit, help him keep his distance from the events.

"The celebration was about a dog," I said, then stopped. They could ask me questions, and those questions might tell me how much they knew.

"Which is why you're involved." I didn't

like Wayne's smirk but couldn't do anything about it.

"Exactly," I admitted.

"So tell us about that dog," he prompted.

"It's a happy story about a really pretty black Lab." I smiled back at him but said nothing else.

"And what happened to that black Lab?" Wayne's tone no longer sounded as pleasant.

Well, what the heck. That part of the story was the good part.

I took a deep breath, then briefly told them how I had inadvertently, yet happily, reunited Janelle with her dog Go — or so it appeared — while visiting Mountaintop Rescue. "She was absolutely thrilled, and the interaction between her and the dog made me feel certain he was the pup who'd been stolen from her," I said. Almost certain, at least.

"By Ada Arnist?" Bridget asked in a pleasant tone. Her smile wasn't a smirk, but I still didn't trust it.

"I have no idea," I said. "It seemed like an amazing coincidence that Janelle would have come so far away to try to deal with her pain about losing the dog, only to find him here. I have no explanation for it." And I wouldn't speculate, not to these two.

"But you were there at that celebration when Ms. Blaystone confronted Ms. Arnist, weren't you?"

"Well . . . yes." I stared around them, hoping for a customer or two to walk in the door. I really didn't want to talk about this part of the story. But for the moment, Icing's only visitors were these two. Maybe I could somehow get Dinah or Vicky to come in here — but even if ESP worked, which I completely doubted, I really didn't want them involved.

"And what was your impression of that conversation?" pressed Bridget.

"I didn't understand it." I realized I probably sounded grumpy and continued more calmly. "In any case, if I said anything at all about it now, it would be speculation, and that won't help you figure out what happened, will it? You couldn't use it against anyone you decide to accuse of the murder."

"The murder," Bridget repeated. "Then you have heard what happened?"

"Only somewhat." I again wished that I could just walk away. "I heard that Ada Arnist apparently drowned last night and that some people are speculating it might not have been accidental. But that's all."

"A celebration gone bad thanks to a strange argument, and an apparent homicide soon thereafter? Don't parts of that sound familiar to you?"

In a way, they did. Myra Ethman had been murdered after she and I had argued at the opening party for my shops. But their mentioning this was a good thing, at least in a way.

"Yes," I agreed, "it does sound familiar. But if you're reminding me about what happened the last time, let me remind you, too, that the obvious conclusion isn't always the right one."

"Oh, and who do you think is the obvious suspect here, Carrie?" Bridget asked.

I rolled my eyes. "I don't care to speculate, detectives. Do you?"

"Oh, I think you've got the same idea that we do," Wayne said with that smirk back on his face. "And just because what was obvious last time turned out not to be the case, remember, we conduct a lot of investigations — and most of the time, what appears to be the truth is, in fact, the truth."

I looked from his gleaming eyes into those of his commanding officer, whose expression was much too similar.

Oh, Janelle, I thought. *I hope you have a good way of proving where you were last night.*

But if she did, would they then focus their suspicions on Neal?

Nine

"Hi, Carrie," said Reed's voice as I lifted my cell phone to my ear. To my surprise, I smiled. Or maybe I wasn't surprised. Reed provided a hint of sanity in this increasingly insane day.

I was back in the kitchen attempting to catch my breath, hoping to rid my mind of the panic and concern the detectives' visit had stirred up in me — which was partly thanks to my recollections of the last times they'd hounded me here.

But not entirely. Like it or not, I was involved in another murder, or it seemed that way.

At least the detectives had finally left. I'd wanted to run right into the Barkery to hug Biscuit for moral support. But I'd heard voices there, figured my assistants were inside with some customers, and didn't want to see anyone — or have them see me, not just yet. I assumed I looked awful.

Instead, I'd come in here.

As I'd been leaning on the mid-kitchen counter, my cell phone had rung. And now I managed to speak brightly. "Hi, Reed. How are things at the clinic today?" My next shift wasn't till tomorrow, unfortunately; a visit there might also have helped to lift my crumbling spirits.

"Just fine. Look, I — I've heard some things and want to know . . . I mean, are you aware —"

It wasn't like Reed to stammer, but I realized he was doing so out of a desire to protect me. If I somehow didn't know what was going on, he didn't want to hit me over the head with it.

Sweet guy.

"I assume you're referring to Ada Arnist," I broke in. "I really don't know what happened to her, although my buddies the police detectives were just here asking questions that made me figure they thought otherwise. All I know is what I've heard — that she was found in Knobcone Lake this morning, and she seemed to have drowned near the resort. And, before you ask, yes, I've heard rumors that she had some bruising or whatever that could indicate it was murder, not an accident."

A nearby sound startled me and I looked

up. I'd been staring at one of the wooden surfaces we used to roll dough on, on the Icing side. Now, glancing up, I saw that Dinah and Vicky had entered the kitchen and stood near the door into the Barkery. They both stared at me, eyes large and interested and curious. Vicky had the same expression as Dinah, so I assumed that the two had been discussing the situation — hopefully with no customers present.

"I need to run," I told Reed.

"Fine. Me too. But are Biscuit and you available to join Hugo and me for dinner tonight?"

"Absolutely," I breathed. The idea sounded like a lifebuoy thrown at me to save my sanity.

Bad analogy, I realized immediately, considering how Ada had died.

"We'll talk later, decide where to go."

We said goodbye, and I hung up.

I stood up straighter, needing at least to act around my employees as if I was okay. "I guess you heard what I was talking about with Reed."

"What else would you be discussing?" Dinah spoke first. "We were waiting on some customers in the Barkery and when they left, I watched out the window and happened to see those two cops leave Icing.

Were they asking you questions this time, too?"

Dinah had been one of my assistants when I was interrogated after the last murder. And with her glistening blue eyes wide and focused on me, I could almost see her mind churning away. Had she already come up with some kind of related story plot?

"I think they're trying to talk to everyone who was at the resort bar last night," I said. "Ada was there."

"Alive?" Vicky's black eyebrows were arched high above her deep brown eyes, enough to be seen over the tops of her thick glasses. She wasn't my prettiest helper but she was smart, planned things well, and knew the retail business. She was mid-thirties and new to Knobcone Heights, although she'd apparently lived in nearby Lake Arrowhead for most of her life. The clothing store she'd worked in for years had closed and she'd wanted to try something different, so here she was. And she'd already started working on the schedule I'd asked her to prepare today.

"Yes," I said. "I don't know how long she was there, let alone what happened to her."

"We can guess part of it," Dinah said. "Or at least what the cops think, after that argument your brother mentioned."

"I'm not guessing anything." I looked from her face to Vicky's and back again. "That's just speculation. What the authorities need is some hard evidence, or eyewitness testimony beyond that argument, or something to really prove, if Ada was murdered, who actually did it." I knew I sounded preachy as I glared at them, but these two hadn't even been around for the argument, let alone anything else connected with what had happened — at least not as far as I knew.

"Oh." Vicky looked down at the floor, clearly uncomfortable.

"Hmmm," Dinah said. "What if the killer was someone like one of us, who didn't even seem to know Ada Arnist? Her family has some connection to this town, though, including that big vacation house. What if —"

"It's fine to plot a book you want to write," I interrupted. "But please do that on your own time. We have some more dog biscuits to bake — ones with cheese."

We actually had plenty, but I hadn't heard the bells in either shop ring and I wanted to get my assistants busy with what they were really supposed to be doing here.

I was sure that, like it or not, I'd be spending too much time myself considering who could have killed Ada.

I was glad when Reed offered to pick Biscuit and me up that evening.

He arrived a little after six, when my shops were closed and my assistants gone for the day. We'd decided to go to Arrowhead Diner, one of our favorite eating places. It was, unsurprisingly, near Lake Arrowhead, a diner car converted long ago into a restaurant. It was a popular family-style restaurant with an outdoor eating arca that welcomed dogs.

It was also a good place to go to flee Knobcone Heights for a while, even though I really liked my town . . . most of the time.

We now sat on the patio in the warm and humid mountain air of a July evening. Our dogs, as always, had gotten along fine in the rear of Reed's sedan on the way here and now both lay under our table, heads up and noses in the air as they took in the scents, sights, and sounds of our surroundings. For the moment, they were the only dogs around, but experience had taught us that canine visitors came and went frequently at this diner.

A server in the standard diner uniform — a green knit shirt with a white, trailer-shaped Arrowhead Diner logo on the chest pocket — came over for drink orders. Needing some bolstering, I chose the same dark beer that Reed chose.

Then we were left alone, if you called being surrounded by other chattering diners alone.

"Are you really okay?" Reed's expression was solemn, his deep brown eyes scanning me as if I was a dog who couldn't verbally answer that kind of question.

Did I feel insulted? Not at all. I knew how much he cared about dogs.

"You asked me that in the car — I don't know — five times? And what did I say then?"

His smile was wry. "I guess your multiple yeses didn't convince me, given how quiet you were. But in some ways — well, I know we had some issues to get past when you were a murder suspect yourself, so maybe I didn't pay enough attention to how you were feeling, but somehow you seem even sadder now."

"Not really. Maybe some of it is reliving what happened before, at least a bit. And . . ." I didn't really want to get into my real fear here, even with Reed. I'd no reason to believe that Neal would harm anyone for any reason, let alone consider killing someone for arguing with a person he was attracted to . . . but the fact that someone might focus on him had continuously crossed my mind, and I was even more terrified for him than I'd been for myself when I'd been a suspect.

Yes, Neal had been a suspect then also, in part because he'd known the murder victim a lot better than I did since she was his boss at the resort. But there'd really been no logical reason for him to have harmed her, except that she'd argued with me, so the police didn't pursue it.

His supposed reason this time was just as illogical, and very similar.

So why was I worrying?

"You're worrying about Neal, aren't you?" Reed's question slammed into my thoughts, and I nearly stood up.

"I thought you were a veterinarian, not a mind-reader," I grumbled.

He laughed just as our server placed our drinks in front of us — plus a bowl of water on the patio for the dogs. The guy then took our orders. I chose a small steak, mostly because of my lack of hunger. If I didn't finish it, Reed might — and if he didn't, Biscuit and Hugo definitely would.

When the server left again, I waited a few seconds, listening to the undercurrent of conversations from the many tables around us. I couldn't make out what anyone was talking about, so I hoped no one would be able to eavesdrop on us, either.

"You're right about my concern for Neal," I finally said after taking a long swig of beer. "And as I think I told you, I've hired Janelle as a part-time employee at my shops, too. I don't know her well, and neither does my brother despite his attraction to her. I like her so far, but I don't like the fact she decided to throw a party, then made accusations and threatened one of the people who came to it. Does that make her a murderer? No. But —"

"But it does make her a possible murder suspect." Reed nodded, then sipped his own beer. "And now you, and your brother, are connected with her. I get it. I also understand why you're involved, even if you didn't intend to be."

"It's not just Janelle and her connection to Neal," I said. "There's another mystery underlying all this. Assuming that Go really is Janelle's dog, how did he get here? Would she have brought him here herself for some reason? If so, why? And if not, who did — and, also, why?"

Reed's laugh was brief, and the look he leveled on me seemed caring — which warmed me more than the evening air. "I know you well enough, Carrie Kennersly, to believe that figuring out the mystery surrounding that dog is even more important to you than getting the murder solved, as long as your brother's protected."

I smiled back. "Am I that obvious?"

"You're that much of a dog lover."

Takes one to know one, I thought, but kept it to myself.

We tacitly decided to change the subject then. Or at least we didn't talk more about the apparent murder or who the suspects might be or even about my brother.

Our dinners were soon served. Sure enough, despite getting some of my appetite back, I didn't feel hungry enough to finish my food — which made the two dogs beneath our table very happy. The steak was delicious enough for me to feel comfortable feeding them table scraps, and I gave Reed a couple of healthy bites, too.

That meant everyone was happy. We two humans were even smiling at each other — a lot — for the rest of the meal and as we left.

In the parking lot, we first walked the dogs just a little to make sure they'd be okay on the ride back to Knobcone Heights. Then Reed opened the back door of his car for them to jump in.

I'd reached for the handle of the passenger door in the front but he rushed around me, beating me to it — and using the opportunity to pull me closer so we could have one great kiss — the sexiest we'd ever indulged in.

"I don't suppose that you'd want to stop at my place for a while," he said against my mouth. "Another drink, some music, some discussion about dogs . . . or whatever."

It was finally time.

After all that had been going on, and to help bolster my wavering state of mind, I thought that dessert, or whatever, would be a great idea.

"I suppose that I do," I said with a smile.

Ten

Biscuit and I returned home in the wee hours of the morning. I didn't see Neal but figured he was in bed.

Good. I didn't really want to talk about my evening — even though I was having a hard time thinking about anything else. Although with the exercise I'd gotten, I assumed I'd sleep well.

I was right. But even so, I had no trouble waking on time to head to the shops. And despite my mind being focused on Reed, I realized that, in some ways, nothing had changed. We were definitely physically closer, and in the beginning of a relationship, but that was all. For now, at least. No discussions about the future, except looking forward to seeing each other more in the clinic . . . and elsewhere.

Good thing Janelle had been scheduled to come in at six a.m. that morning to learn more about how to bake for both shops. She would be a great diversion — assuming she showed up. With all that had been happening in her life, I anticipated a phone call to tell me she was going to be late, if she was coming in at all.

She might be under suspicion. Maybe even under arrest, although surely word would have gotten out about that if it was the case. But in any event, she might not want to be anywhere in public till the situation played out.

To my surprise, though, she arrived a few minutes early, opening the rear door from the parking lot with her new key. "Good morning, Carrie," she called. "Can you let me into the Barkery? I have Go with me again today and I'll want to leave him there with Biscuit while I work."

I was glad she'd remembered our no-dogs-in-the-kitchen rule. "Sure," I said. "Head toward the front and I'll meet you there."

When I opened the door, Go first came over to me and sniffed my outstretched hand. "Good to see you, boy," I said. By that time Biscuit, still loose since we hadn't yet opened, had joined us and was jumping around on the tile floor, her fuzzy golden coat a contrast to Go's straight black fur.

Go turned and looked at her, and they

traded sniffs. All was fine between them.

And the humans? I hadn't spoken with Janelle yesterday so I wasn't sure how much she knew, but I figured that, since the cops had been here, they'd spoken with her, too.

"So how are you?" I began without explaining why I asked. If she knew what had happened with Ada, she'd easily be able to guess that.

"Pretty much okay." Janelle certainly looked okay. Better than okay. She was definitely a pretty woman when she wasn't hurting over the loss of her dog. Her blue eyes sparkled and her pink, glossy lips kept smiling, revealing her white teeth. I'd already given her a green Barkery and Biscuits T-shirt, and she wore it now over beige jeans and her regular purple athletic shoes.

"But if you're asking whether I know what happened to Ada, yes, I heard," she continued. "And some detectives came to our hotel room yesterday and questioned both Delma and me about my argument with Ada at the bar, and our whereabouts that night and all that."

"I don't suppose either of you killed her, did you?" I'd pasted a big, sarcastic smile on my face to hopefully make it appear that

I was kidding — even though I wasn't. Not entirely.

"Not hardly," she said, laughing lightly. "Hey, I know we need to get some more baking in. I'll attach Go's leash to Biscuit's crate, like before, and we can go back into the kitchen and talk."

I should have been the one to say that, but one way or another that's what we needed to do. "We can leave the dogs loose for another forty-five minutes or so," I told her, "as long as the outside door's locked." I checked to confirm that it was, then we both patted our dogs in brief goodbyes and went into the kitchen.

I gestured for Janelle to follow me to the large sink against the wall near the door from the Barkery. There, we both stood washing our hands for a good, long time before we started touching ingredients.

I wasn't about to waste this opportunity. "So tell me," I said, loudly enough to be heard over the gushing stream of water. "Do you know anything about —"

"Ada's death? Only what I heard." She looked straight at me, her light brown hair skimming her shoulders as she shook her head. "It's really terrible, and I understand why the people who heard me confront her at the bar could wonder if I had anything to do with it. But I didn't." She stopped scrubbing, rinsed her hands, and reached for a paper towel from the roll hung on the wall beside the sink. I did the same.

"Of course not," I said, hoping that was true, "but —"

Once again she interrupted me. "And you're one of those people who wonders. I get it, Carrie. I was there and heard myself threaten her." Her grin disappeared and the expression that replaced it reminded me of when she'd first told me about her loss of Go. "I'm trying to put on a good front, even though I'm worried. Of course I am. I threatened the woman, and then she was found dead. I'm not surprised I'm a suspect. But, honestly, that rant got my animosity out of my system."

"Really?" I didn't mean to say anything, but that made no sense to me.

"Really. Look, I'll explain, but let's get some baking started, shall we? I don't want to focus on this any more than I have to."

Once more she was right. I'd already started gathering the ingredients for carob and oatmeal dog cookies, and I waved for her to follow me to the counter on the Barkery side. There, I showed her the recipe and we began measuring and mixing the fixings.

Once we'd gotten it into dough form, I

glanced at Janelle, wondering if she really intended to explain what she'd just said.

Her smile returned, although a bit half-hearted. "Okay, here's what I meant," she said. "I'd had Go back for a day before that confrontation. I was so relieved. So happy. Really intended to celebrate with everyone that night. But I'd come here, to Knobcone Heights, because I'd seen Ada Arnist at the dog parks I'd visited, those where dogs had disappeared. She'd bragged so much about her family home up here, and when Go was dognapped — well, I admit I jumped to hasty conclusions about her, especially after I heard rumors about her financial situation. But it's not like I received a ransom demand or anything, even though some people whose dogs were stolen did. I realized, once I got here, how unlikely it was that Ada would be involved just because I'd run into her often. But then I saw her here and she saw me, and when Go showed up at the shelter, my first reaction was to assume I'd been right in the first place. Was I positive about it? No, but it definitely seemed possible. I assumed she'd dropped Go off at the shelter so I wouldn't spot her with him."

She paused, seeming to concentrate on kneading the dough on the wooden board ahead of her. I glanced her way, inhaling deeply and trying not to be tempted by the cinnamon aroma wafting over from some Icing treats now baking in the oven. "I can understand that," I prompted. "And so even though you got your dog back, you still felt angry. So you confronted Ada."

"Yes." Janelle stopped her kneading and looked back at me. "Sort of. Despite how it probably looked, I wasn't really angry anymore. I was relieved. But I knew not everyone who'd lost their best friends that way would feel the same. So, just in case it really was Ada who'd been doing some dognappings, I attacked her — but only verbally. Honest. And once I'd gotten it off my chest, I can't tell you how happy I felt — and even more relieved, and as if I'd done complete strangers a big favor by warning this woman against ever doing such a terrible thing again. Assuming, of course, she'd done it in the first place. I'm just sorry I stomped out of there for effect. I didn't even see Neal again that night, or he'd have been able to vouch for my complete change in mood once that was out of my system."

Not to mention act as her potential alibi. But I didn't suggest that, either.

Still, I did think that what she'd said made sense. And why kill Ada after she had gotten her dog back? It would seem more likely that someone whose dog was still gone, and who now suspected Ada after hearing Janelle's accusations, would confront and kill her.

"I get it," I said. "I just hope everyone else who saw you there understands."

She stopped kneading and looked at me again, her head tilted and her lips taut with irony. "I haven't told everyone else, of course. And when I told all this to the two detectives, they listened and nodded and took notes and probably recorded what I said. Then they left without arresting me. But did they believe me?" She shook her head slowly. "I doubt it. I'm afraid I'll see them again, and they'll have more than questions next time."

I couldn't disagree with her, but I hoped, for her sake, that she was wrong. Been there, done that. At least in my case, the truth had finally come out that I definitely wasn't a murderer. Who knew what would happen to Janelle — or whether she was, in fact, telling the truth?

We both got back into baking after that. I pondered what she'd said even more as I rolled the dough out and used some cookie cutters in the shape of dog heads to form the biscuits. Did it make sense? Sure. Did I believe it?

I wanted to . . . for Neal's sake as much as anything. Assuming he still was interested in this woman who could change moods so quickly. And assuming the cops weren't focusing on him.

Personally, I was beginning to really like Janelle. She seemed to be a good bakery assistant and more. And as much as I hated the idea of a murder having occurred, whether or not she was guilty, her outburst might have prevented further doggy kidnappings — at least if Ada had in fact been guilty and was killed by someone else who was angry with her for what she'd supposedly done.

For now, I'd keep an open mind — and an open door for Janelle as one of my helpers.

I had a shift at the vet clinic that afternoon and left early for it. I'd been thinking too much about murder and Janelle and Neal and doggy kidnappings. I needed to spend some time with caring people who had nothing to do with any of that.

Especially, hopefully, with Reed.

Biscuit and I headed to Cuppa-Joe's first, though, where I'd have lunch and coffee and my pup would have water, attention, and treats. Cuppa-Joe's was on Peak Road, at the far side of the town square from where my shops were located on Summit Avenue. It was owned by two people I adored, who were almost like substitute parents to me, and to Neal, too: Joe and Irma Nash, both great-looking seniors who were highly active running their family restaurant.

When Biscuit and I arrived and sat down at a table on the busy patio, the first person who came to greet us was server Kit, wearing her usual large, toothy smile. "Hi, Carrie. Hi, Biscuit." My pup stood and wagged her tail, but wisely Kit didn't pat her or she'd have had to wash her hands again. Like the rest of the wait staff, this young server wore a knit shirt with buttons and a collar, with a steaming coffee cup logo on the pocket. Today's shirt was red, but as with all the other servers, I'd seen Kit in lots of different colors.

"Hi, Kit. Are the Joes here?" That was the nickname given to the Nashes by a lot of their customers, including me, punning on how Joe's name was also a slang term for "coffee."

"They sure are. I'll let them know you're here. Would you like your usual?"

"Yes, please." These days I sometimes had

a hamburger with a cup of vegetable soup, along with my coffee. That gave me a meat treat I could pass portions of to Biscuit, while also feeling that I was indulging in something healthy and more sensible for myself.

"Great. I'll bring your soup now."

Before Kit returned, both Joe and Irma came out of the restaurant door, huge smiles on their faces. Joe, with his gray hair, receding hairline, and deep facial divots, appeared like the sixty-something guy he was, but Irma, who was around his age, kept her hair stylishly cut and a gray-free brown, and her mostly unlined face made up like a model's. They, too, wore Cuppa-Joe's knit shirts, both black.

"Carrie, welcome!" Irma bent down to kiss my cheek. "And you, too, Biscuit." She didn't hesitate to hug my pup, but she wasn't handling food.

Joe did the same, and Biscuit responded happily with licks and a frantically wagging tail.

Joe straightened up first. "Good to see both of you," he said. Without asking, he circled the crowded patio and dragged another empty chair over to my table. He and Irma sat down and smiled at me.

"Hi to both of you, too," I said. "Everything okay around here?" I looked around at the busy eating area and assumed it was.

"Sure is. And with you?" Irma leaned across the table toward me. "I don't suppose you're involved with that latest murder that I heard about, are you? I heard it had something to do with a dog."

My dear friends knew me very well. "Not exactly," I hedged, but that was enough to set them off.

"Then how?" Joe asked, as Kit came over with a tray containing my soup as well as three cups of coffee. She set one in front of each of us.

The conversations of other diners surrounding us gave me hope I wouldn't be overheard, but I nevertheless looked around and made sure no one nearby was sitting alone and unoccupied. Then I proceeded to give them the highlights of how I was remotely involved, including Neal's interest in the young lady who'd found her missing dog and threatened the murder victim about it.

"Wow." Joe shook his head when I'd finished, taking a sip of coffee as if it was something stronger. He regarded me with brown eyes set into folds on his face that were nevertheless astute and intense. "And you want to help clear her? You do have some experience in such things."

"I did get questioned already by my detective buddies from before, and I also hired Janelle as a part-time assistant at my stores, but —"

"But, yes, you'll try to figure out the truth, for Janelle and for Neal," Irma said. "And undoubtedly for her dog, too, to make sure that the found pup still has his family. Am I right?"

Both of the Joes regarded me with hints of smiles and deep interest on their faces, as if the answer I'd give would be an earthshaking pronouncement.

"Yes," I said with a sigh. "You're right."

Eleven

So much for attempting to get my mind far away from the latest murder situation. *But my friends brought it up to me,* I thought as Biscuit and I left Cuppa's.

At least it had kept any smile off my face that might have given away to those dear and insightful people the other situation that was filling my mind . . . Reed.

And I didn't have to dwell on the murder, either. I had work to do — in my other profession.

A short while later, Biscuit and I arrived at the Knobcone Veterinary Clinic. It was a block behind the town square that my shops fronted, but close to it nevertheless, so it remained convenient to all townies who needed veterinary care for their beloved family members. It even looked attractive enough for the most elite townsfolk to feel comfortable frequenting it, designed to resemble a textured, blue Swiss chalet with a tall, sloped roof and a comfortable front porch where people and pets waiting for appointments could stay for a while, as long as the weather was good — as it was that day.

At the rear was the door to the doggy daycare facility, where I always left Biscuit while on duty as a vet tech. It, too, was comfortable, with a large area where dogs could hang out together as long as they got along well, but the walls were lined with crates for those too nervous or too belligerent to indulge in games and sniffs together.

The chief daycare manager, Faye, was busy talking with a person holding a pug at the reception counter when Biscuit and I walked in, so I edged up to one of the regular workers, Al, who stood near the edge of the room observing the dogs at play. His usual counterpart, Charlie, wasn't far away, but appeared to be cleaning up someone's accident.

Both were college students who worked here when they could, which would help them decide whether or not to go on to veterinary school. As always, both wore red shirts that said Knobcone Vets Rock over their jeans.

Al grinned toothily as I handed him Biscuit's leash. He was short-haired, tall, and strong enough to wrangle ill-mannered larger dogs. I'd seen him in action. "What's her — er, your — schedule today, Carrie?"

"My shift's for three hours," I told him. "So Biscuit's in charge now."

"Got it." Al bent to pick up my dog and give her a big hug. "So, Biscuit, do you want to play first or sleep?"

I left my pup in his good hands, knowing he would listen to whichever she chose. I slipped through the inside door and into the hallway to the clinic. There, I clocked in and headed for the dressing room to grab my blue vet tech scrubs and put them on, leaving my other clothes in my locker. Then I hurried to the central area where I was given my first assignment of the day by the chief vet, my dear friend and mentor Arvie. I was to help him spay a year-old husky mix.

I kept my eyes open for Reed, but learned he was busy with a dental procedure, and another vet tech was helping him. So, I hurried to join Arvie.

Like my other senior friends the Nashes, Arvie was in his sixties. He had gray hair. "You ready to work?" he asked me, his expression serious. But I knew he was just joking. He knew me well enough to realize I was always ready to work, both here and at my stores. He was one really good guy, not to mention a wonderful, caring vet.

"Gee, do I have to?" I whined, then laughed. "Let's do it, boss."

The day progressed well after that. I helped to give shots to some cats as well as dogs, then got to assist Reed in another neutering. Considering our increasing attraction for one another, especially after the night before, the looks we gave each other during noncritical parts of that procedure consisted of eye rolls and teasing grins.

I wasn't the only tech on duty that day. There were several of us, in fact, but it was Yolanda I was working with when an owner brought two dogs into our crowded reception area.

That owner looked familiar, and I realized he was Tim something, who had been at Janelle's non-celebration party at the bar. Ada had said he lived somewhere locally, but this was the first time I recalled seeing him come in with his pets. Since I wasn't at the clinic all the time, though, it could have been one of many visits for all I knew.

His dogs both appeared to be purebreds, although not the same breed. One was an English bulldog, and the other a schnauzer, and they had injuries that suggested they'd gotten into a fight.

The receptionist for the day took one look

at them and told us to immediately take the dogs to the back for treatment.

"Are they both yours?" I asked Tim as Yolanda and I approached him.

"Yes."

"Then do they fight often?"

He shook his head, his brown eyes, still sunken into his long face, large and sad. "No. Never before. But I guess they both wanted the same bone this time. Are they going to be okay?"

"We'll take care of them," was all I said. I thought so, of course, but no guarantees. "What are their names?"

I carried Waldo, the schnauzer, from our reception area, already examining the teeth marks around his neck. Yolanda had immediately picked up Butch, the bulldog, whose injuries appeared to be all over his body. Since Yolanda and I weren't the best of buddies, I wondered whether I should have tried to get the more difficult dog to carry first, to ease some tension between us.

As always, I thought Yolanda's uniform looked in better condition than mine — newer and crisper. She was dark-complected, with black hair that was pulled as always into a bun at the back of her neck. She was a good vet tech. She also carried grudges, valid or not. She'd been angry with me a while back because of a situation at the clinic that had appeared to be of my making, during the time when I was also a murder suspect. Even after I was cleared, she never seemed to get back to the same minor degree of friendliness that we'd previously shared.

But we still had to work together. And I could at least admire her caring and efficiency around animals.

"You take Waldo to Dr. Jensin," she ordered. "I'll take Butch to Dr. Regles.

That sounded fine to me, so even though I wasn't used to taking orders from Yolanda, I did so now.

Both Dr. Paul Jensin and Dr. Angela Regles were senior vets who, though younger than Arvie, had been around here equally long and had helped to found the Knobcone Veterinary Clinic. Paul was tall, thin, and rather gaunt-looking, but although he kept his face fairly expressionless when talking to people, particularly when imparting a dire diagnosis, he always smiled at the pets and even talked baby talk to them.

"Who's this?" he demanded, immediately after walking through the back door into the examination room into which I'd brought Waldo.

I introduced him to the injured schnauzer,

who wagged his tail slowly, as though every movement hurt. The vet started examining, then cleaning the injuries. Since Tim hadn't come in here with this dog, I assumed he'd gone with Yolanda and Butch.

It appeared that, despite their bloodiness, the injuries weren't too deep and just required cleaning and bandaging, plus an antibiotic to prevent infection. Then we were through.

Something struck me, though, as I assisted my vet in taking care of the dog. Tim had apparently been a friend of Ada's. I'd no reason to think he had anything against her, of course. But what if Janelle had been right in the first place and Ada had dognapped Go? The two dogs Tim brought in might not be purebreds, of course, even though that was how they appeared. But out of curiosity . . .

When Paul told me to take Waldo back out to the reception area, I agreed — but instead of taking him straight out there I headed for one of the other nearby rooms, where we kept one of the clinic's microchip sensors. I turned it on and waved it along Waldo's back.

Yes, the dog was chipped. But the information on the electronic read-out was just gibberish. Billi had told me there'd been a similar problem here at the clinic reading the chip in the dog believed to be Go. Was there something wrong with the our scanner? But the same thing had happened at Mountaintop Rescue.

I headed back into the hallway and was glad to see Yolanda coming down it with Butch on a leash at her side — but Tim, the owner, wasn't with her, either. That also made me somewhat suspicious of him.

"Could you come in here?" I asked Yolanda. "There's something we need to check. It's in the dogs' best interests." I figured that would get her to listen to me a lot better than if I just insisted or said it was something I wanted. We traded dogs and I had her keep Waldo close to her, although the two dogs appeared to have entered into a truce even if they'd fought hard before.

Sure enough, Butch, too, was chipped, and his chip was also unreadable.

"Thanks," I said to Yolanda. "I'd really appreciate it if you let me take them both back to the owner." That way I didn't have to beg her not to mention the chip discrepancy.

Fortunately, Arvie came into the room just then and said he needed one of us right away. Yolanda didn't bother looking at me before volunteering.

That might have irritated me under other circumstances — and, in fact, it wasn't the first time, and it usually did bother me. Not this time, though.

I just watched them leave, then carefully took the two dogs back to the reception room, keeping one on each side of me. Fortunately, they continued to ignore each other.

Tim stood up as we entered and rushed to us. "Are they okay?"

"They'll be fine as long as they don't start fighting again," I said.

"Of course. And will they be scarred?"

"Possibly."

I watched him head to the receptionist to pay. Still holding onto the leashes while he was distracted, I knelt on the floor and hugged the dogs, one at a time.

"I wish you could tell me whether you're really his dogs and why you were fighting," I whispered so no one in the still-crowded room could hear me. But I knew there was something I could follow up on while I was here — nothing definitive, but something that might nevertheless be interesting.

I soon turned both dogs over to Tim and watched him help them into his car. They seemed almost to ignore one another now

— which boded well in terms of fighting.

When he drove away, I went down the hall, away from the reception area, and pulled my cell from my pocket and called Janelle.

"Can you tell me who Go's vet is in LA?"

"Sure, but why —"

"Just a question I wanted to ask them." So much for being casual and finding the right time to ask her. *This* was the right time.

Without hesitation, Janelle told me. After hanging up, I checked on the office computer to get the phone number of the place. I called and acted very serious and concerned, saying I was a veterinary technician here in Knobcone Heights and a dog named Go had been brought in by his owner Janelle Blaystone, and so forth. I was able to answer questions that helped to verify I was who I said I was. I said that Janelle had approved my call — and I was sure she would say she had, if they checked with her — and asked for information related to any treatment of Go. Medical privacy might not be quite as strong in veterinary practice as it is with human doctors, but there are definitely restrictions.

I was able to get the LA clinic to tell me about Go: that he had been neutered, what his weight was, and that he'd been brought in once for an abscess on his right rear leg, near the top of his thigh. Its removal had left a scar.

I thanked them profusely and said it was useful to know whether Go might be prone to developing abscesses. I fortunately didn't need to explain any further.

But I now knew that I had to examine the black Lab Janelle said was Go . . . and see if he had a scar on the inside of his right thigh.

Fortunately, my shift was nearly over. I only had another half hour there, which was quickly taken up by yet another set of inoculations, this time on a Shih Tzu who hadn't had any shots for more than a year.

Then it was almost time to leave. I first waited for Arvie to finish his latest exam and said goodbye, confirming that he was okay with my next shift being in two days.

Next I waited to say goodbye to Reed. We grinned at one another and made plans to meet for dinner at my house that night.

Finally, I went to pick up Biscuit at the doggy daycare room, and we walked quickly back to the shops.

I passed the Icing window first and looked in, seeing Dinah there along with Vicky, and both were busy with customers. Biscuit and I entered the shops by the Barkery door.

Janelle was there waiting on a customer with a Westie.

Biscuit traded nose sniffs with the visitor dog first, then headed over to where Go was leashed to the crate. I followed her, patted Go's head, and then pushed him slightly so he rolled onto his back for a tummy rub.

This way, I was able to see the inside of his thigh.

His black fur was thick, though not so much on that part of his legs. I was able to sweep it back . . .

. . . and saw a round, pinkish scar, right where the person I'd spoken with from Go's vet clinic had said it would be.

Now I was convinced.

"You're a good dog, Go," I said.

TWELVE

"Is Go all right?" Janelle — whose customer was reaching into her purse, presumably searching for the means to pay for her dog treats — had slipped around the counter toward us.

"He's fine." I gestured with my glance back toward the lady with the Westie. "We'll talk later."

Maybe. Did I want to reveal my thoughts to my new assistant?

Did I even know what those thoughts were? Or how they might, or might not, relate to what had happened to Ada Arnist?

But circumstances in the shop suddenly began to tell me I needed to take Biscuit out again, right away, and allow Janelle and Go to accompany us. Although a new set of customers — a family consisting of a mother, ten-year-or-so-old son, and a middle-sized mixed breed light brown dog — entered the Barkery, so did Dinah, from

Icing. "Vicky's got things going just fine in there," my full-time assistant said, gesturing with her head in the direction of Icing. Without asking, she approached our newcomers with a big smile and an offer to assist them in picking out the best treats ever for their pup.

At the same time, Biscuit surprisingly started pawing at the thick plastic frame of her enclosure, usually an indication she wanted to go outside, even though I'd just put her in there.

It wouldn't hurt to take Go out, either. I mentioned the possibility to Janelle, who seemed both pleased and relieved. "Yes," she said. "It's been a while since I've had him out."

I grabbed some biodegradable plastic bags from behind the counter in case our dogs did something we'd need to pick up, and then we hurried outside with them. In a minute, there we were, with both dogs leashed and walking ahead of us along the sidewalk.

"Let's go across the street to the town square," I suggested, since it was a good place to walk dogs on gentle hills and along grass beneath — what else? — knobcone pine trees. Janelle was fine with that.

The day was warm, but overcast and

muggy, and I wondered if we'd get some rain. Not many people were on the side-walks, but the park was crowded with kids and pets.

As we crossed the street, I noticed a guy standing alone. As with Tim, I recognized him from the party at the resort bar. What was his name? Gary? Garvy?

At the bar, I'd thought he was flirting with me, but maybe I'd just imagined that. In any case, I didn't need to talk with him again, so I steered Janelle and our dogs toward another part of the square.

"Tell me what you were doing with Go," Janelle insisted. "And why you needed his real vet's name. You're a vet tech. Do you think something's wrong with him?" Her tone was urgent, and I hated for her to be worried about a nonexistent health issue.

But did I want to tell her I'd been attempting to find a way to prove to myself whether she was lying or telling the truth about this dog she'd claimed was hers? Not especially. Particularly not now, when I was convinced she'd been truthful.

Which of course brought up all those other issues I'd been contemplating — such as whether or not Janelle currently believed that Ada had dognapped Go. And since she'd come to town assuming that Ada might be here with Go, at the Arnist family home, had she also had a plan to get her dog back?

But she'd gotten her dog back by accident.

None of this meant she'd hurt Ada, of course. Maybe, as she'd said, she'd just decided to issue a warning to Ada and anyone else who might consider hurting others by stealing their beloved dogs.

The core issue for me had been the beautiful black Lab's real identity, and now I felt confident that no matter what else Janelle might have been thinking or feeling, she was right about that.

I turned away from where our two dogs were sniffing the turf and relieving themselves. I needed to reassure Janelle. "As far as I can tell, Go is fine. And," I added, "he is Go."

"Then you contacted his vet to check up on me?" Janelle's face, so pretty and calm now, squeezed up a bit as if I'd hurt her feelings.

"Well —" I really hated to admit it, but —

"Hi," came a male voice from behind us. For a moment, I felt relieved at the interruption.

Until I turned and saw it was the man who'd been standing on the corner, the one

I'd recognized.

"Hi," I returned unenthusiastically, then continued walking with Biscuit, gesturing with my head slightly to encourage Janelle to join us with Go.

"We met at the resort bar the other night," the guy continued. "And, well, forgive me for being nosy, but I was told you own that great couple of shops across the street, those two bakeries."

If I'd been concerned he was flirting, now I was sure of it. I wasn't particularly pleased, especially when he hurried ahead and planted himself in our path. It didn't matter, on the negative side, that he was ten or more years my senior, or, on the positive side, that he was a good-looking man. I just wasn't interested.

Not with Reed and me getting closer. I wasn't even about to follow up with the other men who'd seemed inclined to enter my life recently, even when they occasionally called.

Although there was some hint of the debonair about this man. Maybe it was his white shirt and dark trousers, given that he just appeared to be hanging out here, not hurrying off to some kind of meeting like a well-dressed businessman would.

"Like I told you then, my name is Garvy

Grant," he said. "And you're Carrie Kennersly, right?" He didn't wait for my response before saying, "And you're Janelle Blaystone. I was there during your argument with Ada Arnist." His tone was low and sad now. "I heard what happened to her, but from all I've also heard about you, Janelle, I'm sure you didn't do it."

Why didn't I believe him? And why was this guy so insistent on talking to us?

As I attempted to find a polite but unrelenting way to tell him to buzz off, Janelle said softly, "Thank you, Garvy. I appreciate that."

"Are a lot of people giving you a hard time?" he asked. "Just because you argued a little doesn't mean you'd have hurt her. And from what I heard, you were just protecting your beautiful dog there." He moved from his position directly in front of us so he could kneel on the ground and gently wrestle with Go. At the same time, he reached over and patted my little Biscuit on the head. "I certainly understand that," he said. "I love dogs."

Okay, the ice in my heart shouldn't start melting just because this guy professed to love dogs, but somehow I no longer felt as urgent a need to get away from him.

"Yeah, me too," I said. "Do you own a

dog?" If so, I'd invite him across the street to the Barkery to buy some treats.

"Not now." Garvy rose, his expression sad. "Mine recently passed away. I'm taking some time to grieve before I get another."

Now I really felt for the guy. Not that I wanted to get any closer — or flirt with him in response.

That did seem to get Janelle's attention, though. "I'm so sorry," she said, her tone suggesting she really meant it. "Do you live around here, or are you just visiting?"

"Just visiting."

"Well, if you start thinking about getting another dog while you're here, Carrie knows the people at Mountaintop Rescue. You can always go take a look and see if you fall for any of the dogs there." Janelle knelt down beside Go this time and hugged him. "It's where I got my dog back. He'd been missing before."

"That's what you were arguing with Ada about, wasn't it?" Garvy asked. "You thought she had something to do with your dog's disappearance?"

"Well . . ." Janelle was standing again and looked concerned.

As well she might be. I didn't understand, either, why this guy was acting so friendly yet asking so many difficult questions.

Time to interrupt. "Glad you agree that Janelle had nothing to do with what happened to Ada," I said. "But we were just taking a doggy break. We need to get back to our stores." My stores, really, but they were now part of Janelle's life, too.

"That's great," Garvy said. "Let me walk back with you. I unfortunately don't need any dog treats right now, but I've heard really great things about the baked goods at Icing on the Cake. I want to buy some cookies or something. You can advise me on what's best."

"Everything's great," I told him wryly. "But you don't have to come now just because —"

"Oh, I want to."

I tugged gently on Biscuit's leash and saw Janelle do the same with Go. I couldn't really tell this guy not to come to my bakery.

Well, okay, I could, but I chose not to . . . at least for now.

There wasn't a lot of traffic that late afternoon, so we quickly crossed back to the retail side of the street. "We need to put both dogs in the Barkery," Janelle told Garvy. "Then I'll take you next door to Icing and see what people treats look good to you."

"Wonderful!"

Biscuit and I were first to reach the Barkery door. I was delighted, initially, to see that the place was full of people, some with dogs and some without.

I wasn't at all delighted when I saw that two of the dogless folks were my dark-suited detective non-friends, Wayne Crunoll and Bridget Morana.

Or when they immediately made their way through the crowd toward me.

No, toward Janelle. Wayne nodded at me while Bridget didn't even spare me a glance. "Hello, Ms. Blaystone," she said to Janelle. "Would you step outside with us for a few minutes? We have some more questions."

"Oh, I can't possibly spare her," I said hurriedly. "We had to take the dogs out to do . . . well, you know, what dogs do. But you can see how busy we are here. We need to step right in and help the staff members who are waiting on customers."

"We'll only take her away for a few minutes," Wayne said, but the sparkle in his eyes told me that he was hoping she'd confess and they could arrest her right then.

"Can you tell me in just a few words what you want to talk about that we haven't already discussed?" Janelle's voice was higher than usual, but she sounded calm.

"A couple more things have come to mind

about how we can find some of the other people who frequented the dog parks with Ms. Arnist in LA," Bridget said.

"Honestly, I don't know the names of those people. The dogs are another story."

"Well, you can tell us which parks and which dogs," Wayne said. "We'll work it out with the local authorities to visit the individuals or get them to assist, if necessary."

"Can we do it another time?" Janelle asked, catching my eye. "We really are busy here."

"You can visit the station tomorrow," Bridget replied. "Step over here and we'll set up a time."

Before that time, whatever it might be, I'd introduce Janelle to Attorney Ted Culbert. He was one of the men I'd been somewhat avoiding, in the hopes that my relationship with Reed would grow stronger. But he'd been a great help, and given me good advice, when I'd needed some legal assistance of my own.

For now, I walked away as Janelle went into a corner with the detectives, presumably to schedule a time to talk tomorrow.

I glanced around, remembering Garvy. He'd seemed to believe in Janelle. Not that his opinion would matter. But maybe, by bribing him with a free cookie, I could get him to mention to the cops how he'd decided Janelle was innocent despite her argument with Ada — for, no matter what the detectives said, I still believed they were hoping for her to confess.

But when I made my way through the Barkery's crowd, I didn't see Garvy. Of course not. Just being around dogs and dog treats might make the grieving former dog owner feel bad. I headed into Icing.

We had a crowd there, too, whom Vicky was waiting on.

But I didn't see Garvy there, either.

Strange.

Still, I didn't care whether he was around. And I figured I might see him again when he was ready for some baked treats.

THIRTEEN

Speaking of treats, Reed called later that afternoon, interrupting my not-so-deep concentration while I did some accounting in my small office at the back of the kitchen. He reminded me about the dinner plans Biscuit and I had with Hugo and him. I needed something both to distract me from all that was going on and to cheer me up, so I was looking forward to it.

Just after finishing up with an Icing customer, I heard from a clearly dejected Neal. Janelle hadn't answered when he'd called her, nor had she responded to the messages he'd left. I worried that I might have to postpone my plans with Reed.

I told my brother about the visit from the detectives that day and how they had apparently scheduled a time to meet with Janelle tomorrow — along with the fact that I had given Janelle information about the attorney I'd talked to during my own days as a murder suspect. Once Neal had an explanation for her mood, he seemed to feel a little better. When he said his work behind the reception desk at the resort that day would end at five, I told him that Reed was coming over to our place for dinner and that he was invited to join us.

I called Reed back to tell him that Neal would be there as well. "I'll bring Chinese food for all of us," Reed promised.

"Except the dogs," I said. "I'll have food for them."

"Treats, too?"

"Of course."

I considered inviting Janelle also, but I didn't want to do that without checking with Neal first. From what he'd said, she might refuse anyway. Besides, what I really wanted was just to hang out with the two topmost men in my life, along with the dogs. Maybe that was selfish on my part — but I liked the idea of having a dinner with no emotions to deal with except for those related to the two men who'd be there.

When Biscuit and I arrived home around six thirty, Neal was already there and had surprisingly set the kitchen table for the three of us. I'd already walked Biscuit, so I sat down at the table with Neal to await Reed, Hugo, and our food.

"So are you doing better?" I asked my brother. His usually glowing blue eyes looked dull, and he was moving slowly.

He must still be thinking a lot about Janelle — unless the detectives had now also bothered him. Unlikely, though. He'd have mentioned it.

"Kind of," he said. "But, you know, when Elise said she had a couple of guests say they wouldn't mind a hike tomorrow night, I jumped on it."

A hike. Depending on where he would go, that might actually fit really well in the agenda I'd been considering for myself. "Will it be similar to the last one?"

"Sure, it could be. Why? You want to go, too?"

"Yes," I said, without explaining why. But my on and off thoughts about Ada's death — and the dogs — had been tumbling all over the place, and I'd even been coming up with some odd scenarios. As a result, I had an urge to visit the Arnist mansion again just in case that guy Tim was hanging out there by himself. What if those dogs he'd brought to the clinic were like Go, and he and Ada had brought them all to Knobcone Heights after dognapping them? Maybe he and Ada had been staying there, even though the place appeared unoccupied, and now, with her gone, he was still living there? And . . . well, I was jumping to too many conclusions.

But I wanted to reassure myself that the home where Ada had stayed while she was here — and before she'd been murdered — wasn't a hangout now for lost dogs.

If it wasn't, I wanted to track down where Tim was staying with the dogs he'd claimed were his. Unfortunately, I hadn't checked in the clinic files for the address he'd given. Assuming it wasn't the Arnist property, I'd look it up when I went to the clinic the day after tomorrow.

Then I blurted out something I'd been holding inside for a while. "Neal, I have to ask — you seemed so interested, before, in Gwen . . ." My good-looking brother, who'd always had more than his share of dates, had lately been zeroing in on one woman at a time. Maybe he was looking for a real relationship.

"I still like Gwen," Neal said with a wry grin. "But I told you, she said she has a boyfriend somewhere else. So when Janelle appeared in town, I found her really pretty and nice and sad and all."

On top of everything else, Neal was a nice guy. But I hated to see him hurting over either of these women — or anything else, for that matter.

The doorbell rang then. Biscuit stood up and woofed, and I hurried to the front door.

It was Reed, arms laden with plastic bags with the logo of a local Chinese restaurant on them. Hugo was with him, and the two dogs traded their usual nose sniffs as well as butt sniffs.

"Come on in," I said, reaching for one of the bags and smiling at him. "Mmm. Smells good."

"I hope you like what I got," he said.

"Definitely." I kept my voice low as our eyes caught and held in a suggestive gaze.

"I meant food," he finally said, raising his eyebrows.

"Of course." I backed off. After all, he knew that Neal was here, too.

But before Reed could start reeling off the names of the dishes he'd brought, I said, "And I hope you'll be in the mood for another Neal-led hike tomorrow evening."

Fortunately, Reed was. Once more, we'd assembled at the resort — Hugo and Reed, Biscuit and me, and, to my surprise, Janelle and Go.

There were others, too, in athletic gear and carrying backpacks, who were paying the resort and Neal for the experience. They included Garvy Grant, who was dressed now in jeans, a blue Knobcone T-shirt, and large white athletic shoes and looked all prepared to go on an intensive hike.

This was going to be interesting.

But as we started out, walking along the beach as before to circumnavigate the loop around Knobcone Lake, Garvy stayed away from me. Maybe he recognized that I preferred being with Reed.

Janelle and her dog hiked at the front of the group, along with Neal. They'd kissed each other briefly before we started, so hopefully Neal was no longer concerned about how she felt about him. I'd already told Neal part of my purpose for going on this outing, and he was all for it.

Reed and I, and our dogs, stayed beside one another, which made me feel good. He knew I had a hidden agenda for this walk. Plus, we were together.

Janelle hadn't worked at the shops that day, and she'd made it clear, when I'd asked, that her interrogation at the police station hadn't been fun — but she hadn't been arrested, either. And, yes, she'd hired Ted Culbert to be by her side. I was glad that Ted must have adjusted his rates, since I felt certain this photographer, and my part-time employee, didn't have a lot of money to spend on legal fees.

As we hiked, Neal turned often and walked briskly backwards, using his red staff to point out sights along and above the lake as he had before. But I thought he was moving the group more quickly, since it didn't take long for us to reach the residential area across the water from the resort.

Last time, it had been Janelle who'd wanted to scale those elite residential roads. Maybe she did again, although she hadn't mentioned it to me.

This time, I was the one who wanted to check out the Arnist estate. It hadn't been obviously occupied last time, and the most likely scenario now was that it still wouldn't look occupied — since, at the moment, it most likely wasn't.

But to my surprise, when we'd headed up Pine Lane and passed the other large mansions up the hill, then made the turn onto Vistaview Place, the metal gate across the driveway that led to the ornate gray stone house stood open.

Interesting. Was my remote and off-the-wall suspicion true? Had Tim, that guy with the dogs, been living here with Ada and now stayed here alone?

But there was an older couple there, getting out of a new-looking white Mercedes near the house.

Maybe others in the Arnist family had come to town, possibly because of what had happened to Ada.

Clearly I wasn't the only one who was wondering about it. Garvy waved one arm in the air toward the house, then started hurrying through the gate and up the driveway.

"Hey," Neal yelled at him. "Come back here." Hikers were supposed to sightsee on their excursions and not trespass, or that's what I'd understood from Neal.

But Garvy ignored him. And since Neal had all the other hikers to wrangle, I decided to play the helpful big sister. I hastened after Garvy.

Instead of looking grateful, Neal glared at me, too. But I was interested in what was going on. And it was certainly better for me to check things out than for him — or Janelle — to do it. I might get some insight here into what Ada's family believed had happened to her.

Or not. But it wouldn't hurt to find out.

Garvy had reached the couple. "Hello," he said. "Do you live here?"

The man was dressed as nicely as I'd seen Garvy dressed before, but he was at least a couple of decades older, and his shoulders were slumped forward. I guessed he was, in fact, an Arnist, and in mourning.

At Garvy's question, he stood straighter and glared with moist hazel eyes that were partly hidden by age-lined skin folds. "Yes, this is our property. What are you doing here?"

Garvy hung his head, regarding the man from beneath lowered brows. "Then you're related to Ada Arnist," he said quietly. "I'm very sorry for your loss."

The man swallowed. "Thank you." At a quiet wail from the other side of the car, he hurried over and put his arms around the woman who stood there crying. She was probably his age and dressed in a nice, fashionable pants outfit with a white scarf draped around her shoulders and dangling earrings that appeared to be large, appropriately shaped tear-drop diamonds.

Garvy joined them. I stayed in the background, not wanting to interfere — but still interested. "My name is Garvy Grant," he told them. "If there's anything I can do, please let me know. I'm in real estate but I'm here on vacation. I met your daughter and was sorry to hear what happened to her."

The woman's wail grew louder, but the man pulled slightly away, holding out his hand to shake Garvy's. "We're Sheldon and Sondra Arnist." His raspy tone indicated that he, too, was holding back tears. "If this place hadn't been in our family for . . . well, we weren't spending much time here before and will probably never come back after this. Ada was . . . well, she liked this place. Liked the view of the lake and . . . I doubt we'll want to sell for a while but you can give me your card just in case."

"Oh, I didn't mean to presume . . ." Garvy let his words trail off as he pulled a card container from his pocket, extracted one, and handed it to Sheldon Arnist. Of course he meant to presume. Weren't real estate people always on duty — like veterinarians and vet techs?

Now I knew the reason he'd hurried to meet these grieving people. If I hadn't already determined to ignore any flirtation on his part, I certainly would have now.

On the other hand, I had reason to say hi to these people, too — not that I would. Not yet, at least. But I'd have loved to ask if they'd been aware that their daughter was visiting here. Whether she had come with any friends. More important, whether she had been collecting any dogs, and, if so, whether she traveled with them.

Did they know that Ada might have

brought Janelle's dog Go up here, at least? Or that Janelle, who was with the hiking party still in the street, had confronted their daughter in front of a lot of people just before she was killed?

I didn't hear any dogs barking from inside the house, so I made the assumption there weren't any. I wasn't sure, though.

But I couldn't ask any of that. And when I looked back toward the street, the crowd of hikers remained there, with Neal closest to the gate, his gaze on me.

I wasn't sure what he was trying to impart to me, but I knew what needed to be done.

"Excuse me." I approached the three people, Biscuit at my side. "I couldn't help overhearing some of what you said. I'm very sorry for your loss, too. And right now, my fellow hikers are eager to go." I planted a nonnegotiable glare on Garvy.

I wasn't happy when he leveled one of his flirtatious smiles on me. "You're right." He turned away. "And let me repeat my condolences." He joined me, and I hurried off down the driveway.

"We're not supposed to bother the residents," I hissed toward him as we neared the rest of the gang.

"I don't think expressing our condolences bothered them," he said mildly.

We'd reached where Neal stood, and he, too, glared at Garvy. "Let's go," he said.

"Sure." Garvy started leading the pack of hikers farther along Vistaview toward where we'd grab the next road going back down toward the lake.

Neal hung back, along with Janelle and Reed. "Did you learn anything . . . helpful?" He stole a glance at Janelle and Go.

"Yes and no," I said. "I still have a lot of questions, but I gathered those were Ada's parents who've just arrived here, and they don't spend a lot of time here in Knobcone Heights despite owning that house."

"Was Ada staying there before . . . before?" Janelle asked.

"She said she was, some of the time." I recalled how Mr. Arnist had talked about his daughter liking this place and its view of the lake.

"I assume they didn't tell you who they believed killed their daughter." That was Reed, and his tone was droll. He clearly didn't believe I'd gotten that information from them, and he was right.

"Nope," I said. "One thing I did learn, though."

"What's that?" Neal asked.

"That Garvy's in real estate. I figure he can find things out about our house pretty easily. Yours too, Reed. And given a hint of encouragement, he might try to find a buyer for either of us."

"Well, I'm not interested," Reed said. We started following the other hikers, side by side as our dogs walked with us, and Neal and Janelle hurried to get to the front of the pack again. I met Reed's gaze. He apparently wanted to know my degree of interest — in Garvy? In Garvy's profession? Both?

"Me neither," I said, and he smiled.

Fourteen

As good as it felt to walk beside Reed, I'd hoped to get a chance, sometime on the hike, to speak with Neal alone. Failing that, even talking to Janelle might get me what I wanted to know: whether she really had been avoiding Neal, and, if so, why she appeared so glad to be with him now.

But they were together throughout the rest of our outing. They acted quite friendly with one another, even flirtatious, so either Neal had been wrong or Janelle had changed her mind about interacting with him.

Or maybe she'd simply not had time yesterday to talk to him, since as well as being busy at the shops, she was probably worried about her meeting with the detectives today.

In any event, I didn't want to ask those potentially uncomfortable questions when they were together. I'd hopefully be able to learn later.

When the hike was over and we were all back at the resort, I couldn't ask then, either. Reed and Hugo had picked Biscuit and me up at home, and he drove us back there without lingering.

When he parked on the street in front of my house, I hopped out and opened the back door to get Biscuit. "Stay," I said to Hugo, and the Belgian Malinois naturally obeyed, although he looked a little sad since Reed had exited the vehicle, too.

But Reed only accompanied Biscuit and me on my dog's brief and final walk of the evening, then escorted us to the front door. There, he pulled me into his arms. We shared a very pleasant good night kiss — as we had privately last night, after our Chinese dinner at my home — but nothing more at that time.

Neal was here now, as he'd been then. I supposed it would be okay if he knew that Reed and I were growing closer, but I wasn't comfortable with that yet.

"See you tomorrow," I told Reed. I had a shift scheduled at the clinic in the afternoon, but because of something I now wanted to do there, I'd have shown up anyway.

"See you tomorrow," he repeated, and Biscuit and I walked into the house.

■ ■ ■ ■

I did get the information I'd wanted from Janelle early the next morning, when she showed up to help me start baking for the day. I'd checked the calendar, and our official scheduler Vicky had, in fact, penciled Janelle in that day, even though I'd thought Frida was due to be scheduled early.

"I get to bake those cinnamon apple dog treats?" Janelle asked with excitement after leaving Go in the Barkery and joining me in the kitchen.

"Sure." I let her start mixing the ingredients before I began asking my questions about her and Neal.

Her first reaction was to look uncomfortable, but she did respond. "I really like your brother, Carrie. And I think he likes me. If things go well, my intent is to stay here in Knobcone Heights for a nice long time. But . . . well, the past few days, I thought things weren't going well at all. Those detectives backed down a little yesterday when I told them I'd lawyered up and Ted Culbert arrived at the police station. Thanks for the introduction, by the way. After that, their questions all seemed to center on who I'd seen at the dog parks in LA at the times dogs disappeared, and how often Ada had shown up then. I could only give rough estimates, but they seemed okay with that. They stopped pushing me about how well I'd known Ada, and how much I might have hated her if I thought she'd stolen Go. That kind of thing."

"Then does it sound like the cops will lay off you now?"

"I don't know. I hope so. I felt so relieved after it was over that I returned Neal's calls. Turned out he was scheduling that hike for last night, so I asked to come along."

"Glad you did." I meant it. I liked seeing Neal happy. Plus, having Janelle around and talking meant I could continue to eliminate her from my list of murder suspects.

Or so I hoped. We seemed to be becoming friends, in addition to her interest in Neal. And I definitely appreciated her photography and promotion of my shops on the Internet.

That made me rethink the other potential suspects I'd come up with as I worked opposite her in the kitchen the rest of that early morning. I was baking some Icing treats to start the day, although my concentration wavered.

I knew the killer wasn't Neal. And there was an entire world of people out there I hadn't met who might have known and disliked Ada.

There were two people, though, whom I wondered about and could possibly look into more. One was Janelle's friend Delma, who'd been staying with her here. I hadn't seen her since the party that night and didn't even know if she was still in town.

Might she have done something about Ada in support of her buddy Janelle and her dog? Delma was also apparently a dog lover, although I hadn't yet had an opportunity to meet and pat her little Boston terrier. She could also have wanted to stop Ada from further dognappings.

Assuming Ada really had been a dognapper. Plus, there were some big assumptions if I was genuinely considering Delma a suspect who was angry enough to do something to back up her friend and maybe save some dogs . . . that the something she could do was to commit murder.

The second possibility I still pondered was that guy Tim, whom I knew had dogs with him. Were they his — or stolen?

He'd known Ada, but did he have a motive to kill her? Did he kill her?

I assumed Janelle would know more about Delma than about Tim. "So how is your friend Delma enjoying her visit here?" I asked casually as I picked up a rolling pin and started rolling out the dough I'd been working on. "I take it she's not much of a hiker, since she didn't join us last night either."

"She's been mostly staying in our hotel with Shobie." Janelle's nose crinkled as though she smelled something bad. "Delma's come down with some kind of stomach bug, although she's tried to stay away from me as much as possible, especially when she's needed to throw up. Good thing our hotel has a nice-size lobby with restrooms. And she's even seen a doctor."

"Oh, that's a shame," I said. "When did she start feeling bad?"

"The night of the bar fiasco." Janelle was arranging round balls of dog cookies on a metal tray before putting them into the oven. Good thing she was studying her work and not looking at me. She might have been able to read my thoughts from my face.

Interesting timing to start feeling ill. Had Delma eaten something that didn't agree with her? Gotten an infection of some sort?

Or did murdering Ada make her sick?

It hadn't been that long ago, after all. Today was Friday, and Ada had been killed on Monday night. A lot had happened since then, and it felt like ages had passed.

But if the killing had in some way affected Delma's tummy, she could easily still be feeling it. And if she'd stayed away from Janelle to throw up that night, she might not be able to vouch for Janelle's presence at the hotel overnight, and Janelle might not be able to vouch for her either.

"I hope she feels better fast," I said, cleaning my hands off with a paper towel so I could go around and open the oven door for Janelle's tray.

"Oh, she's much better now. In fact, she promised she'd come in to Icing this morning, first thing. Now that she can eat again, she wants to try some of the scones and other people treats."

Interesting. It seemed like my mentioning her had conjured her up.

In fact, it was now seven o'clock, so I washed my hands in the kitchen sink to prepare to open the shop doors. Dinah would arrive to help at any minute.

But Delma preceded her, holding a little black and white Boston terrier who was undoubtedly Shobie. She was waiting outside when I opened Icing's door. "Hi," she said. "I want some sweets, and I want them fast." Her forty-something face grinned at me, and I smiled back.

"Let's put Shobie in the Barkery first, and

then you're welcome to come into Icing." I reached over to pat her dog's head, and the little fellow turned to sniff my hand.

I went outside with them and led them in through the Barkery's door, then showed Delma how to hook Shobie's leash to Biscuit's crate right beside Go. The three dogs traded sniffs while wagging tails — Shobie's was tiny and stubby. I laughed.

"Okay, come on into Icing." I led Delma through the Barkery into my human bake shop. Once inside, I paused, stepping out of her way. "How are you feeling?" *And did you happen to get sick because you committed a murder?*

"Oh, did Janelle tell you I was sick? Not sure what caused it, but thank heavens I'm over it now, and I'm really hungry. So you can sell me a lot of stuff." That grin widened even more.

I found myself liking this woman with her short black cap of hair, friendly personality, and sensitive stomach. If she happened to have killed Ada to protect dogs and her friend . . .

Well, I didn't want the killer to be Delma, but I'd rather it be her than the person I hoped to clear — Janelle. Unless, of course, Janelle had actually been the murderer.

If so, I'd rather know than not know —

and be there to pick up the pieces once Neal found out, too.

Siblings stick together.

It was past noon. Delma hadn't stayed long, but she'd done as she'd mentioned and bought a substantial number of Icing treats, as well as some from the Barkery for Shobie.

Later, she had come back without her dog to go to lunch with Janelle. "After all I ate, and since I'm just recuperating, I'm surprised I have any appetite left," she'd told me as I worked behind the counter in the Barkery. Then she'd winked. "Of course, I've saved some of my treats for later, too."

She and Janelle left then, since Dinah and Frida were there to watch the shops. A good thing, since Biscuit and I were heading to work at the clinic.

I thought about stopping for lunch and coffee at Cuppa-Joe's, but decided not to today. I had the thing I wanted to do before starting my shift, and I didn't want to be late. I allowed my pup to take her time sniffing and doing what she needed to in the town square. But soon we got past it and reached Hill Street, where the clinic was.

As always, I stopped in the back with Biscuit to leave her with the doggy daycare staff. Then, hoping I'd see Reed, I hurried through the hallways to the clinic's office before heading to the room to change into my scrubs. I would lock my purse in my locker in a few minutes — after doing some quick research, jotting down what I found, and sticking it inside my bag.

We vet techs often took turns staffing the welcome desk facing the reception area. Behind it was the general office we all used, complete with computers. Fortunately, the tech staffing the area at the moment was Kayle, an enthusiastic guy who'd recently decided to go to veterinary school. He was still applying, but he was so committed and smart that I figured he'd have his choice of where to go.

I was glad to see him there, though, since I intended to look on the computer and didn't think he'd be terribly curious about what I was doing.

Yolanda, on the other hand, would undoubtedly shuffle by and look at the page I was studying.

I didn't intend to take long. In fact, I could justify my search somewhat, since I'd worked with the dogs purportedly owned by the guy whose records I was hunting: Tim Smith. I could simply tell anyone who asked that I was just checking to see if he'd been back for a follow-up with his injured dogs.

What I really wanted, though, was the address he had given us for our records. I just hoped he'd used one that was local and real, rather than make something up.

The address I found for him was in Blue Jay, a small mountain town near Lake Arrowhead, not far from Knobcone Heights. At least the town was real. I did a quick check on my smartphone and determined that the rest of the address was real, too — although whether the house there was occupied by Tim and his dogs remained to be seen.

And I did intend to see it, as soon as I could.

I made the trip there early that evening, after I'd closed my shops. With Biscuit in a doggy seat belt in the back of my car, I headed in that direction. I figured I could grab dinner in a fast food place somewhere along the way.

The bad news was that the house at that address was small, with a relatively flat yard, and when I passed slowly by, I saw a few kids outside playing ball on the lawn. They were watched by adults I assumed were their parents.

I didn't see Tim, and as far as I could tell, there were no dogs around.

Drat.

I kept my windows open nonetheless and hung around, continuing to patrol the area. Every time I heard a dog bark I headed in that direction.

My slow sleuthing eventually paid off. Perhaps I'd written the house number down wrong, but I doubted it. A couple of blocks down on the same street, I heard a bunch of dogs barking. When I drove by, I saw several in a fenced-in yard.

I didn't see the two that Tim had brought into our clinic. Those I did see — six of them — were of different shapes and sizes: a pug, a Rottweiler, two Scotties, a cocker spaniel, and an Australian shepherd.

I couldn't tell for certain, but if I had to guess from this distance, they all appeared to be purebreds to me.

Fifteen

This part of the neighborhood was interesting. The homes were spaced far apart, with large, fenced-in hilly yards. This was the mountains, after all.

A couple of homes had gardens, but most seemed unoccupied, or at least their yards were full of weeds.

Not a particularly busy block, I figured, although it did have some damaged sidewalks. But it wasn't a bad place to hoard dogs since there weren't many people around to complain.

Maybe, like some of the estate houses, these were second homes to the owners, perhaps people who liked to come up into the mountains to enjoy winter weather. They weren't here now, since this was July.

But that was speculation. Maybe all the homes were occupied at the moment, no matter how they appeared. And whether they were didn't really matter much to me.

I pondered what to do next. All I had was suspicions and suppositions. There could be a perfectly legitimate reason for those dogs to be at that house. Maybe it was another doggy daycare facility. Maybe Tim had nothing to do with it.

I hadn't, after all, seen the two injured dogs he'd brought to the veterinary clinic there.

And with all the dogs and the noise and the possible smells they caused, why hadn't even the few neighbors there complained?

There was a lot I didn't know and wanted to find out. But if I parked and got out of my car and started knocking on neighbors' doors asking questions, Tim, or whoever lived there, would undoubtedly find out. If there was something going on that shouldn't be — like the housing of dognapped canines — that house would undoubtedly be quickly vacated, too.

What should I do?

I decided to use my phone to take pictures of the place and its behind-the-fence occupants. I attempted to be as unobtrusive as possible, but if anyone was looking in my direction they would probably have spotted me aiming my phone. As a cover, I did hold it up and pretend to be typing in a text message. But that wouldn't really be much of a cover, since any observer could also assume I was texting pictures I'd taken to someone else.

Okay, enough here. "Ready to go?" I asked my sweet, calm Biscuit, who, despite her harness, was standing up in the back seat in reaction to my stopping and all the dog barks. She'd let out an occasional woof but mostly remained nice and quiet. Now she looked at me, her ears forward and tail wagging, responding to my question. I took it as an affirmative answer and slowly drove off.

I asked myself again, what next? This could be a criminal matter — or not. It might have something to do with Ada's murder — or not.

I didn't view the two detectives who'd grilled me and were now after Janelle to be friendly, so I didn't want to ask them for advice.

There were a couple of people I knew, though, who weren't in law enforcement but in government, and they might be able to give me some suggestions.

The easiest to find and talk to was Billi Matlock. Using my car's Bluetooth as I headed along one of the winding mountain roads back toward Knobcone Heights, I called her.

Fortunately, she was at Mountaintop Rescue helping to socialize some of the newest residents, rather than giving classes at her day spa, Robust Retreat.

She promised to meet me in twenty minutes at Cuppa-Joe's.

A short while later we sat on the patio at Cuppa's, Biscuit at my feet. Kit had already brought us our coffee, and we'd ordered some croissants and jelly — not sweets to compare with what I sold at Icing, but okay as a late-afternoon snack.

The Joes had come out to greet us when we first arrived and made a fuss over Biscuit, but they were hosting a party inside so didn't stay long. Just as well. As much as I loved being with them, I wanted to be alone with Billi for this discussion.

I'd already told Billi what was on my mind. The pretty and astute City Councilwoman appeared concerned, her deep brown eyes pensive as she looked at me. She was dressed casually that day, not in spa apparel but in dog rescue T-shirt and jeans.

"If nothing else," she finally said slowly, "we have some jurisdictional issues. I agree that the situation bears looking into. If that place is occupied by the guy who hung out with Ada Arnist, our local police should at least be able to question him — although I assume they already have. But if he's got dogs that are possibly stolen property . . ."

I knew full-well that pets were considered property and not true family members by the law. But kidnapped or stolen, the outcome should still be the same. If it were true, the perpetrator should be arrested and prosecuted, and the dogs returned to their owners — their families.

"You realize, of course, that this is all about my suspicions, thanks to my meeting Tim with Ada, and Janelle suspecting Ada of dognapping Go, and then Tim showing up at the clinic with apparently purebred dogs, and —"

"Yes, I know you have no proof. But you're a very astute person, Carrie." Billi smiled at me. "You may be way off-base. But in case you're not, someone should look into it."

"Someone?" I prompted.

"Well, I'm thinking that we need some good advice." She paused. "Have you ever met Chief Loretta Jonas?"

"Yes," I said. Chief Loretta had recently adopted a dog from Mountaintop Rescue and I'd briefly spoken with her when she brought the little schnauzer mix to the vet clinic for an exam and shots. But we'd not talked much. I had heard more from her when she was being interviewed on local television now and then, including when I was a murder suspect, and once since Ada was killed.

But from Billi's suggestion and determined expression, I suspected I was about to talk more with her now.

As she did in TV interviews, Chief Loretta Jonas wore a formal police uniform, complete with a dark jacket and medals of different sorts, none of which I could interpret. She also wore a frown.

But she had agreed to see us right away when Billi had called — and I was certain that was because her caller had been Billi. Did she try to suck up to City Council members? That I didn't know, but keeping on the Council's good side probably didn't hurt her.

The chief was likely in her fifties, with medium brown hair all in one shade that suggested the color wasn't natural. She must have frowned a lot, since the lines on her dark-complected face seemed right at home given her current irritated expression. She sat behind a desk, but I could tell she was slender. Maybe she worked out with those under her command.

In all, she seemed an impressive officer. I prepared to tell my story and concerns to her, figuring that she'd listen, thanks to Billi's presence, before telling me nicely to get lost — or get back to the clinic and help save a dog the usual way.

That was how things seemed to start out. I appeared to be a nonentity to her. "What's going on, Ms. Matlock?" the chief asked, barely sparing a glance toward me first.

We sat in her roomy but sparse office in the Knobcone Heights Police Department. Billi and I had chairs facing a sharp wooden desk that had nothing on top of it. There weren't even any file cabinets in the room. The poshest thing I saw was the chief's own plush golden desk chair.

"I'd like Ms. Kennersly to explain her concerns to you, Loretta," Billi said. So they were on a first-name basis after all. Or at least that was the more informal way Billi intended to play it. "They have something to do with your murder investigation of Ada Arnist, although maybe only peripherally. In any event, they have something to do with a crime that's being committed down in the LA area."

Loretta's dark brown eyes rolled again in my direction. The rest of her face appeared a touch disgusted, although I didn't know her well enough to determine if that was her usual expression. She'd looked more pleasant at the clinic, but she'd been off duty then. And of course she had looked solemn but benign during the TV interviews. Maybe her disgusted look now was how, as police chief, she got people on the defensive, which encouraged them to tell her everything so she'd start looking more approving.

"All right, Ms. Kennersly, what do you have for me?"

"First," I said, "how's your cute little schnauzer mix. What's his name?"

Her expression thawed for an instant. "Jellybean. He's great." Her serious expression returned. "But let's discuss the reason you're here."

I, too, grew more serious. "Okay. I know that as part of your looking into Ms. Arnist's murder you're apparently considering Janelle Blaystone as a suspect, since she and Ada had a public argument." I purposely put as much confidence in my tone as I could. "I'm not sure whether you know what the argument was about, though." Maybe she did by now, but in any event I proceeded to tell her about Go.

She nodded curtly a couple of times, so I

assumed that this wasn't new to her.

But I continued, mentioning that among the people who'd been at the bar that night was a friend of Ada's, Tim Smith. "I don't know all the details, but Janelle had seen Ada visiting some dog parks where other purebred dogs were stolen from in LA. I believe that Ada's mentioning Knobcone Heights may be one reason why Janelle came here." I chose to keep that somewhat fuzzy to give a semblance of protection to Janelle, since I wasn't sure what story she'd told the police.

The police chief said nothing.

After exchanging glances with Billi, who continued to appear supportive, I went on. "Then, after Ada died, Tim brought a couple of apparent purebreds to the clinic while I was on duty as a technician. It might have meant nothing, but I was curious, especially after both had microchips but neither chip was readable by the clinic's scanner, which was in fine working order."

I didn't mention how I'd searched for Tim's address, in case it was an improper delving into his supposed privacy, but told her I'd tried to figure out where he might be staying now and in the process had discovered a somewhat remote house, outside the small town of Blue Jay, where there were a bunch of apparent purebred dogs. Then I showed her the photos on my phone.

"So you think that makes Mr. Smith a suspect in Ms. Arnist's murder?" The chief finally spoke, nearly startling me. Her tone sounded not only skeptical, but irritated, too. "Since you were formerly a murder suspect and apparently conducted your own investigation before, that now makes you some kind of detective?"

"She did help to clear herself," Billi said firmly. I could have hugged my friend for standing up for me, especially with that unswervingly challenging expression on her face as she regarded the chief.

"I'm just attempting to inform you of some information I obtained," I said. "Whether it's relevant to your investigation of Ada's murder, I have no idea. But don't you law enforcement agencies work together to help each other solve crimes? If nothing else, the dogs at that house in Blue Jay might all be stolen from people down in Los Angeles. Maybe not, but shouldn't you look into it?"

Loretta nodded slowly. "As you mentioned, there might be a number of law enforcement agencies involved — those in the areas where the dogs allegedly were stolen, plus possibly the San Bernardino

County Sheriff's Department, since Blue Jay doesn't have its own. And the only way we might be involved here in Knobcone Heights is if there is some potential link to the murder we're investigating."

"You have some obligation to check with the other departments and let them know there are some possibly suspicious circumstances here, don't you, chief?" Billi's tone did not invite a negative answer. I read into it that the Knobcone Heights City Council might find a way to ensure that the local police department cooperated with those others — even if it meant chastising or otherwise punishing the local officer in charge.

I suspected that Loretta interpreted it the same way. "Whether there is an obligation is irrelevant. All law enforcement agencies generally attempt to help one another, and I certainly intend to look into this."

"And you'll keep City Council informed about what the other agencies report to you?"

Loretta's glare suggested she wanted to shout something negative at Billi. But her tone, when she responded, was held carefully in check. "Of course, Councilwoman Matlock."

■ ■ ■ ■

Chief Loretta had one of her officers show us into an adjoining room, where a cop named Sergeant Himura, who had a similar irritable expression as his boss, took down the information about the dogs and the address where I'd seen them. Fortunately, he didn't ask about why I'd happened to be looking in that area.

At least my two detective buddies didn't appear at the station to give me a hard time.

But I was nevertheless surprised to see someone else I knew there: Garvy Grant. As Billi and I finally headed down the wide, well-lit hallway containing the police department's executive offices toward the exit, I saw him exit from another door.

He saw us immediately, too, and hastened toward us. He was dressed once again in his white shirt and dark trousers. "Hi," he said, lifting his light brown eyebrows high enough on his expansive forehead to create wrinkles. "What are you doing here?"

Exactly what I'd intended to ask him. "We just had a meeting with Chief Jonas about some dogs," I said, having no intention of getting into any specifics. "And you?"

I glanced toward the identification plaque

beside the door he'd exited and noted that the office was occupied by the department's chief information officer.

What kind of information was a real estate agent looking for?

"Oh, I always check out the towns where I'm vacationing," he said vaguely as we continued down the hallway. "You never know when a client will start asking questions about the neighborhoods, and I always like to have answers." He glanced at his watch. "Not quite dinner time, but would you two like to join me for coffee?"

"Sorry," I said quickly. "I need to get back to my shops."

"And I have to hurry back to Mountaintop Rescue," Billi said. "I always like to find out who's been there expressing interest about some of our rescues."

"Well, I'll invite you both again soon," Garvy said in a tone that suggested he felt sure we'd want him to. He then hurried ahead of us through the police station's busy, citizen-filled reception area.

"Thanks," Billi said, her tone more ironic than genuine.

We followed him out the door, and I no longer saw him as the crowd swallowed him. Billi and I walked together for a short distance until we were on the opposite side of Hill Street from Mountaintop Rescue, joking a bit about our opinions on whether Chief Loretta or her minions would actually look into the dog situation.

"Oh, I think she will," Billi said. "It'd be an interesting thing to bring up at a Council meeting if she didn't. Not that anyone's likely to do anything about it other than ask her."

"Well, thanks at least for that," I said. "And thanks for getting me the audience with Her Highness so quickly." We both laughed. "Anyway, I'll bring some of our leftover treats for your charges to enjoy soon. And let's get together for coffee at Cuppa's again soon."

"Of course. And then we can talk about your brother's love life — and yours, too. How's Reed doing?"

I felt a flush rise up my face. "He's fine. I think." I paused. "I'd better find someone interesting to introduce you to. It's not enough to be a member of one of the town's most elite families. You need to expand your empire."

"And who says I'm not?" she asked cryptically, then dashed across the street.

SIXTEEN

I hadn't wanted that invitation from Garvy Grant. But the next afternoon, he nevertheless appeared in Icing.

The morning had been fairly uneventful. Frida had been the earliest of my assistants to arrive, and she had happily settled into the kitchen preparing dog treats, even though she specialized in creating human dishes at home. When she was done baking some new pup-cakes for us, she took over the people baked goods that I'd been working on.

Now the glass-fronted display case in Icing was filled with our usual delicious products with Frida's extra touch. She was an artist with icing — the actual sweet topping, not just the store — and so a lot of our cookies and cupcakes, including our special red velvet ones, were adorned with tiny sweet roses and other floral touches and even some really cute and unique smiley faces. I couldn't help smiling back at them.

Frida hadn't brought her dog Zorro in for a while, but she knew he was always welcome in the Barkery.

As usual, I'd been moving back and forth between my shops. That way I could also admire the dog treats in the Barkery. They looked the same as always today — scrumptious, for canines.

It was Saturday, so Dinah was here, too. At the moment she was staffing the Barkery. If all went as currently planned, she would have the next two days off. Janelle had been in for a while this morning but now Go and she were out for lunch.

So, for now, Frida and I were the ones helping human customers in Icing, and there were a lot of them, which was a good thing. I was ringing up a customer's large order of our cupcakes and sugar cookies for a kids' party that afternoon when the bell on Icing's door rang.

As always, I glanced up, prepared to smile at whoever was entering to assure them that they were noticed and would be waited on as soon as possible.

My smile this time was a bit forced, though, when the person who entered was Garvy. His grin didn't look at all false, though.

He still looked all professional-real-estate-guy in his dark trousers. Was he here to try to convince me to sell my shops and let him be the agent for the sale?

He might as well leave right away.

More likely, though, he was here to buy some of Icing's products. He'd told me before that he'd do so, before he'd so oddly disappeared.

Since I was the one currently helping a customer, Frida hurried toward our newcomer, her hands out slightly in welcome and a smile on her attractive face. Her medium brown hair was pulled back into its usual ponytail, which added to the appearance of roundness of her cheeks. "Would you like some of our special baked goods today, sir?" she asked.

"Absolutely," I heard him reply, but then the customer I was waiting on asked for a dozen more of our chocolate chip cookies, so I had to concentrate once more on what I was doing.

That was the last of my customer's order, though, so after I'd packed up her treats and rung them up on the register on the counter, I glanced around as she walked out the door and set off its bell again.

I saw Frida right away, gesturing for a customer to join her in front of the glass case. The customer wasn't Garvy this time. He stood near the closed door that led into the Barkery. And his gaze was on me.

Since there weren't any other customers in Icing, I had to approach him.

"Hi, Carrie," he said effusively, brows raised so high in greeting they nearly pointed at his forehead. "It's nice to get a good look at this place. Can you give me a tour of both shops?"

As I recalled, he'd said he'd lost his dog recently, but he might have friends with pets that he could buy Barkery treats for. Or maybe he could help ease his sorrow by eating human sweets himself.

"Sure." I attempted to sound a lot more enthused than I felt. "This, of course, is Icing on the Cake." I waved my hand around, gesturing toward the small tables at the front and then toward the display case.

"Lovely," he said. "I'll want to try some stuff from here. But I'd like to see your other shop first, before I pick anything out. Okay?"

"Sure," I said again, wondering if I should ask about how he was doing after the loss of his dog. Instead, I decided to approach it differently. "You can go right through this door. My dog Biscuit stays in the Barkery pretty much all the time when I'm working.

She's got her own area and an open-topped crate. And she's probably not the only dog there." I paused as he reached for the door knob. "I hope it won't be too hard on you to go in there. I mean, after . . ." I let my voice trail off. I figured he'd interpret my silence the way I wanted him to.

"Thanks," he said solemnly, and so softly I had to strain to hear him. Maybe that was also because he'd gotten the door open and some dogs in the Barkery were woofing at each other. I recognized Biscuit's voice, and Go's louder one, so I knew that Janelle had returned from lunch. There were also some yappier ones I didn't know offhand.

I followed Garvy inside and closed the door behind me. There were two Yorkie mixes near the area where Biscuit was confined and Go was leashed. A person I assumed was owned by the small yappers stood between them, scolding them fruitlessly. They continued to talk.

I glanced at Janelle, who stood behind the counter with Dinah, and nodded. She interpreted it correctly and reached into the back of the glass case to extract a couple of small biscuits.

She moved around to join us on the tile floor, handing the biscuits to the Yorkie-mom, who turned to look at her gratefully.

Sure enough, the treats were enough of a distraction to silence the little dogs, at least for now.

"Thank you so much," their owner said. She looked down at her babies and smiled. "Whatever those are, I want a bunch of them. They love them!"

"Absolutely," Janelle said. "They've got apples and carrots in them. We've got some other great stuff, too. Come on over here and we'll figure out what you want."

Dinah had just rung a purchase up at the cash register but didn't join us since there was a short line near the counter. That left me to continue to entertain my buddy Garvy on my own.

Well, not entirely on my own. He walked over to where Go and Biscuit remained by themselves, now that the Yorkie-mom had picked up her little ones. "They're beautiful," he said. "Of course I met them before, but I just love dogs."

Which made me feel even worse for him. I found it hard to dislike dog lovers. And this particular one had recently lost his best friend.

"Me too," I said quietly. I considered asking him if he was thinking about getting another dog — not as a replacement, of course, but as a new friend. Instead, I just asked gently, "What kind of dog was the one you lost?"

Garvy had been kneeling to pet Go, who sat quietly on the tile floor. Now he rose. "A bulldog. They're such wonderful creatures. I — I'm considering getting another one." His narrow lips curved into a sad grimace. "Maybe. I'd have to find one who bonds with me, of course. Just because they're the same breed doesn't always mean they're the right dog for you, you know."

"Yes," I said, "I do know. You can tell fairly quickly, though, if a dog can become your new family member. That's what happened with Biscuit and me."

"And with Winston and me," Garvy said. "That was my dog's name."

"Appropriate for an English bulldog," I said, smiling sadly.

Now that I no longer had the sense that Garvy was attempting to come on to me, I liked him better. Felt sorry for him. Even wanted to help him.

"I thought so," he responded. He cocked his head slightly. "I haven't been to the shelter here, but do you happen to know if they have any bulldogs available?"

"They don't," I said, "unless one has come in during the last day or two since I was there."

"I don't suppose you've seen any other bulldogs around, have you?"

"There are a couple I see occasionally at the vet clinic or shop, but if you mean am I aware of any available for adoption, the answer, unfortunately, is no." Of course, I still had no idea about why those dogs in the yard in Blue Jay were there — whether they'd been stolen, whether they'd be confiscated once the authorities checked into them, or whether, somewhere on that property, was the English bulldog that Tim had brought into the clinic. But there was no reason to mention my speculations.

"I'll be in town for a while," Garvy said. "I like this area, and it's a good place to get away from home so I don't think as much about Winston."

I thought about how Janelle had come here supposedly for a similar reason — because of losing her dog.

But Winston hadn't been stolen, or at least that wasn't what Garvy said. The poor thing had passed on.

"The thing is," Garvy continued, "as much as I miss Winston, I'm thinking that the best way not only to get over his death but to honor him is to get another dog as soon as possible. And I loved him so much that I definitely want to get another bulldog."

"Even though I know of some people around here who own bulldogs, I'm not aware of any breeders," I told him. "You might want to check with Mountaintop Rescue to find out if they can tell you about other shelters that might have one. Or you could look online. There are some sites where available dogs are featured by type and location."

"Yes, I'm aware of those. And I will be checking around. You can be certain of it. But you'll be sure to let me know if you see any bulldogs that are potentially strays, or up for adoption?"

I realized then that not only was I standing near Garvy, but he'd inched up toward me — and though we had a nice crowd of customers at the Barkery, that wasn't the reason for it. We weren't very near the others, but Garvy was too close to me.

Once again I felt uncomfortable with the guy.

Very obviously, I checked my watch. "Unfortunately" — not — "my shift at the vet clinic is going to start soon, so Biscuit and I will have to go. But I hope you'll go back to Icing and pick out some treats for yourself." I didn't offer him any freebies, though. I didn't especially want him to come back.

"I definitely will. Thanks. And thanks for listening to me. It helps to talk to a fellow dog-lover while I'm trying to deal with my loss of Winston. Really. And I appreciate that you'll let me know if you see any bulldogs that might be available. Right?"

He was really harping on that. The way he was pushing bothered me.

"Thanks for stopping by," I said anyway.

And as sorry as I feel for you about Winston, I hope you don't stop by here again, I thought.

SEVENTEEN

My mind remained somewhat on bulldogs, so when Biscuit and I reached the clinic, I glanced around the doggy daycare area just in case any visitors happened to be that breed or a mix that had some resemblance to bulldogs. None were there. Even if there had been one, its visit to this center would indicate to me a caring owner, not someone who wanted to give their dog up.

And with my mixed feelings about Garvy Grant, did I really want to help him find a new pup? I'd worry about that new family member of his and how Garvy might treat it.

Not that I'd any indication he would do anything but love a new dog. But the guy somehow rubbed me the wrong way with his pushiness on so many levels.

"What's going on, Carrie? Are you okay?"

Arvie's voice startled me. I had just begun walking down the clinic's well-lit main hall toward the locker room to change clothes, but I'd barely noticed where I was, my mind still hovering around bulldogs.

Our chief vet had just exited one of the examination rooms. He wore his white medical outfit with a stethoscope around his neck and black athletic shoes. I wanted to hug him for the concern written all over his face.

"I'm fine," I told him. "But I'm thinking about a conversation I just had with a guy who recently lost his dog. He's considering adopting another, so my mind keeps circling the possibilities." I looked into Arvie's eyes, which were narrowed in concern, and decided it wouldn't hurt to ask. "I don't suppose you know of anyone with an English bulldog available to a new home, do you?" In other words, *Is that guy Tim the person I'm concerned he is, and has he brought that injured bulldog back here for any reason?*

"I'm not aware of any, but I'll let you know if I hear of one," Arvie said. His expression now appeared more bemused than concerned, and I gave a brief laugh.

"Thanks." I hugged him. "It's a long story, and I'll tell you about it when we get some time together."

"It's about your brother and his new

girlfriend and her dog, I'll bet. Or is it about that woman who was murdered near the resort?"

"You've always been one of the most perceptive people I've ever met," I told him, stepping back. "It's about all of that."

The expression he leveled on me now seemed both caring and dismayed. "You're going to try to solve *this* murder, too? Last time I understood why, since you were being ragged on as a suspect. But this time —"

"This time," I broke in, "they're looking at Janelle, and you're right, Neal is interested in her. And I like her. She's a dog person and is working for me now. Can I swear she's innocent? No. Not yet, at least. But there are a few people I think the authorities should be looking at more closely than her."

"And that has something to do with a bulldog?"

"In a way," I said. "And — do you remember that guy who was here the other day with two injured dogs who'd been fighting with one another? One of them was a bulldog."

Arvie nodded. "He's one of your suspects?"

"Could be. In any case, I'm concerned

about how he treats those dogs and others." Like, *Does he dognap them and hold them for ransom or resell them? And had Ada been his accomplice or enemy in it?*

But that would be TMI — too much information — to bombard Arvie with here and now, especially since Yolanda had just poked her head into the hallway. "Oh, there you are, Arvie," she said. "Are you ready to examine this cat?"

"Be right there," he told her, his eyes not leaving me. He lowered his voice. "I don't have to tell you to be careful, do I?"

"Nope. I can figure that out on my own."

"I hope so. I'd rather that you figure out to stay away from it, but I know better. So . . . keep me informed."

He turned and strode down the hall toward Yolanda, who was watching me expressionlessly — which let me know she was peeved.

My first assignment of the day involved working with Reed to help him examine a pit bull with stomach issues who lay on one of the metal tables in another examination room. Yes, I'm strong enough to hold one, and this girl was one of the sweetest dogs, clearly not intending to bite anyone helping her, no matter how much it hurt.

When we were finished, the owner, a

young woman in tank top and shorts who looked physically fit enough to handle any kind of dog, gushed, "Thank you so much," and hugged her pitty. "She'll be okay now?"

"Keep her on the meds we'll send home with you and limit her diet for the next few days, as on our instruction sheet," Reed said. "And we'll want to see her again next week. But, yes, she should be fine."

The woman next hugged Reed — it was probably inappropriate, but I understood it, and not just because I was dating this good-looking, nice guy. He was one really excellent veterinarian, and the kind of attention and feedback he'd given her was worth a lot more than a hug. Of course, she would pay for services rendered on her way out.

When she and her dog were gone, I was alone with Reed till the next patient was sent in. We'd talked by phone since the night of the hike, and of course I was glad to see him now.

"You seem a little preoccupied," he said. "What's new in the Janelle situation?" The guy was beginning to know me well.

"Not much, but on an unrelated topic — most likely — I did ask Arvie to let me know if he hears about any adoptable bulldogs."

Just then, one of our other techs opened the outer door to the room and a guy with a small cat crate entered. I knew it was a cat crate because I heard an effusive meow.

"There's a lot to tell you," I told Reed hurriedly. "Talk later."

It seemed I never got even a few minutes of alone time with Reed when I was at the clinic, but we could always call each other later. I retrieved Biscuit from daycare and we set off to walk back to my shops.

A slight rain misted over us, so for part of the way I used an umbrella I'd had in my locker. Biscuit didn't seem to care and in fact appeared quite happy sniffing things along our walk. Maybe the rain enhanced the smells.

We passed the end of the town square and Summit Avenue. Soon we were at the door to the Barkery.

I didn't see any customers when I opened the door for Biscuit to enter. That wasn't a good thing. Dinah was on duty, and I saw Go attached to the crate at the side of the room. "Hi," I said. "All okay?"

"All's fine. Janelle's over at Icing, in case you were wondering."

I was, but not a lot. I'd jumped to that correct conclusion already.

"That's fine." I went behind the counter and rested my closed umbrella against the wall near the door to the kitchen. Then I grabbed a couple of paper towels from a shelf behind the display case to go wipe Biscuit's damp feet. As I did so I looked again at Dinah, who was at the front of the case apparently counting what was left. When she paused for a moment, I asked her, "Were we busy while I was gone?"

"Yes. This is the first lull."

It wasn't a long one, since by the time I'd secured Biscuit into her comfy enclosure and tossed away the paper towel, the bell on the door rang and a family with two kids and two spaniels walked in.

"I'll take care of them," Dinah assured me quickly. "I think you'll enjoy seeing what's going on next door."

She didn't tell me what that meant, and since she immediately started helping our newcomers, I didn't ask.

I approached Icing by way of the kitchen, though, since I wanted to give my hands a thorough washing after wiping off dirty doggy paws. First I put my purse and umbrella in my office. When my hands were clean, I entered Icing by way of its door into the kitchen.

Unsurprisingly, Janelle was there, and so was Frida. No one else was, which made me wonder whether this shop also was just having a momentary lull or a bad business day. But before I could ask Janelle, whose back was to me as she stood on the tile floor facing the store's front, she turned. Her official-looking professional camera was in her hand.

"She's so great!" Frida exclaimed, coming from the far side of the glass case. She clapped and moved her head so her ponytail waved from side to side. "Janelle has been taking pictures of the cookies and cupcakes and everything that I decorated this morning and posting them on the Internet, with lots and lots of plugs for Icing on the Cake. And in case you're worried, she took a few shots of Barkery treats before, too, and posted them. She's amazing!"

Janelle's smile looked almost shy. "It's what I do — besides helping out here, of course."

"Of course. But it's obviously a good idea for bake shops to have assistants who decorate and photograph the products. Thank you both."

A middle-aged couple entered Icing then, and Frida hurried to help them. I approached Janelle.

"So, everything else okay?" I asked her. I didn't want to be specific, but after my own experience I was wondering if my buddies the detectives had taken up hounding her in hopes she would blurt out a confession at last.

"Yes, thank heavens." She sounded relieved. She apparently understood what I hadn't specifically said, since she added, "Maybe I said something helpful to make them look elsewhere."

I certainly hoped so, for her sake. And mine, so I could continue to employ this helpful assistant and wouldn't have to try to make things better for Neal as he worried about her.

My phone rang then. I felt fairly certain I knew who it was.

I was right. "Hi, Reed." I moved away from Janelle and the display case toward the far side of Icing, away from where everyone was now hanging out.

"Hi. Would Biscuit and you like to come to my place for dinner tonight? It's too wet outside to grill anything but I'll cook some spaghetti and meatballs."

"Sounds great. What time?" It was almost six o'clock now. I'd be closing the shops soon.

"Make it seven. And I hope Biscuit and you will hang around for a while."

I got the message. His house, so we wouldn't have to worry about Neal coming home. We could stay there for a while with the dogs.

I had a feeling that tonight would be fun. And memorable.

It started out even more memorable than I'd anticipated, but for far different reasons.

After saying good night to all my assistants, I locked the doors and put everything financial away in my office, which I locked, too.

Then it was time for Biscuit and me to leave.

I walked my little girl first, across Summit Avenue and onto the paved paths of the town square. The cloudy sky and thick humidity threatened more rain, but at the moment no precipitation was falling. That was good, since Biscuit and I took our time as she did what she needed to. Then we crossed the street again and went around to the back of the stores where I'd parked my aging white Toyota sedan. Anticipating rain, I'd thrown a rag towel on the floor of the backseat that morning, and I used it now to wipe Biscuit's paws.

Then I harnessed her in and got behind the steering wheel to drive to Reed's.

There wasn't much traffic that evening. There seldom was in Knobcone Heights unless there was some event going on, like a holiday celebration. The threat of more rain had probably kept people off the roads, too.

Reed's house, like my house, was south of the main downtown area, not in the various mountainous areas where some of the town's elite lived. On the other hand, his place was in a different set of hills, in quite a nice area — more upscale than mine but not the highest caliber.

I'd found this out over the last few months, on other occasions when I'd gone to his home for dinner before returning to my place. And even though our relationship was heating up a bit, I still wasn't considering staying all night at his place — at least not yet, since even if Neal suspected that my relationship with Reed was becoming warmer, I wasn't ready to confirm it to him. Not yet, though maybe soon, depending on how things continued to develop.

It took me less than ten minutes to drive to Reed's usually, so I took my time.

But as I prepared to pull out onto Summit Avenue, a silver SUV drove by. At first I hardly paid attention to it — until I noticed the driver.

It was Tim Smith. And I thought I saw some movement in the backseat. A person? Or a dog or two? He'd gone past too fast for me to be sure.

Well, so what? Tim lived around here. For all I knew, perhaps he had a job unrelated to canines.

I didn't know if the house where I'd seen the dogs was actually his, or if he was those dogs' owner or caretaker or had any relationship to them at all.

I didn't know if he wasn't, either.

I figured Reed's spaghetti could be reheated if I didn't get to his place immediately. Instead of turning right, as I should have, I waited until another car passed by, then turned left.

I fortunately still saw the SUV in front of me, but by a couple of blocks now. I had to go a little faster to catch up.

It was interesting to me that the direction Tim was going would lead to the best route to Blue Jay. Was that where he was heading?

And why was I so obsessed with finding out? With finding him?

Because he'd known Ada? Because they might have been conspirators in dognapping?

Because he might have murdered her?

That was all complete speculation on my part. Even if Tim had more than the two dogs he'd brought to our clinic, that didn't mean he'd stolen them — or conspired with

Ada to do so if she, in fact, had been the thief Janelle suspected.

Plus, even if he had, that didn't mean he'd killed her.

All this kept circulating through my mind, even as I continued to follow him.

He did turn onto the route that would take him to Blue Jay.

But I didn't get through the traffic light fast enough. I lost him. When the light changed, I didn't see him ahead of me, nor on any of the roads that led from the one I was on.

Obsessed or not, I decided to check the house with the dogs. "Hang on," I called to Biscuit in the backseat and sped up a bit.

It took another ten minutes for me to reach Blue Jay, then pass through it to the residential area where I'd seen all those dogs in the yard.

Tonight, I saw no dogs — but of course it had been raining.

I also saw no lights on inside the house.

Most of all, I didn't see the SUV that Tim had been driving.

Obsessed? Oh, yeah. Maybe I was nuts.

But I did that a lot when I worried about dogs.

Did I really want to get completely involved in potentially solving Ada Arnist's murder? I'd no idea if this guy was really a viable suspect. And today, at least, Janelle hadn't been harassed by the cops as if she was their only suspect.

"Let's go to Reed's and Hugo's right now," I said to Biscuit.

I needed a diversion — and being with Reed for the next few hours would undoubtedly provide a really good one.

Eighteen

Reed was in fact a good diversion. A great one.

Although I did have to dissemble a little with him about why I'd come a little later than we'd discussed. I just told him that time had gotten away from me.

That was close enough to *Tim* getting away from me.

Our pasta dinner, with some really good wine, was delightful. So was our conversation, and our walking the dogs afterward, and — Well, I definitely had a night to remember before Biscuit and I headed home to bed.

I was quite glad to remember it the next morning, a few hours after opening my shops. I happened to be staffing the Barkery with just Biscuit's assistance at the time when Jack Loroco walked in.

I hadn't seen Jack for months, even though when I'd first met him he had taken several trips up here to Knobcone Heights to see me. Because he was romantically interested in me? I thought so, and in fact I'd been somewhat attracted to him. Still, he came to town a lot anyway for recreation — snow and water skiing, boating, hiking, and more.

And of course, he was mostly interested in my Barkery and the wonderful dog treats I'd developed myself. If VimPets would let him buy my recipes, we'd work together as his company promoted my treats on the mass market. But so far, his bosses had decided against buying them, which was a good thing. It meant I didn't have to worry about whether I really wanted to sell my recipes.

"Carrie, hi," he said effusively as he came through the door, the bell ringing above his head.

I was waiting on a local customer, Sissy, who'd been a long-time patron of Icing before I bought it. She'd recently acquired a rescue Yorkie from Mountaintop Rescue and frequented the Barkery part of my shops a lot now. She gave me a quizzical look, then aimed her middle-aged glare at my new visitor as if irritated at his intrusion.

"Oh, sorry," Jack said. "I don't mean to interrupt. But it's good to see you, Carrie."

He ambled over to pat Biscuit on the head through the open top of her enclosure.

"Hi, Jack," was all I said, giving him a brief wave and finishing up with Sissy. "Now you can go next door to Icing," I told her. "Vicky and Frida are there right now and they'll make sure you take home as many red velvet cupcakes today as you want." That was Sissy's favorite.

"Thanks, Carrie." She tossed another glare toward Jack before heading over to Icing.

"Sorry," he said again, approaching me. Jack was a good looking guy, with a deep summer tan on his face and on his bare arms beneath his blue, short-sleeved dress shirt. His straight nose was prominent over his wide, smiling mouth, and his light brown hair looked longer than I'd seen it before. His slacks were khaki, his apparent favorite color for casual pants, and he wore white athletic shoes beneath them. I had a suspicion he wanted to hug me. That was fine as long as it was brief and friendly.

I made certain that it was, pulling away quickly.

"So what brings you here?" I asked.

"Just a visit for now. Oh, and I need to go say hi to Harris Ethman."

Harris, the widower of Myra Ethman and

the owner of the Knob Hill Pet Emporium, had joined his wife in giving me a hard time when I'd first opened the Barkery, claiming my shop was inappropriate competition for their pet store. But after Myra's death — and, mainly, after I was cleared of her murder — Harris and I had slowly developed a fairly civil truce, and now even recommended each other's stores to customers when appropriate.

The Emporium hadn't carried VimPets products before, but it had begun stocking some lately. I'd been in contact with Jack about it when I first saw his stuff there. He'd been aware of it, but he hadn't visited town again until now.

"Seeing Harris sounds like a good idea," I said.

"Hey, why don't you come with me? You don't look that busy this Sunday morning, so why not?"

I wasn't that busy, and I did need some more of Biscuit's regular gourmet food — which was, in fact, manufactured by VimPets and now available at the Emporium. I could get one of my assistants to come over from Icing.

And I could take Biscuit for a walk.

Did I want to spend more time in Jack's company? Well, we could talk business. And

I did like the guy, even though nothing romantic had developed.

"Sure," I said. "Let me get someone over here to staff the Barkery and I'll be ready to go."

The Knob Hill Pet Emporium wasn't far from my shops, just across the town square and down twisting Peak Road.

"Too bad you don't have Rigsley with you," I told Jack as we walked. Rigsley was his dog, a large gray mixed breed whom Jack mostly left at home when he came to Knobcone Heights. He'd told me before he had a great sitter and loved his pet. I figured I'd believe this more if he didn't leave his pet at home so much.

"Yeah," he agreed. "I miss him." His momentarily sad expression looked genuine, and I realized that he had reasons not to have his dog along on trips that were mostly business related — like this one apparently was.

It didn't take us long to get to the Emporium. Jack held the door open for Biscuit and me, and we walked in.

The Knob Hill Pet Emporium was as elite as its name, from the neon sign outside that blazed its crown logo to the areas within, where expensive items — from rhinestoned leashes to pet clothing — were displayed on rows of gold-hued metal racks. There were a few patrons there now, as well as a couple of employees whom I recognized.

Harris Ethman himself stood in a far corner talking with someone I couldn't see. I knew where the dog food I needed was displayed and could have just gone there to pick some up, but the friendly thing to do would be to say hello. So I headed with Biscuit in that direction, toward the shelves where balls of every shape and size for dogs and cats to play with were on display, passing a couple of people discussing the pros and cons of dog collars versus harnesses.

Harris's conversation must have been engaging since he didn't look around, not even, initially, when Jack reached him first.

"Hi, Harris," Jack gushed, holding out his hand to be shaken. Harris did turn then, the edges of his always downturned eyes folding even more into a scowl. But he must have liked Jack now that he was selling Vim-Pets products in the store, since his frown changed immediately into a smile on his edgy face beneath his receding hairline. He wore a black cotton shirt with an Emporium crown logo sparkling on the pocket.

His move to shake Jack's hand revealed who he'd been talking to: Garvy Grant.

"Hi, Carrie," Garvy said, in a tone almost as effusive as Jack's. His smile was huge, the corners of his mouth pointing up toward his minor comb-over. He wore a Knobcone Heights T-shirt today over jeans.

"Uh, hi, Garvy," I said with much less enthusiasm in my voice. "Have you found a new dog to buy things for?" That felt a little cruel since when I'd seen him only yesterday, he was still searching for his new bulldog. I glanced down at Biscuit, who now sat beside me on the shining, wood-looking floor.

"No, but I'm here to try to find one. I thought a nice pet store like this would have contacts, and people here might know of dogs available for adoption, including bulldogs."

Jack had stepped back and now watched us as we talked.

So did Harris. He added now, "We do sometimes hear online or in person when someone has pets up for adoption, primarily breeders looking for the right new home for their puppies."

"As I told you, that could be great," Garvy said. "But I'd really prefer an adult dog, one I might not have to train as much."

"And I thought you said that bulldogs were on your list but you might be willing to adopt another breed," Harris said.

"It depends." Garvy kept his gaze away from mine, and I wondered what that was about.

"If that's the case," I said, "be sure to check Mountaintop Rescue, like Janelle mentioned. Most of the dogs there are mixed breeds." I glanced down and smiled at my own mixed breed, who stood up on her hind legs and put her paws on my knees. I petted her.

"I've looked, but none struck me as being right for me." Garvy now sounded uncomfortable, and I had the sense that while he didn't want to insult rescue dogs, neither did he want to adopt one.

"Well, when you find the right dog, whatever breed or mix he might be, be sure to feed him VimPets food," Jack said, leaning toward Garvy to hand him a promotional brochure. "You can buy it right here at the Emporium." He again grinned toward Harris, whose return smile looked ironic, especially as he moved his head to regard me.

"Yes, you can," he said, "but be sure to buy your special treats at Barkery and Biscuits."

I laughed aloud, then said, "Thanks. And I'm always glad to tell people to buy the best non-handbaked stuff ever for their pets right here at the Emporium."

Despite my smiles and laughter, I felt uncomfortable. First of all, two of the three men had attempted at times to flirt with me. Second, I had a sense that there was an undercurrent flowing around me that I perceived but didn't understand.

Jack probably just wanted to sell more of his company's product here, and maybe hang out with me a bit more. Harris was being friendly with me now, and that seemed fine. But was there something else on his mind?

And Garvy? I wished I did have access to a bulldog breeder with puppies available so I could accompany him there and see his reaction. Maybe he'd fall immediately in love and go through the process right there to take one home.

But . . . well, I didn't know why I didn't trust the guy.

Maybe he'd come here to see Harris in an attempt to list his property for sale rather than to talk dogs with him. Maybe he felt sleazy to me simply because, as a realtor, he was in sales. Although, in some ways, so was I. Jack and Harris were, too.

It didn't really matter. The men were engaging now in a conversation about dog food and why VimPets ruled. I didn't need to participate.

I backed away, pulling gently on Biscuit's leash so she would follow me. I slinked my way to the shelves where VimPets food was actually for sale, picked out a bag of premium kibble and some cans of Biscuit's favorite wet food, and inched my way to the cash register.

None of the guys seemed to pay attention. I was a bit surprised, especially regarding Jack, but it felt good just to pay one of Harris's staff members and slip out, a couple of large plastic bags of food in my hands.

Biscuit and I didn't get far, though, before we were joined by Jack. "Sorry," he said. "I didn't mean to ignore you, but you know I can't disregard a chance to promote my products."

"That's okay," I said. "I need to get back to my stores anyway, so feel free to stay here and promote." I shot him a smile I hoped looked perky and encouraging since I actually meant what I said.

"Well . . . if you don't mind, I can always pop in and see you later. I'll be around town a couple of days, promoting, visiting people, boating, and whatever."

"Sounds good," I said. That didn't mean

I'd take the time to talk much more with him, though.

"Oh, and that guy . . . what's his name? Garvy? Does he sell pet products, too?"

"No, real estate," I said. "I just gather that he likes dogs."

"Well, the way he talked . . . Anyhow, maybe I can give him more advice on how to find another dog. I had the sense he lost one recently, right?"

"Right," I agreed. "And again, if you happen to know where he can find an English bulldog, let him know. That's his goal, or so he told me."

But had Garvy changed it, expanded the horizons of his search since yesterday, after not finding any likely sources for bulldogs here?

I didn't know. Didn't really care.

But while Jack returned to the Emporium and Biscuit and I started walking more briskly toward our shops — or as briskly as I could with bags of dog kibble and cans in my arms — I found myself wondering what Garvy Grant was really doing here.

If he wasn't trying to sell our properties for us, maybe he was representing a client who wanted to buy all the shops in Knobcone Heights with pet-related themes . . . and I shuddered as we started walking along the sidewalk at the edge of the town square.

We entered the Barkery first, as usual. Placing the bags of dog food on a shelf behind the glass display case, I was surprised to see that Go was already there, leashed to the enclosure. Janelle hadn't been scheduled to work today, or at least I didn't think so.

Vicky was staffing the Barkery just then. She stood behind the counter totaling the order of the two women who stood before her, one cradling a fuzzy Chihuahua. They were locals. I recognized them although I didn't know their names.

"Hi," I said to them, and the dog, too, of course.

"Hi. This place just gets better all the time." That was the woman holding the dog. "Morocco, here, just loved the sample biscuits she was given. We bought a bunch for her."

"That's great," I said with a smile, which I then moved from the customers and dogs to Vicky, who was doing such a great job.

As the two ladies left, I approached Vicky. "It looks like Janelle's here." I gestured toward Go, who had settled down on the floor with her nose pressed up to Biscuit's crate. Inside it, Biscuit also lay with her nose near where Go's was. I was delighted that they were such good buddies.

"Yes, she's in the kitchen now. She brought someone with her. I hope it's okay."

I wondered who it was. But I didn't want to disturb Vicky so I just said, "Sure. I'll go say hi."

I maneuvered my way around the counter to the door to the kitchen, which I pushed open.

Janelle was on the Barkery side of the dividing shelves. I half expected her to be taking pictures again, but I didn't see a camera.

I did, however, see Delma with her, her hands out as if to try to slow Janelle's pacing. Not that there was a lot of room for pacing in my well-designed but packed kitchen.

"Hi," I said, my tone pleasant but firm. "I didn't expect you today." I looked first at Delma but landed my gaze on Janelle.

"I didn't expect to be here, either, Carrie." Janelle's voice sounded uneven and moist, as if she was crying. Her big blue eyes were, in fact, a bit wet.

"What's going on?" I asked.

"It's those damned cops," Delma said, running her fingers through her cap of dark hair. I wanted to tell her to stop, that I didn't want loose hair fluttering around the kitchen, but at the moment it was more important to learn what she was talking about.

I also wondered where Delma had left Shobie, but figured her dog was at their hotel.

"What cops?" I asked, assuming I knew the answer.

But before either had the opportunity to explain, I heard the bell go off over the door to the Barkery. Customers were always a good thing. But then I heard the voices. Familiar ones.

"Hi. I'd like some treats for my little dachshunds, here." That had to be Detective Wayne Crunoll, who had brought his doxy mixes here before.

"And I'll go next door for some goodies from Icing." That was Detective Bridget Morana. "Oh, and by the way, is Janelle Blaystone over there?"

Janelle let out a small gasp as Delma threw her arms around her in a hug.

"I think they're here to arrest me," she cried.

Nineteen

"What makes you say that?" I asked. Before she answered I added, "When they considered me a murder suspect they just dropped in here now and then, sometimes individually and sometimes together. I think it was more to unnerve me than anything else. They often succeeded. But I kept maintaining my innocence and not talking much about what they wanted. And eventually the truth came out."

"Really?" Janelle's hopeful expression made me regret my optimistic description, at least a little. Every situation was different.

"Don't count on it," Delma told her with a look of distaste and mistrust on her face. "Just be careful what you say. To everyone."

Like me? Well, I didn't trust Delma, either. In fact, I had a sudden urge to point at her and demand that she provide all the information as to where she'd been at the time of the murder, hopefully as the two detectives walked in.

Maybe I had no reason to mistrust her. I was just trying to add more suspects to my mental list.

Both detectives came into the kitchen, flooding it with their in-charge attitudes. Good thing I wasn't baking anything, or kneading any dough. I'd have feared that their unwelcome presence might add an unwelcome smell.

I assumed that Wayne had appropriately left his dogs in the Barkery. I quickly decided how to play this game.

"Hi, detectives." I maneuvered around Delma and Janelle down the thin aisle between the dividing shelves and the ovens and plastered a smile on my face as if delighted to see them. "Have you come in here to see how we bake? Or would you like some lessons?"

"Neither." Bridget's voice was curt, even though she, too, smiled — a cruel one, I thought. "We just wanted to talk to Ms. Blaystone, get her input on some information we received from the authorities in the dog park locales."

"This seems a strange place to discuss that," I said. "Let's go into the Barkery." I motioned for them to turn around, and, surprisingly, they complied, leading the way back through the door they had just entered. Them, obeying me? How unheard of.

"Can I just run out the back?" Janelle whispered frantically.

"No, that would just make it worse. Let's see what they really have in mind. But let me take the lead, at least for now."

"Gladly."

Vicky was still in the Barkery. She was waiting on a group of customers, including, apparently, the parents of three kids who were making a fuss over the four dogs in the corner — Biscuit, Go, and Wayne's Magnum and Blade, which always seemed to me like strange names for little doxy mixes. I regarded the group warily, but the parents appeared to be watching, too, and the kids were gently patting the dogs and talking to them.

"Let's sit down here." I pulled a couple of small metal tables together and started to move enough chairs around them. I considered placing only four there, to exclude Delma, since she didn't need to be here.

"Why don't we go outside with Janelle for a few minutes? We just have a few questions we think she can answer." That was Wayne, looking all friendly-cop. I didn't trust it.

"How long can you stay?" I asked. "Janelle

obviously needs her attorney with her if you're going to question her, and I don't know how long it might take him to arrive."

"It won't be those kind of questions." Wayne's expression soured fast. "We just want some more information."

"I think a lawyer can determine what kind of questions or information his client can safely provide," I said sweetly.

"It's just about the damned dog parks," Wayne said through gritted teeth.

His superior officer waved her hand toward him over the table where we were all now sitting. "Detective Crunoll is right," she said smoothly, "but I can understand your concern, Ms. Blaystone. If you agree with Ms. Kennersly and would rather come to the station again with your attorney, that's fine. We'll figure out a time for tomorrow."

Janelle looked trapped, her gaze going from me, back to the cops, then to Delma, as if her friend could provide assistance.

That lady appeared nonplussed, as if she wasn't used to not having answers to dilemmas like this. Apparently feeling she had to say something, she spoke. I was surprised when what Delma said made sense. "Why don't you ask your questions, detectives? If there's anything about them that worries us at all, Janelle can do as you said and schedule a time to talk at your station with her lawyer."

"Fine." Bridget looked at me as if for my okay. I raised my brows and didn't disagree.

Then she looked toward Janelle, who appeared like a deer in headlights with her blue eyes huge, but she didn't disagree, either. "Okay." She sounded tentative and not at all comfortable.

"Okay," I repeated, deciding to try to stay a bit in charge here. "What do you want to ask her?" I leaned forward, resting my elbows on the table as I stared first at Bridget, then Wayne.

What they asked really didn't sound as if they were using it to get Janelle to implicate herself in Ada's death. Maybe just the opposite. They wanted more information about which dog parks she had seen Ada in when, and who she'd seen talking to her.

"The local authorities have started asking the same kinds of questions at those parks," Bridget said, "but the more data we have, the better for trying to determine what actually occurred, and who might have had a motive to kill Ms. Arnist."

"Who *else* might have had a motive," Wayne said with a smirk. I saw Janelle flinch as I rolled my eyes. Delma looked almost ready to stand and confront the guy.

Maybe she really did just want to help her friend. Although . . .

"Maybe you could provide some insight, too, Delma," I said to her. "I assume that you sometimes met Janelle and Go in some of those parks with your dog — what's her name?"

"Shobie," she said through gritted teeth. "I really didn't know Ms. Arnist, not any more than I knew other people who brought their dogs to the parks when I was there. Shobie and I went wherever Janelle and Go did, so Janelle would be better than me at coming up with names and such."

Should I be suspicious of her? I wasn't about to assume her innocence, at least.

"Not that I'm really involved here," I said, "but maybe it would be helpful for Janelle to do some kind of list of whatever new information she can provide about the parks where she saw Ada, and what other people she saw talking to her. Assuming you can remember things that specific, Janelle?"

"I'm not sure, but I can try — more of the people, and their schedules that I can remember, too. Would that help?"

I heard what she didn't add: would that help the cops focus on other people and get off her back?

"It wouldn't hurt." But Wayne's smile was again so smug I wondered whether this was a good idea after all.

It would also give more specifics about when Janelle saw Ada.

"Well, then," I said, "Janelle can contact her attorney and run the idea by him. If it sounds okay to him, she can start putting the list together soon. Okay, Janelle?"

"Fine with me," she said, and the smile she aimed at me was full of gratitude.

The detectives were gone. So were Detective Wayne's cute dogs. I'd given them a couple of peanut butter biscuits to see them on their way. I'd be happy if the dogs came back, just not their owner or his police force compatriot.

Was I now certain that Janelle was innocent? Not really. But I still hoped so. And I still hoped to zero in on that Tim guy.

I needed more information about him and his relationship with Ada. They'd known each other. From what Janelle had said, Ada had had a thing about pedigreed dogs — so she certainly might have been the dognapper, especially considering the Go situation.

The two dogs Tim had brought to our clinic appeared to be purebreds. So did the few pups I'd seen in the yard of that house

— which might or might not be where he was living.

None of that was enough to convict Tim of killing Ada. And she must have known zillions of other people, from the dog parks or elsewhere.

Including her parents, who'd put in an appearance here.

I was able to wrest Janelle away from Delma for a few minutes to call Ted Culbert. I accompanied her back to my office so she'd have privacy — from everyone but me.

I wanted to hear what he said.

Standing near the door, I let Janelle sit on the small chair behind my compact desk to use her cell to make the call.

She must have had his number programmed into her phone already, since she just pushed a couple of buttons and put it up to her ear. She had to wait for a minute, but then Ted apparently got on the phone.

"I'm at Carrie's shops," she told her lawyer. Then she related the visit from the detectives and how they'd said that the questions they asked couldn't be used against her, so she didn't need to have her lawyer present.

She held the phone away from her ear for

a minute, and even I could hear Ted's shouting.

"Okay," Janelle said when he was done, sounding chastised. "I won't talk to them at all unless you're with me. But I did agree to make a list of the times I saw Ada in the various dog parks I've told them about, and who she was talking to then, and what I can remember about the times."

Once again, Ted's response was loud. Once again, Janelle sounded chastised when she responded. "Well, I wasn't going to give it to them without letting you look at it, but I won't give it to them at all now." Another pause from her end. "Okay, I'll go ahead and see what I can come up with, and I'll give it only to you. And you'll let them know we've talked and that I won't be handing them anything. I got it." Another pause. "Yes, Carrie's right here."

She held out the phone. Apparently Ted wanted to talk to me.

I felt fairly certain it wasn't to try to indulge in our occasional light flirtation.

I leaned against the frame of the closed door and held the phone against my ear. "Hi, Ted."

"So you are there, Carrie. I assumed so, since Janelle said she was at your shops. Were you there while the detectives were harassing her?"

"Well, yes. It did sound to me like they weren't asking her questions about herself, so I didn't completely discourage them. But I guess I was wrong."

"I guess you were. I thought you'd learned better when I was representing you. In any case, people who are suspects in any kind of crime who are represented by counsel shouldn't talk to anyone about the case except that counsel, and especially not cops. Got it?"

"Yes, I get it."

"And you'll make sure Janelle gets it, too?"

I couldn't promise that. But what I could promise was, "I'll tell her what you said and won't encourage her to talk to the detectives or anyone else in authority without your being there. Is that okay?"

My eyes were on Janelle's, and she gave a tiny, understanding smile, followed by a gesture with her thumb and forefinger together that suggested agreement.

"Now . . . When are you and I going to get together for dinner?" Ted asked. The change in subject startled me — enough that I didn't immediately tell him not in the foreseeable future.

Not only was there my relationship with Reed, but I figured this would be a bad idea if I wanted Ted to continue representing Janelle to the best of his ability — and that certainly was in my brother's, and possibly my stores', best interests.

"I'm not sure," I dissembled. "Soon, I hope, although I've got some things going on at the shops — oh, and a friend who wants to do some business with my Barkery products is in town, so I just can't commit to anything at the moment."

"Well, soon it is. Give me a call if you think you'll have some time — and I'll be calling you, too." He paused. "Oh, and Carrie?"

"Yes?"

"I know you did a good job figuring out who killed Myra Ethman when you were the primary suspect, but that doesn't make you a licensed and skilled detective. I appreciate your wanting to help my client, and I understand you have reason to. But keep out of it. You hear?"

"Yes," I said. I heard.

But that didn't mean I agreed.

Twenty

I purposely had a nice, calm rest of the day, glad when it was finally time to close my shops.

We'd had a good day of business. I'd had an odd day dealing with people on a non-business basis.

When Reed called and suggested we get together for dinner, I asked for a rain check, and he mentioned that rain was predicted for the next night.

"That may be when I'll cash it in," I said.

"Then let the rain come down," Reed said, and I smiled as I hung up.

I was in the Barkery closing up and looked down at Biscuit. "Now let's go home and veg out," I told her, and we did.

I talked to Neal a bit when he came in later. I wasn't surprised to hear he'd gotten together with Janelle, nor that Delma had joined them, along with both their dogs. Neal escorted them all on a nice walk that would have been better, he said, if it had erased all that Janelle said she'd been through that day with the detectives and her lawyer.

I didn't disagree, but I did go to bed early, which helped me wake up very early the next morning.

At least my day at the shops started off well. Frida came in first thing and helped with the baking, and everything was ready for me to open both shops on time.

A few hours later, I had just entered the kitchen to check on some scones baking for Icing when my phone rang. I pulled it out of my pocket and looked to see who was calling.

It was Billi Matlock.

"Good morning," I said, walking slowly toward the Icing oven. I smelled the luscious aroma of blueberry scones and inhaled as I spoke. "How are you this morning? *Where* are you this morning — at your spa or at Mountaintop Rescue?"

"I'm actually at City Hall right now since we're preparing for an impromptu lunch meeting of City Council. But I just came from the shelter, and — well, have you met a visitor to town named Garvy Grant?"

I sucked in my breath. That guy was apparently getting around. And why was Billi asking me about him?

"Yes," I said. "I gather he's looking for a new dog since he recently lost a pet. Did he ask you about English bulldogs?"

"Yes. It apparently wasn't his first visit to the shelter but I hadn't seen him there before. I was the one to talk to him this time, though. He seemed quite interested in seeing what other dogs we had in residence when I confirmed to him that we didn't have any English bulls. And no, before you ask, I didn't tell him that my fellow City Council member Les Ethman happens to have an English bull. I'm not sure where Les got Sam and didn't want this guy bothering him about it."

"Good choice," I said. "Now, would you please hold on a minute? I need to get something out of the oven, but I want to continue this conversation." I wasn't sure why, except out of curiosity. At least Garvy was apparently listening to my suggestion to really look around our local shelter to see who was there. On the other hand, he was holding out for the particular breed, which was fine, but in that case he should be hunting online for rescues or breeders. "Okay," I said after taking the pan of scones from the oven to cool and picking up my phone again. "Back to Garvy Grant. I don't suppose he was interested in adopting Sweetie, was he?"

I was sure I knew the answer, since the little dog resembling Biscuit didn't look at all like a bulldog. But adorable Sweetie hadn't been swept up into a family yet, and I felt a bit guilty for not adopting her myself. On the other hand, I'd worry if I heard that someone like Garvy had adopted her.

"I think you know the answer to that," Billi said dryly.

"Okay, then, why did you call to ask me about him? Did he say something about me?"

"Yes, he said he'd talked to you and you'd sent him to my shelter."

Oh. Okay. "And is he going to check for breeders now?"

"I got that impression."

"Good." I prepared to change the subject somewhat, to ask if Billi had engaged in any good rescues since we'd talked last.

But before I could, Billi said, "Did he strike you as a little . . . well, let's say, odd?"

Rather than just shouting "Yes!" I wanted to hear Billi's rationale first. "In what way?" I prompted.

"Well, he kept asking questions — not only about where we rescued our dogs, which public shelters and all, but he asked to see a list of all the dogs we'd brought in lately, and whether any appeared to be purebreds. And then he asked if anyone had tried to dump any dogs off here, and if so, what their backgrounds were. I thought of Go, of course, but by then I was freaked out enough about the guy to just answer generically and not entirely truthfully. Is he some kind of over-the-top animal rescuer?"

"He's apparently in real estate. I don't suppose he made an offer to sell the property that Mountaintop Rescue is on, did he?"

"No. Not at all. How interesting." But Billi didn't sound interested, just more bemused by the situation.

I was glad I wasn't the only one who didn't quite get Garvy Grant.

Maybe I could find out more about him.

After I hung up with Billi, though, I heard the bell over the door ring a couple of times in Icing. This wasn't one of Dinah's regular working days, but Vicky had requested that she come in and Dinah had agreed. I poked my head in to see if she could handle the crowd, since I only had one part-timer on duty that morning, Frida, and she was in the Barkery.

All seemed fine in Icing. Dinah was waiting on one small crowd of customers, and another man and woman were peering into the glass display case and discussing what they might want to buy.

I nevertheless strolled in and raised my voice. "In case anyone's interested, I just pulled a really nice, fresh, and delicious tray of blueberry scones out of the oven."

"That sounds perfect," said the woman, and the guy nodded.

Dinah's crowd, too, also made excited noises, and I wondered if I'd made enough new scones.

I went into the kitchen again, itching to go into the Barkery but knowing I'd better deliver the promised scones first.

Which I did. And five minutes later, I at last got to head to my other shop.

Frida seemed to be doing fine there, too. Biscuit, in her enclosure, was trading nose sniffs with a Lhasa Apso on the outside, and that dog's owner was busy instructing my assistant which doggy treats she wanted, to go. Two more crowds of people were there, a couple sitting at one of the small tables with their coffee and a couple of goldens on the floor beside them, chewing on something.

The others — three women in nice outfits, suggesting they were on a break from their jobs — appeared to be waiting to be helped, so I helped them. One looked familiar, probably had shopped here before, but I didn't recognize the others. I gave all of them sample treats for their pups at home, then gathered the products they wanted to buy.

Fortunately, my phone didn't ring again until after I'd rung up their purchases and they'd all left the Barkery.

It was Neal, who invited me to join him for dinner at the resort. That was highly unusual. My brother rarely invited me out anywhere, let alone his place of work. Not that he would necessarily pay; I realized this after I'd hung up.

I figured I knew what was on his mind: I was being nosy again regarding a murder situation, and, since we'd just discussed it last night, he knew my latest involvement. But apparently, not only were Ada Arnist's parents now eating often at the resort restaurant — Neal had mentioned this before — but they'd made dinner reservations for that very night.

Did Neal even have access to dinner reservations at late notice, or was he still — or again? — friends with waitress Gwen? It didn't really matter.

"Maybe you can get some additional insight from them about their daughter and her friends and dogs and all," he told me.

"While you and I eat dinner there?"

"Well, it won't hurt to try. And you're better at it than I am, although we can hopefully get a table near them so we can at least eavesdrop."

"Well, okay." I made myself sound reluctant, though I was a bit intrigued.

Before I hung up, I heard noise from outside the Barkery. Rain.

I recalled my rain check, and thought it wouldn't hurt at all to have someone else at the table with us.

"I hope it's okay with you," I said, "but Reed will most likely be joining us."

"Sounds good," Neal said.

No, I thought. *Sounds like rain.*

We were busy for the rest of the day, and I only had the two assistants on duty. That meant I didn't have time to look on the Internet and see what I could find out about Garvy Grant and his real estate transactions . . . or anything else.

But I planned to do so soon.

I finally closed both stores for the evening and Biscuit and I headed home. Despite the rain, I walked my little girl outside after pulling into the driveway, then dried her paws as we entered the house through the kitchen. She had a good dinner of VimPets food plus a couple of Barkery treats.

Since it was Monday, Jack had already headed back down the mountain to his home, but he'd called and promised to come back soon.

I hoped he'd give me some notice next time — although I wasn't sure I wanted to spend any more time with him.

Reed soon picked me up at my house, and I greeted him with a kiss. We were dogless for the evening, partly because of the ongoing rain shower, which wasn't very heavy but definitely steady. We wouldn't want to sit outside on the resort restaurant's patio.

I didn't want to do so in any case, since I'd no indication that Ada's parents would come with a dog or would otherwise wish to eat their dinner outside.

I did, however, explain to Reed as he drove why we were eating with Neal, and at that particular restaurant.

"You're determined to find out who killed Ada Arnist, aren't you?" he asked when I was done.

I watched his face for disgust, admiration, or whatever he was feeling as I responded, but he simply looked alert as he drove. "I'm concerned about my brother," I said. "He cares for Janelle, and she's a suspect like I was before. If I can learn the truth, or at least attempt to, I'll either help him further that relationship or nip it in the bud — if it turns out she really is the killer."

"And who do you think it is at this moment?"

I waited before responding, pondering the possibilities. "I'd like to think that it's Tim, the guy who brought those two purebred dogs to the clinic. Maybe he and Ada were conspirators in the dognappings that included Go, and had a falling out, and . . ."

"And he killed his accomplice? That sounds like a good theory. But I gather the cops haven't pounced on it. Any idea why?"

"I've mentioned that situation to them, especially the whole dognapping thing and the house I found with dogs in it where Tim might be living. But I don't think they've talked to him to check him out. Janelle's still a convenient suspect because of her argument with Ada."

We had reached the resort and Reed took the ticket to enter the parking lot. I'd check with Neal about whether he could get it validated tonight. After all, we were here primarily because he'd set things up so I could listen to, and possibly talk to, Ada's parents.

Reed had to hunt for a spot in the crowded

lot, but we soon parked and headed into the lobby — busy as usual. I hurried to the reception desk to let Neal know we were here.

"Go ahead into the restaurant and use my name," he said. "I'll join you in just a minute."

Reed and I followed his instructions and, despite how crowded the restaurant was, we were seated fairly quickly, taking up one of the few empty tables.

And, sure enough, the senior man and woman I'd last seen at the Arnists' mansion were at the next table.

I hadn't gotten a really good look at them previously, but it seemed to me that they now looked even a bit older. I wasn't sure whether Ada's body had been released yet so they could have it transported to whatever funeral home they'd chosen.

They both had on clothing that appeared expensive and dressy, and Mrs. Arnist wore a lot of jewelry, as she had when I'd seen her before.

For the moment, I just settled in at the table. Reed and I each ordered wine and glasses of water. Our server wasn't Gwen but a guy I didn't recognize, and I was glad I didn't have to make conversation with the woman Neal had previously been interested in.

As I studied the familiar menu, I said nothing but kept my ears perked up. The Arnists didn't seem to be conversing with each other. They must have ordered, though, since there were no menus on their pristine white table cloth, but there was a basket of rolls.

I wasn't quite sure how to handle this and was glad when Neal finally joined us. We all three placed our orders fairly quickly after that. Both Neal and I chose rainbow trout, which could have been caught right in Knobcone Lake. Reed selected a chicken dish.

When our server left, I looked first at Neal and then let my gaze rove tellingly to my right, where the Arnists sat, and back again. What I didn't do was ask what I should do next.

Neal gave a brisk nod in their direction, silently telling me to approach them.

And do what? Well, offering my condolences wouldn't hurt.

I stood and walked toward the table. "Mr. and Mrs. Arnist?"

"That's right," the man said, and they both looked up. The woman's gaze looked wary.

"I was one of the people on the hike near your house the other day, but I didn't get much of a chance to talk to you. As I said then, though, I'm sorry for your loss. I'm a real dog lover, and I heard that Ada was, too."

"She didn't steal that woman's dog," Mrs. Arnist — Sondra, if I remembered correctly — hissed.

"I'd really love to have whoever hurt her brought to justice," I said, without actually responding to her statement. "I'm sure you've talked to the police about it, but did you have any idea Ada was in trouble? That someone might harm her?"

"She had a lot of friends," Sondra wailed. "Everyone loved her. It just doesn't make any sense."

"Why are you asking?" her husband — Sheldon? — demanded. He peered past me toward the table where Reed and Neal still sat. I turned enough to see they were both watching. "The police told us not to talk to anyone here but them. But if you're that nosy — did you know our Ada? Do you know who killed her?"

Time to back off. Instead of getting more information here, I was only getting more frustrated.

TWENTY-ONE

Since Neal was with us, he drove me home, which meant I said good night to Reed at the resort — but not before we got off on our own for a few minutes while Neal went back to the reception desk to sign out or whatever he did. He also, fortunately, was able to validate Reed's parking ticket.

Which was a good thing, since Reed insisted on paying for dinner for all of us.

Our few moments alone together in a hallway allowed us to kiss good night. It seemed I could really be getting serious with the hunky veterinarian.

The rain had tapered off into a mist, so the drive home beneath the Knobcone Heights street lights was wet and shiny.

"Where's Janelle tonight?" I asked my brother. I'd half expected her to join us for dinner but realized that could have been a bad idea, since the main purpose of the outing was to try to learn something from or about Ada's parents. Not that I'd been successful.

"She and Delma said they were just going to stay at their hotel with their dogs and order in a pizza. I've already called to tell her we didn't get anything too exciting from the Arnists."

"Oh. Did she hope we'd learned something?"

Neal was silent for a moment. When I glanced over at him, my brother was looking out the windshield toward a stop sign. We were, in fact, stopped. But I didn't think his grim expression was completely due to trying to stay safe on the wet roads.

"That's part of the problem," he finally said. "I'm not sure what Janelle's hopes are about anything. Her expectations don't seem very high or optimistic. I think she believes she'll be arrested at any moment."

Okay, I might have been unsuccessful at my attempt to wrest some information from Ada's parents, but maybe this would lead me into learning something from my brother.

"I'm sorry to hear that. She's doing a great job helping out at my shops, and she's even providing me free publicity on social media. I like her." But I couldn't swear she was innocent of murder.

Could Neal?

"Yeah, me too. A lot." We started creeping slowly forward in the mist. "But . . ."

He hesitated, and since I didn't see anything dangerous outside the car, I asked, "But what?"

"She really loves her dog, which I understand. And she'd already gotten him back when Ada was killed, so I really don't believe she'd have any reason to have hurt her then."

Oh. So my brother had at least some of the same doubts I had. "But you're not sure." I didn't make it a question.

"I'm pretty sure," he asserted loudly and immediately. "I'd be more likely to think her friend Delma did it. They're good buddies, you know. I've spent some time with them together, on short walks and having dinner and all, and that Delma does seem to have a temper."

"Enough to kill someone she got angry with for maybe doing something awful to a friend?" I really hadn't gotten to know Delma well at all, so although I considered her as much of a suspect as anyone who'd appeared to know Ada — especially those who'd met Ada elsewhere — I hadn't really focused on her much.

Neal slumped a bit in his seat. We were

nearing our house, and, fortunately, he was driving slowly. "I don't know. Maybe it's just wishful thinking because no one's been arrested yet and I really don't want it to be Janelle who did it." He paused. "I know you think it might be that Tim guy. But do you have anything you can take to the cops about him?"

"Beyond what I've already done — told them I thought he might have been her accomplice in stealing dogs — I have no proof of it. And I'm not sure if they've looked at all into the place in his neighborhood where the dogs were. Even if they're taking me seriously without telling me about it, I don't know if he's a killer or just a possible dog thief."

"Right." Neal pulled into the driveway, so this conversation was over. We even said good night then, since he planned to go straight to his room.

I soon had Biscuit out for her last walk of the night. She didn't seem to mind the dampness and neither did I. In fact, it seemed appropriately sad, as if the world around us was crying a bit over the dilemma of Ada's murder.

Boy, was I developing an imagination. I'd have to tell Dinah about how wild my thoughts were getting. Maybe my creative assistant could use them in a story.

Back in the kitchen, I dried Biscuit off with a towel, especially her wet paws. Then we both headed upstairs to bed.

I wasn't surprised not to fall asleep quickly. Too many questions still circulated through my mind.

Did the Arnists know anything that might help determine who killed their daughter?

Was Delma Corning's attitude any kind of sign that she could have had something to do with it? Or was she acting that way in protection of a guilty Janelle?

Was I right that Tim Smith was a dog thief, an accomplice of Ada's, and her murderer?

I couldn't learn any of that just lying in bed. And that stuff wasn't all that I wondered about. There was one thing that I'd already decided to research that might have nothing to do with Ada's murder — but was scratching at my mind, making me curious.

I had planned to do some Internet searches on bulldog-lover Garvy Grant. Maybe by learning something on this tangent, I'd be able to shove everything else aside, at least for a while.

No matter what, I was determined to Google him tomorrow.

■ ■ ■ ■

That didn't happen first thing, though.

I got a call from Arvie at the veterinary clinic begging me to do a shift that morning. I'd already been at my shops for a few hours and all the baked treats for both of them were ready for the day to begin. Janelle was there early, and I had her working in the Barkery. Dinah was in Icing. Both said they wouldn't mind if I was gone for the rest of the morning, so Biscuit and I left soon afterward.

Fortunately, the problem at the clinic was more of a scheduling error than having an abundance of really ill pets, so although the time passed quickly, I was able to help in a bunch of non-life-threatening situations.

Afterward, Biscuit and I took the time to stop at Cuppa-Joe's for a quick bite of lunch out on the patio and short visit with the Joes.

When we returned to the shops and I was about to take my dog into the Barkery, I was surprised to see who was walking up the other side of the sidewalk toward me: Chef Manfred Indor. He was one excellent chef, who'd been fired pretty much unjustly from the resort restaurant a few months ago.

He and I had bonded after his firing, and although he had found a couple of other jobs nearly immediately, he had promised to provide me with some additional dog treat recipes of his own making.

He had done so already, and that was apparently why he was here again. The rotund guy was wearing a long white jacket over jeans and was carrying a large plate with a metal cover over it. He was accompanied by his partner, George Sackson, who had come with him before. George was carrying a second covered plate. He was nearly as large as Manfred, and had brown hair much longer than Manfred's kinked dark hair.

"Hi," I said to both of them, stopping on the sidewalk just outside the Barkery door. Biscuit sat down at my feet, wagging her tail, her nose up in the air, which showed that she smelled whatever treats these men had brought. "Are those for me?" I grinned.

"No, for some of your customers," Manfred said. "If you like what they contain I will give you the recipe, as long as you give us both credit for creating it. It was George's idea first, and we've both refined it."

"And what is it?" I asked.

"Organic gingerbread dog cookies," George responded, revealing large white teeth as he smiled. He was more prone to smiling than his partner, or so I'd noticed before.

"That must be why Biscuit's so exited," I said. "She can smell the gingerbread out here. But come on inside and she and I will both try them."

They entered the Barkery with us, and all four of us, plus Janelle who'd been running the shop, took tastes of the gingerbread dog cookies.

"Delicious!" I exclaimed, and Janelle seconded it. In her way, so did Biscuit, standing up on her hind legs and digging a bit at Manfred's long jeans for more.

Now, we will do this the same way as last time," Manfred said. "You go ahead and sell the cookies on these platters at whatever amount you want to charge. Then, if you're happy with the results, you can pay us half of what you bring in. If you like them well enough, you can have the recipe — and, again, you can pay us half of whatever you net on selling those you bake."

"Of course," I said. "And like last time, I'll give you both credit for creating these wonderful dog treats." I sometimes labeled my various dog and people products by placing small flags with the names of the treats on the display platters. I had done that before with Manfred's and George's excellent creations — peanut butter last time.

"Is it okay if I take pictures now and put them up for everyone to see?" Janelle asked, looking first at me and then at Manfred.

"Of course," the chef boomed.

"Sounds great to me, as long as you mention both the Barkery and the creators of the treats on your online sites," I added.

"Of course," Janelle said.

While she took photos of the platters with their lids removed, then of Biscuit and a couple of customers' dogs who'd just come in — after I got their written okay about doing so — I made a pot of coffee for the people in the store, including the customers. I made sure the two women left with bags of gingerbread treat samples, as well as a couple of cookies from Icing.

Dinah had come in to the Barkery, too, after finishing with some Icing customers, to see what all the excitement was about. She promised to listen for the bell in case others seeking people treats entered Icing, and of course I would, too.

So we wound up having an impromptu dog treat party. I enjoyed it — even as I realized it was delaying what I'd hoped to accomplish that day.

But sometimes spontaneous fun and treats

had to come first.

And then we had more customers. Mostly on the Icing side, and I learned that the crowd was a busload of tourists who had come from San Francisco to visit some offbeat areas in Southern California that they might not have seen before. But not just offbeat areas; since they considered themselves traveling gourmets, they were trying out, on their journey, restaurants and bakeries and other places selling foods that were new to them.

Somehow, Icing on the Cake had gotten onto their list — from Janelle's online promo? — and I could only cheer, offer them samples, and suggest some of our favorite people sweets to buy, such as the former owner Brenda's wonderful red velvet cupcakes.

Janelle stayed in the Barkery, which had a good regular turnout, but this tour bus contained only people, not their dogs.

I did manage to ask a lot of them — primarily middle aged to senior women — if they happened to have left their canine best friends at home. Some did, so I sent them over to the Barkery side to see what we had to offer there, too, and to get samples they could bring home to their dogs. Better yet, to assuage their guilty consciences about leaving their dogs by buying them a nice bagful of special Barkery treats.

All in all, it was a busy, productive, and profitable afternoon. When the tour bus left, I had to hurry into the kitchen to bake another round of people cookies and cupcakes for customers who might come in during the rest of the day.

I didn't make a large amount, though, to avoid having too many leftovers. Even if I did have leftovers, the freshest items would still be saleable tomorrow. Those that were still good and edible but I preferred not to sell, I would save for the charities down the mountain that came up weekly to pick up leftovers from my shops and other bakeries around here. They then made our slightly unfresh products available to low-income families near them who happened to have a sweet tooth.

This was similar to how I made Barkery leftovers available to my vet clinic and Mountaintop Rescue, to assure that nearly none of my baked goods from either side went to waste.

"Everything okay in here?" That was Dinah, who had stayed out in Icing while I got the latest set of trays ready to bake. It was getting toward late afternoon, and a lull in the number of customers, after our wonderful glut before, was probably a good thing.

"Fine. No one in Icing right now?"

"No. All's well, and I peeked into the Barkery before coming back here. There were a couple of young guys there with a golden retriever who was over at the side with Go and Biscuit while his owner bought him treats. Janelle seems to be doing fine there on her own."

"Great. Then would you keep an eye on the oven for me? I need to check something in my office. Keep your ears open for anyone coming into Icing, though."

If only my young-looking wannabe writer assistant knew what I was up to.

But I didn't tell her as I closed the office door behind me, sat down at the small desk, and booted up my computer.

Twenty-Two

Did I really care about this research project? Maybe. In particular, though, it felt good to believe that I might reach a resolution and get some answers about at least something — or someone — in the odd things going on around me.

At least I'd potentially learn which real estate company employed the bulldog-seeker Garvy Grant. Then I could tuck him, or at least thoughts of him, way back in my mind and simply be friendly but even more remote when I saw him next.

Assuming I even saw him again. Maybe his vacation was over and he had headed back down the mountains to the real properties he was familiar with and intent on selling.

Besides, in a large city like Los Angeles, he was much more likely to find an English bulldog who needed to be rescued. He could certainly find breeders there. Then he could hook up with a new canine family member. That was what people did — nice people. Good people. Was Garvy Grant among them?

Sitting on my narrow, wheeled desk chair, I booted up my laptop, the same one I used for keeping track of the accounts of both my stores.

Then I did my Google search. There were a couple of people with similar names as Garvy Grant but different spellings.

I did find a website for a Garvy Grant in real estate in Los Angeles, but there weren't many details about transactions he'd been involved in. I didn't stop there, though.

Interestingly, where the search engine suggested other similar names, I found that there were men named Grant Garvy — with variations on that spelling, too. Some had photos associated with them, so I could rule them out, but some did not.

One of those Grant Garvys apparently did live in Southern California.

The best I could tell from the information about him, he was a private investigator.

Was this the man who was visiting Knobcone Heights and looking for English bulldogs?

If so, why?

■ ■ ■ ■

I stayed at the computer a while longer, looking up Grant Garvy the PI, but I didn't find anything much about him or his background or any investigations he might have conducted. I supposed that if I was more of a techie and could dig deeper into the couple of sites where I did see his name — one was a list of licensed private investigators where you had to be a member of the organization to dig into it, and another asked you to sign up as a potential client and apparently then get bombarded by PIs looking for clients — maybe then I could find out more about him.

Till now, I'd been cordial enough to Garvy Grant — if that was his actual name. I'd seen him around town, often at locations that had something to do with dogs, such as at my Barkery and Knob Hill Pet Emporium, and I knew he'd been to Mountaintop Rescue.

I hadn't been eager to get to know more about him, or to get to know him better, especially since I found his occasional attempts to flirt with me utterly off-putting.

As a result, I had no idea where he was now. Was he still in or around Knobcone

Heights? If so, where was he staying?

Did it really matter? Sure, I was curious to learn if my slight bit of snooping was accurate and the guy was a detective — of a different sort, of course, than my non-buddies in the Knobcone Heights Police Department.

And if he was, why had he come here? Was his presence additional evidence that dognappers down in Los Angeles were using little Knobcone Heights as some kind of headquarters?

I shifted then to another search engine. Maybe it would have something different, another way to find out more about Garvy.

That didn't corral the many directions my mind was taking.

I was jumping to a lot of conclusions about Garvy without any reason or evidence, or anything else but suppositions. Maybe he wasn't either of the people I'd found through that first search engine, the Garvy Grant in real estate and the Grant Garvy who was a PI.

Even if he was, though, his interest in dogs in his own life could be genuine, a diversion as he either enjoyed a vacation here or investigated something else altogether.

On the other hand, if he did have something to do with the dogs and was trying to find out what Ada and any accomplices of hers might have done with them . . . well, did he know who those accomplices were? Were there more besides Tim?

Maybe he would know of a whole additional bunch of people who'd had a motive to kill Ada.

As a result of my unstoppable musings, I really wanted to find the guy and talk to him. Maybe he would help me clear Janelle of suspicion in Ada's death.

Unless the opposite was true, and he could instead show why Janelle was the most likely killer.

If all went well, though, maybe we could collaborate. Or I could at least learn something from him. I didn't want to be a private investigator, but P.I. skills might come in handy to help clear Janelle — I hoped.

Okay. I had spent more than enough time on the computer. I needed to get back into my shops and help my assistants wait on any customers.

And ignore what I felt certain would be floating around in my mind: *How do I find Garvy Grant and talk to him now?*

I spent the rest of the afternoon going back and forth between my stores waiting on shoppers. I had to calm my mind to avoid allowing distraction to prevail over good business sense and customer care.

I considered asking my two helpers on duty, Dinah and Janelle, if they happened to know where Garvy Grant was. I was sure Janelle at least knew *who* he was since we'd been together with Garvy around. But I'd no reason to think she knew where he was these days.

I wasn't sure Dinah had been working the day Garvy had visited my shops, so I'd no idea whether she would even know who he was, let alone where he might be.

During a lull between customers, when things were relatively quiet, I took Biscuit and Go for a walk across the street to the town square. I'd done that before when Janelle was on duty and had brought her dog with her to the Barkery. She, in turn, sometimes brought Biscuit along when she walked Go.

I'd seen Garvy once before in the town square, so I hoped today would be the second time.

It wasn't.

How did one find the location of an almost-stranger? I hadn't found any specifics about him online. Even if I could locate his contact information I didn't think I'd call him, since I didn't want to sound as if I wanted to see him, even though I did — but for reasons of my own that someone as flirtatious as he was might misconstrue.

I could tell him I was looking for a piece of real estate, but I didn't really want him to show me any.

I simply wanted to run into him somewhere, act surprised to see him, and ask my few questions.

Because . . . well, if it turned out he was Grant Garvy, Investigator, I really, really wanted to learn what he knew about the stolen dogs, and if they had anything to do with Ada's death.

Weird on my part? Yes. But it might save me time and energy in clearing Janelle to get any insight he had.

So how could I find him subtly? Call all the hotels in the area?

That wouldn't be subtle, even if they gave out information. And I didn't know if he was even still in town.

Billi Matlock would most likely let me know if Garvy showed up at Mountaintop Rescue again, not because I'd asked her to, but because she might want my further input into what to say to the guy about bulldogs, or about canines who were actually available for adoption at the shelter. I decided not to contact her.

I didn't always know when Neal was taking a group of hikers out next, but even though the rain had nearly stopped, I doubted he'd do an outing that evening. Tomorrow, maybe. I could ask him tonight if he was, and who was signed up for it.

So how else could I find the guy — or shut my own obsession down and simply forget about him?

I considered again where to look for Garvy.

The two places in town where people tended to congregate, both residents and visitors, were Cuppa-Joe's and the Knobcone Heights Resort. I'd not seen any indication of Garvy's presence at Cuppa's, though he might have visited there sometime when I wasn't around.

But one place I had seen him was the resort. Despite having eaten there last night, it wouldn't hurt to spend part of this Tuesday evening there, especially if I had company.

I scooped up after both Go and Biscuit, glad I'd brought a couple of my usual biodegradable bags, gave them a few more minutes to sniff and squat, and then walked them both back across the street. When I had them secured in the corner of the Barkery containing Biscuit's enclosure, I went back outside after removing my cell phone from my pocket. I stood on the sidewalk, smiling at people I recognized even when they walked by without stopping at either of my shops. Residents would come back when they needed something sweet for themselves and nutritious for their dogs. Icing and the Barkery had already developed a reputation in this town for both.

I quickly pushed the button to call Reed. I didn't expect to reach him right away since I figured he'd be with a patient. Although it was getting late in the day for scheduled office visits, things generally tended to run overtime at the vet clinic.

To my surprise, though, he answered. "Must be ESP," he said. "I was going to call you soon and see if Biscuit and you wanted to join Hugo and me for dinner again tonight."

"Yep," I said. "ESP. I wanted to find out if you two could join us at the resort this evening."

"I was going to suggest the Arrowhead Diner, so we're not completely on the same wavelength, but the resort works for me, too. We'll pick you both up at your place at seven o'clock, okay?"

"Okay," I agreed with a smile — even as I continued to watch the town square across the street in the event that my target happened to appear there now, after I'd left it.

But I still didn't see Garvy . . . now. I hoped I would tonight.

I'd called to warn Neal that Reed and I and our dogs would be at the resort once more that evening, though I didn't tell him what I wanted to learn there this time. When we arrived, Neal was still busy behind the reception desk, but I waved to ensure he saw us. Then, at my request, Reed and I headed toward the bar first.

That was the place where I'd seen Garvy here previously. But when I stood at the door and let my eyes get accustomed to the low light, I didn't see him in the crowd.

"Let's go eat," I told Reed.

We sat on the back patio, beneath an umbrella although the only humidity was in the air, not falling as rain or even mist. Tonight Gwen was our server, which became even more interesting when Neal pulled up a chair and joined Reed and me at our table, with Biscuit and Hugo at our feet.

Neal's former romantic-interest-of-sorts was fully cordial, though, and brought us water quickly, followed by the wine I'd requested and the beer the guys had ordered.

Gwen might be a good one to ask whether Garvy had been at the resort. She saw everything and everyone, I figured. Did she know him? I couldn't recall if I'd seen them in the same room together previously. Neal, of course, would know who Garvy was, and Reed, too. I didn't see my target here at the restaurant, either inside or on the patio with us. Maybe, other than being potentially fun, tonight's outing would be a complete bust.

But I could at least ask some hopefully subtle questions about him, and who'd seen him around last.

It didn't turn out nearly as subtle as I'd hoped, though. Not only did Neal join us for dinner, but he had invited Janelle, too. That meant Go was also with us, which was fine. So were Delma and her Boston terrier Shobie.

That added up to five humans and four dogs at the two tables pushed together to accommodate all of us. I decided to wait until we'd all ordered and then try to find a way to subtly start asking for any information about Garvy.

Maybe I shouldn't, though. I was being completely weird about this. What if it did turn out he was a PI? Was I going to run all my suspicions and suspects by him?

Not a good idea.

I decided, despite my rationale for coming to the restaurant tonight with this group, to just drop the whole thing.

But the subject of Ada did come up, especially when Neal mentioned that her parents had been eating there the night before and we'd chatted with them.

"Too bad they didn't tell you who might have been after their daughter," Janelle said to Neal, sounding dejected. "Did they give any hint?"

"No," he said, then glanced at me.

"Unfortunately not." I decided to act as if I was changing the subject completely. "So when's your next evening hike around the lake, Neal?"

"Yes, I want to go next time," Delma said. "Those hikes sound like fun."

We talked about the recent ones then. I gently pushed the conversation into a discussion of who had joined us.

"They were mostly guests from the resort," Neal said. "Some other visitors, too."

"Like that real estate guy — what was his name?" I asked.

"Something like Garvy," Neal responded.

"Oh, he came into our stores, didn't he?" Janelle asked, and I nodded.

"If you get another hike together, maybe you could contact the hikers who came on the last two — like that Garvy," I said. "Do you know how to contact him?"

His answer had to wait for a few minutes as Gwen and another server brought our food to the table. I'd ordered a delicious-looking Cobb salad that night. Reed got a double hamburger and immediately removed one of the beef patties to share with all the dogs.

But when we got back to the prior conversation, Neal had no information about how to contact Garvy. Apparently the guy had paid cash, which happened often since Neal didn't charge a lot for his hikes. And no one talked about having seen him again, even though I tried to nudge the conversation once more in that direction.

Mostly what I got out of the evening was a good dinner with nice people and well-behaved dogs. I noticed how much attention Neal and Janelle were paying to one another. No matter what else was going on, their attraction appeared to be ramping up.

Afterward, since Neal indicated he was going to stay around for a while with Janelle and Delma, then take them back to their hotel room, Reed invited Biscuit and me to his home for a drink before taking us back to my place.

We each, indeed, had one more drink at his house. And engaged in some very enjoyable and personal stuff, too. Soon, though, I had to ask that he take us home because of my usual early hours the next morning.

So that was that. My evening had been wonderful, but I'd gotten no information about Garvy Grant or Grant Garvy or whoever. Maybe it was just as well. I'd do a lot better on Janelle's behalf by going in other directions.

Maybe I could even find a reason to stop in at the police station and talk to the chief. Loretta Jonas had not been particularly excited when I'd given her the information about the possibility of stolen dogs being in the area. Maybe I could bring her treats for her rescue dog Jellybean and find a way to ask how other things were going — like, had any law enforcement organization found out about those dogs I'd been concerned over, or were the cops ready to arrest someone in Ada Arnist's death?

Sure, I could do that subtly.

Once more that night I didn't sleep extremely well, even though I felt very relaxed after being with Reed earlier.

And for the next few days I tried to rein my mind in, since I didn't have any further ideas about how to help Janelle. She hadn't been arrested yet anyway. Maybe all was good with her.

Until Friday. That was when she called me at the shops, sounding utterly upset, to say she couldn't come in that day to help out. She'd been asked to bring her attorney and come back to the police station since they had a few more questions for her.

I was in the Barkery when she called, along with Vicky, who was also helping out that day. Dinah was working in Icing. I hopefully had enough assistance that day, and I had to do something to help Janelle. But what?

More customers entered the shop, so I had to concentrate on them first. A good diversion, and a profitable one, since they were planning a doggy birthday party and wanted a whole bunch of Barkery treats.

When they left with numerous packages in their arms, my mind returned to Janelle's call. I still needed to figure out what to do.

Unless, of course, the cops actually did just need some more information from her about her suspicions of how Go had gotten to Knobcone Heights.

Then why would they advise her to bring her lawyer?

I was standing behind the counter at the

Barkery, my head somewhat spinning. I closed my eyes briefly to try to settle down my thoughts — and the bells at the door rang.

I opened my eyes — just as Garvy Grant walked in.

"Hello, Carrie," he called out effusively, avoiding Vicky and the people she was waiting on and striding straight toward me. "Did I hear that you were looking for me?"

Twenty-Three

Interesting. How had he gotten that impression? Was he some kind of remote mind-reader?

When and where had he heard . . . ? He hadn't been at the resort on Tuesday when we'd had dinner there, had he? Even if I hadn't seen him, Neal would have known if he was there.

Then again, if my intuition was working right and the guy really was a professional PI, he'd surely want to know who was checking him out. Was there some way he could sign up for some kind of notification if his name was searched online — any possible name?

My puzzlement must have been obvious since he laughed, brightening the shine in his green eyes. Yes, he was good-looking. Too bad I wasn't interested.

"Hey, I think we've got some stuff to discuss," he said. "Care to take Biscuit for a walk across the street with me?"

We weren't extremely busy, and I knew Dinah and Vicky could handle the shops. I could keep an eye on things remotely, too, from the town square as I walked Biscuit and talked with Garvy. "Fine," I said. "Let me tell my assistants."

A few minutes later, I hooked Biscuit's leash to my excited pup's collar and we exited the Barkery with Garvy. There was a bit of traffic on Summit Avenue, but we soon got across the street. A few other dogs were sniffing out the busy town square filled with parents and kids, so I let Biscuit slowly wend her way in the direction of these dogs, watching to make sure the nearest ones, a pit bull and a collie mix, didn't appear aggressive. Only the pit bull got close, and Biscuit and he seemed to get along fine.

Then Garvy gestured toward a path leading into the town square beneath some of its knobcone pines, and Biscuit and I began walking in that direction.

Today was one of the days Garvy dressed casually. Did that mean he wasn't on duty — either as a real estate agent or, possibly, a PI?

It was time to start our conversation, but he didn't seem inclined to even though he'd suggested it.

So I took control. "What made you think I was looking for you?" I asked.

"A little bird told me."

I glared at him.

"A little bird at the Knobcone Resort," he amended. "I went there for a drink last night."

I pondered who he might be talking about, who'd been there when I hinted that I hoped to chat with him sometime. Neal and Reed wouldn't have told him. Janelle? Delma? Then the most likely candidate dawned on me. "Was the restaurant server Gwen chirping in the bar?"

"I'll never warble about it," he responded, which told me I was correct. "So now that we're together, what did you want to talk about?"

I only hesitated for a second. "I've been thinking about how to find you a new bulldog," I lied. Well, it wasn't entirely a lie. But I wanted to know more about why he wanted one. Had he told the truth about losing his recently?

"Thanks," he said. "I'm definitely looking for another one. But not necessarily for the reasons I mentioned to you before."

I nearly blurted out my questions about why he was really looking. Did he love bulldogs? Or, if he was actually a PI, did he have some other reason for being here? Like, was he hunting for dogs like Go who'd been stolen — and might have wound up in this area, thanks to Ada or her buddy Tim?

Garvy placed himself in front of me on the path so I had to stop walking. I looked up into his face. There was enough of a light breeze blowing that the hair he had combed over his forehead blew a little sideways. His hairline wasn't too far back, so I assumed it was just a point of male pride on his part. Even if I'd been interested in him, the height of his forehead was irrelevant.

I didn't say a word, just looked up and waited for him to say something.

"I've heard some interesting things about you, Carrie." His smile curved up almost sensuously, which nearly made me wince. Was a continuation of his unwanted flirtation why he'd really suggested we take a walk?

"Really?" I attempted not to throw irony into my tone. "Like what?"

Biscuit gave a little tug on her leash as she strained toward another area of nearby groundcover. Rather than wait for Garvy's answer, I turned toward her and took enough steps to add some slack to her lead.

"Like you happened to solve a murder a few months ago."

I wasn't really surprised he'd heard that. This wasn't a huge town, and gossip got around — especially since the murder victim that time had been a member of one of Knobcone Heights' most illustrious families.

"It's true that I was involved," I agreed.

"And now you're trying to figure out what happened to Ada Arnist, aren't you? I gather that last time you were one of the suspects, but not now."

I sighed. "You already know that Janelle Blaystone works for me part-time. She argued with Ada, so now she's a suspect. Since she's a friend and employee, I'd like to help her if I can. That's all."

"So what do you know about me?" That was definitely a shift in subject.

"Not much. You're a visitor here, you work in real estate, and you'd like to find yourself a bulldog to become part of your family." I turned to look at him to see if his expression changed with anything I asserted.

He only looked amused. "You're right," he said. "Or that's at least what I intend for people to believe."

He turned away and started walking in the opposite direction from where Biscuit's leash was stretching. He'd clearly wanted to intrigue me, then sneak away so I'd have to follow him to learn any more.

I half wanted to immediately lead Biscuit back to my shops. Instead I stood there until Garvy stopped and turned, apparently not happy I hadn't followed his lead. He walked back toward us, sidestepping through what appeared to be a class of middle-grade students and their teachers who had just caught up with us.

He was soon back with me. "Look, I've heard you like to grab coffee at Cuppa-Joe's. Why don't we go there?"

Now I was feeling even more uncomfortable. Why had he gotten all this information on me? How had he gotten all this info?

He must have known what I was thinking, since his grin appeared smug. "Here's some of what I want to talk about. I think you may suspect it. I'm not actually in real estate. I'm a private investigator."

We were at the patio at Cuppa-Joe's, sitting at a table in a far corner next to the fence with my sweet, patient little golden Biscuit lying at our feet.

It was probably a good thing that Cuppa's didn't serve liquor, since I might have indulged. I was feeling a bit discombobulated about being here with Garvy. Not because of his admission — I'd already wondered if he was the PI with the upside-down name. But I didn't know what he wanted, now that he'd made the admission.

Both of the Joes, my dear friends Irma and Joe Nash, had immediately come over to say hello to Biscuit and me. They'd glanced toward Garvy, then gone back into their coffee shop to help other customers. We were being waited on out here by Kit.

I had asked Kit for a mocha; Garvy stuck with black coffee. She had just set our drinks in front of us, aiming her usual toothy smile at each of us in turn, but also sent a quizzical glance at me before walking away.

I was here often enough, sometimes with Reed, to know that the people here thought we were in a relationship. The Joes probably recognized it wasn't a done deal, though — or, dear pseudo-parents that they were to me, they'd have taken me off by myself and questioned me by now.

Although the patio was crowded, Garvy and I were off by ourselves enough to feel comfortable that what we discussed would be private. Taking a sip of my warm, chocolaty mocha, I said, "Okay. Spill it. You're a private eye. What are you doing here?"

"I suspect you can guess. I was hired by some people in Los Angeles to find their stolen dogs — the way your friend Janelle's Go was, before."

"And one's an English bulldog." I didn't make it a question.

"Yes, a white one named Youkay — as in U.K."

I laughed, then grew serious. "So you, like Janelle, thought that Youkay and maybe other stolen pets could have been brought up here because Ada Arnist's family has property here?"

He nodded. "But things weren't as simple as I'd hoped. There weren't any dogs at the Arnist property. Then Ada showed up in town, and all that happened with Go and Janelle . . . and then Ada's death."

"Are you implying that Janelle was the killer?" I half stood and glared at him.

"I know you want — intend — to clear her. Me? I just want the truth. More important to me, I want to recover my clients' missing dogs. I don't suppose you know anything about them, do you?"

Then he didn't know about Ada's friend Tim having some dogs with him? Or did he want to find out what I actually knew?

I wondered whether to hedge a bit, then decided simply not to tell all I knew — which wasn't much anyway. "I don't really have any information, although one of the guys who showed up at the resort bar that night, Tim something, brought a couple of dogs to my veterinary clinic after they were in a fight. I think he was a friend of Ada's." *And my main murder suspect,* but I didn't mention that. "In case you're wondering if he's a dognapper, I have no idea. One of those dogs happened to be a bulldog, by the way."

"Interesting. The bulldog's owners are my primary clients. Have you seen him around since then?"

"No." Which was pretty well true. I'd seen the place he'd given as his address in Blue Jay, and some dogs in the house not too far from there, but I hadn't run into him.

"That's too bad. I'd like to talk to him again but I've lost track of him . . . temporarily."

What did that mean? He'd spoken with Tim before? Had he known he had at least a couple of dogs with him — and might have more? But to find that out, I'd have to tell him about the dogs at the house in Blue Jay, which I didn't want to do.

Instead, I decided to change the subject to something potentially useful to me. "So you really are a PI," I said. "That sounds fun — and more. Tell me what I should know to conduct investigations. I really had to wing it when I needed to clear myself."

I was still winging it, to help Janelle. I didn't need to mention that. He'd already figured it out. But maybe I genuinely could learn something from him.

Taking a sip of coffee first, Garvy started talking about the life of a PI, how he got clients, how he had learned over time to investigate the issues they needed him to figure out.

I found myself fascinated by some of what he had to say — the ins and outs of talking to people, what to do in person and what to look up on the Internet, and more.

I had no intention of becoming an official investigator, of course, but I'd definitely found myself in the difficult position of having to pretend to be one to save myself, and now Janelle, from untenable situations as murder suspects.

"So why did you tell people you're in real estate?" I asked as he slowed down a bit.

He gestured for Kit, several tables away waiting on other customers, and asked her for refills of our drinks.

That felt like a good idea to me. I asked her if she'd bring some water for Biscuit.

In response to my question, Garvy said he'd found it best to take on an undercover persona in as many situations as possible, because if you admit you're a private investigator, people will either tell you nothing or they'll tell you everything — but you won't know if it's true. If they think you're just a new friend, they're more willing to open up.

That made sense.

"And . . . well, do you use your real name?"

He smiled. "I suspect you did some Googling of me, Ms. Kennersly. And if you did, you might suspect the truth. You may even have found the small website I maintain for my cover as a real estate salesman. I do go by Garvy, especially when I'm on a case, but my real name is Grant Garvy, not Garvy Grant."

To my surprise, I found myself liking this flirtatious, somewhat secretive guy.

Even as I distrusted him. After all, he had come to this area seeking stolen dogs. Ada had apparently been involved in their theft, and so, most likely, had the missing Tim.

Ada, one of his targets, had been murdered.

I added him to my list of potential killers, maybe second in line to Tim.

We talked for a little while longer, then I said, "I really need to get back to my shops, but this has been interesting. Not that I want to do what you do, but I'll do what I can to help Janelle if she needs it. Since she hasn't been arrested, maybe the cops are still looking into other people."

"I heard they didn't arrest you," Garvy said with a grin, raising his cup to his lips for possibly his final sip of coffee.

"Nope. I was lucky." Fortunately, my timing had worked well, too.

"Could be, or maybe the cops around here are smarter than in some other places."

To my chagrin, I found myself blurting, "Does that mean they'll arrest you?"

Twenty-Four

Garvy froze, his cup only halfway back to the table. I'd potentially made a big mistake, kind of accusing him of murder, if it turned out he was guilty.

On the other hand, we were in public, so it was safer to accuse him here than somewhere else.

But suddenly he burst into laughter. "Oh, you're smart," he said. "Do you accuse everyone you think might have a motive? If so, let me suggest that you stop doing that. Subtlety works best in most situations during an investigation, especially if you happen to be accurate. A murder accusation is a good motive for someone who's guilty to kill a second time."

"In public?" I challenged, trying to sound as amused as he seemed to be.

"Oh, but a killer can wait till the right private moment. Don't you watch TV shows?"

Kit returned to the table then with our check. Garvy immediately grabbed for it as Biscuit stood up and stretched. "A little more coffee?" Kit asked him.

"Sure, some to take along as we leave."

"And mocha?" She looked at me.

"No thanks." Although revving myself up with more caffeine sounded good.

I could get ready to run, and I'd no doubt that Biscuit could keep up with me.

We argued jovially about who'd pay the check. I finally allowed Garvy to do it even though the success of his current investigation might be in jeopardy — and therefore his paycheck, too.

After Kit refilled Garvy's cup, he leaned toward me over the table. I noticed how broad his shoulders were and got a sense, with him now in his T-shirt rather than dressed up, that he could be one strong dude.

Accusing him of murder, even though I wondered about him, probably hadn't been the best idea.

"Okay, you asked, so I'll tell you," Garvy finally said. "No, I don't think the cops are about to arrest me, although, as you know, I went to talk to them." I remembered I'd seen him in the police station, so that was no surprise. "We talked mostly about the dog thefts, but I did bring up the possibility of Ada's involvement. And that I was looking for those dogs. The cops were astute enough to ask where I was the night she was killed, and I told them I'd gone to the supposed party at the resort bar, then returned to my hotel. I came to Knobcone Heights alone and have no one to vouch for my having spent the night in my room, but that was what happened."

Even having someone vouch for your whereabouts wasn't always enough, I'd learned. For example, Delma had apparently stood up for Janelle as much as possible, considering her illness, but that hadn't stopped the authorities from suspecting Janelle.

"Okay." I stood up. "I'm glad to hear you're innocent." But could I believe it?

I wished I couldn't, since I was still determined to clear Janelle.

"In case you don't believe me," he said, catching up with me as Biscuit and I started wending our way through the patio crowd, "just look at me now."

I turned to glance at him and he laughed once more.

"I didn't mean that literally," he amended. "The thing is, I was looking for stolen dogs."

"Wait till we're outside," I told him. "I can't hear you very well here."

We exited the patio through a door to the sidewalk, and I stooped to pick up Biscuit.

There were plenty of cars flowing by, since Peak Road was a major street on the far side of the town square. Other people were strolling along the sidewalk, too. I didn't feel endangered being with Garvy, at least not now.

When he continued talking, what he said made sense, darn it. I couldn't put him high up on my potential suspect list.

"Here's the thing, Carrie. If you're going to act like an investigator, you do have to look at all the angles."

"Okay, what angles are you talking about?"

We carefully crossed the street, and I put Biscuit down on one of the town square's paths. She immediately started walking with her nose to the ground.

"Mine. What I meant by 'look at me' is that you can see I'm still on this case, searching for those stolen dogs. Ada was my main suspect. She still is, although I believe Tim to be her accomplice. Ada had ties to this town. If she were still alive, I'd have confronted her, solved this situation by now, and gotten those poor stolen dogs back to their owners. I already considered her a primary suspect, so I wouldn't have killed her and cut off my ability to follow and question her, certainly not before I got answers."

"Did you learn where she was keeping the dogs?" I asked. If so, he could have killed her without any bad consequences — well, other than being prosecuted for murder.

"Yes. But not until they were moved out, after her death."

"By Tim Smith?"

"By the man you know as Tim Smith," he amended.

We were now about to cross Summit Avenue to reach my shops. I looked at him. "Don't tell me his name is Smith Tim, like yours is Grant Garvy?"

Yet another smile lit his handsome face. I bet he had women scratching at each other to get his attention — and, in my mind, I blessed Reed. Reed was a calming, and altogether appealing, influence that kept me from feeling attracted to this perplexing man.

"No, I won't tell you that. But his real name is Tim Thorine. He's twenty-six years old, grew up in Fresno, moved to LA to attend college, and that's where he met Ada Arnist."

"You forgot to say he's a dognapper."

Which made him loathsome, as Ada had been, although I hated to think ill of the dead. But I was more worried about the dogs the two had apparently stolen. Were they okay? Where were they? Would they get back safely to their loving owners?

"I may not have said it, but I won't forget it," Garvy growled. I wasn't sure I'd seen his expression this grim before and figured he and I were on the same wavelength — at least about this. "Not until I've found him and returned those dogs to their owners."

I wanted to applaud, but he might take it wrong. But, yes, we were thinking alike, at least about the stolen dogs.

We were now right in front of my stores. I didn't want to invite him in, even though he could enter anyway as a member of the public. And I still felt conflicted about telling him the little that I did know about Tim Smith-Thorine's possible whereabouts.

Maybe I'd use some of the investigative techniques he'd mentioned and check to see if I could find Tim myself, then make a point of talking to Police Chief Loretta Jonas again.

With luck, whether or not Garvy got credit for it, those poor dogs could get back home soon.

■ ■ ■ ■

Dinah was busy in Icing and Frida, who'd replaced Vicky, was busy in the Barkery when Biscuit and I returned. There weren't a huge amount of customers in either store, but enough to make me happy. Frida had brought her beagle mix Zorro that day, although she usually didn't. Biscuit and Zorro got along well, so my pup was fine with heading for her enclosure where Zorro was tethered.

Before I walked inside the Barkery with Biscuit, Garvy had headed away, down the sidewalk. He and I had exchanged contact information first, but I didn't give him anything he couldn't have found online about the phone number and addresses I used for my shops. I got his phone number, though, and promised I'd let him know if I learned anything more about where Tim might be, or anything else about a pack of purebred dogs who might have just recently arrived in the area.

And maybe I actually would, if I learned anything useful — and genuinely believed that Garvy was the best bet for ensuring those dogs got home safely. I wasn't sure about that.

But I was positive I wanted to do all I could to ensure that the missing dogs were found and reunited with their families.

I decided to follow up with my own best resource, as tenuous as that was: Janelle. Maybe Delma, too, since they were friends who'd gone together to some of the dog parks where the dogs went missing.

As a result, I called Janelle and asked if Delma and she would be available to meet me for dinner that evening, preferably at the Arrowhead Diner. No guys to be present this time. Women's night out.

I didn't explain that I preferred to ask all the questions myself, and not get my nosy brother, or even the animal-caring vet I was seeing, involved in the discussion. Not this time, at least.

I arranged to meet them at seven o'clock. They were free to bring their dogs, as I was bringing Biscuit. Winter would arrive in the San Bernardino Mountains eventually, but not for a few months, so I figured I'd keep my dog with me as much as possible on these kinds of outings, while I could.

For now, I left Biscuit to head over to Icing, where I checked things out and hung around for a while, then helped Dinah prepare for that evening's closing. I took the cash register records into my back office, then did the same in the Barkery with Frida.

"I'm working on a really special meat loaf at home tonight," she told me. "It'll have a savory bacon and blue cheese gravy with some special seasonings I've been playing with."

"Sounds delicious," I said, my mouth actually watering. I hadn't realized it, but I was hungry.

"I'll save you a sample," she promised.

Soon, both shops were closed, Dinah was on her way home, and Frida and Zorro had dashed into her car to head for the grocery store — probably the one managed by her husband.

Biscuit and I got into my car, too. Before I drove us to the Arrowhead Diner, I had a long detour to make.

I drove to the residential neighborhood in Blue Jay where Tim Smith-Thorine had told the vet clinic he lived with his two dogs. I wondered, as I drove, if I was doing too much of this investigative stuff. Shouldn't I leave this part to Garvy, and the resolution of Ada's murder to the authorities?

Sure, if I didn't care for dogs or Janelle. Neither Garvy nor the cops seemed to be doing an adequate job of handling their responsibilities.

It was nearing twilight in the mountains,

but the narrow, twisting roads fortunately had reasonably good lighting. I soon got to the street that was my goal. I didn't see any kids outside this time at Tim's address, but neither did I see or hear any dogs. This part of the neighborhood was quiet. But I hadn't really believed, after last time, that I'd find any missing dogs here.

The deserted-looking place down the road was different. I hoped to once again find some dogs at that location. Contacting the police about them hadn't gotten me anywhere before, but if I found them again, I'd make more noise about it.

I slowed down as I cruised along the street, using the control on my armrest to open the passenger-side window.

I heard nothing from behind the fence at the very rundown house I'd noticed before. Just in case, though, I parked and got out of my car.

Ah. Walking toward me, from the direction I'd just driven away from, was an older lady with a small gray terrier. Maybe fellow dog-people could bond and talk about this apparently vacant house.

I unhooked Biscuit from her safety harness in the back seat behind me and snapped on her leash. Then we started walking along the damaged sidewalk in the direction of the woman.

I took my time, hoping it appeared that I was just walking my dog and didn't want anything else. The lady kept approaching, so I must not have appeared threatening. When the two dogs got close, they did the normal doggy thing and investigated and sniffed each other. Biscuit wasn't usually a barker in that kind of situation, and the other dog appeared fine with it, too.

I smiled at the lady. "Hi. I just visited some friends a couple of blocks away and was driving through here. Biscuit seemed to want a walk, so here we are." I paused, watching for the woman's reaction. "I was here a week or two ago and thought I saw a whole lot of dogs in one of the yards around here, so I figured the neighborhood was dog friendly."

The lady smiled beneath her thick, dark-rimmed glasses. She had thin, silvery hair cut short and a sagging chin that went well with the rest of her lined face. "We're definitely dog friendly around here, but the dogs who were here are gone now."

"Oh, then I was right that this is the location?"

"Yes. This house, as I understand it, is under foreclosure, so the guy who brought the dogs here had no business doing so."

"Oh. What was that all about?"

"I wish I knew. The dogs were noisy a lot, but he seemed to take good care of the place, cleaning up after them and all. And I know he must have been feeding them. They looked all right, and a day or so after I realized he was gone, a delivery truck from one of the major companies pulled up with a dog food delivery. I told him there was no one living there."

"I take it he just drove off."

"Well, yes, after calling someone — maybe his office. He stood on the sidewalk, and Gershwin, here, was doing his thing, so I only heard part of what he said."

Was I going to get lucky here and learn something helpful from this nice, chatty lady? She seemed to be waiting for me to ask her.

"What was that?" I asked.

"I gathered that the dispatcher said he'd been given old information or something like that. They had a forwarding address."

Yes! I was going to find out where Tim had gone with the dogs.

"Really? How interesting. Where was it?"

"Somewhere in Knobcone Heights, I think, though that's all I heard." At my urging, she told me which delivery company it was. “Anyway, we need to run,” she said. “Have a good evening.”

Twenty-Five

So what should I do next? I pondered that as I drove Biscuit and myself to the Arrowhead Diner to meet Janelle and Delma.

I'd tell Chief Loretta, that was for certain. It sounded as if Tim and the stolen dogs might be back within her jurisdiction. Maybe that would spur her to find them, both the poor dogs and Tim, who, in my opinion, should be looked at more closely as a murder suspect.

But was that enough? Even if she looked for and found Tim, what would happen to the dogs?

Should I tell Garvy anything and let him search for them? Would he somehow have access to the delivery company's records, or someone who would provide that information?

Did I trust him enough to tell him?

Dinner that night convinced me that I should do anything I possibly could to get those dogs home.

As anticipated, Biscuit and I sat on the patio at the diner with Janelle and Go, and Delma and Shobie. If I ever got tired of patio eating, I'd have to give up dining with dogs, and that was never going to happen — especially with my little Biscuit.

Also, as I often did, I ordered a hamburger, the better to share with my pup. I additionally ordered a glass of red wine to help me relax.

Janelle and Delma and their dogs had come there together, or so they told me. They were waiting when Biscuit and I arrived and had already gotten the table, with a seat available for me.

When I sat down, they'd been talking about their lives in Knobcone Heights. Fortunately, it sounded as if Janelle intended to stay in town indefinitely. Was that because of Neal, or her job at my shops, or a combo?

Or was it because the cops had warned her to stay around?

Considering the look she shared with me as I took a sip of water and listened to their conversation, I figured that my last guess was at least a factor.

"Shobie and I will be heading down the hill soon," Delma said. I hadn't heard what she did for a living, but she'd been here for at least a couple of weeks. Did she have a job?

"You must have a nice, long vacation package at your work," I said, smiling at her.

"I'm a high school teacher, so I've got the whole summer." The smile on her round face was ironic, as if she anticipated a criticism from me. "I sometimes tutor or take on short classes this time of year to earn a little more money, but I didn't this year."

"What do you teach?" I asked, interested now.

"Basic biology, at a small private high school near Santa Monica. In case you can't tell, I love animals." She bent over and patted Shobie on the head. Her dog's muzzle went up in the air in apparent ecstasy at the attention.

"I figured," I said, smiling.

"Then you must also figure that I'm really upset — not only about the dog thefts near where I live, but the fact no one has found any of them. Except Go, here, and that's a miracle. But I've been in touch with other victims and they haven't even received any more ransom notes." She glared at me over her snub nose, as if she blamed some of that on me.

"More?" I ventured.

"Some of them received initial teasers via email," Janelle said quietly. "The emails said they would hear more later and should be prepared to pay a thousand dollars or more to get their pets back." She paused, then said, "I never got one, even though I was ready to pay immediately to get Go back." She got off her chair and knelt beside Go, giving her dog a huge hug. When she looked up again she said, "I'm just so lucky."

She definitely was. The scuttlebutt in the media, of course, was that the dognappers weren't intending to give the stolen dogs back but to sell them. That was why they had all been purebreds or designer dogs.

I mentioned this, and Delma said, "Yeah, you're right. But a few of the people I talked to sent money to some address they were given and still didn't get their dogs back."

So it was even more critical to find the dogs as soon as possible, so they could be reunited with their real families and not sold to new ones — assuming that it hadn't already been done.

So far, at least a couple of weeks had passed that I knew of. Probably a lot longer for some of the grieving families.

Finding Tim-of-the-changing-last-name was even more critical because of this — although I wanted to have him located anyway, since he should at least be interrogated about Ada's murder, if he hadn't been already.

Our meals arrived then, thanks to one of the male servers wearing the typical green knit shirts with the Arrowhead Diner logo on the pocket. "Enjoy," he said, and winked at Janelle.

I considered my brother's romantic interest to be the prettiest one at this table, too, but the guy didn't have to slight Delma and me. I figured that would enter into his tip.

On the other hand, I didn't want him or anyone else to flirt with me, except for Reed at the moment.

But if I needed to, to get what I wanted from Garvy, I might be the one to flirt with him.

On the whole, dinner was pleasant. I didn't mention anything about Ada or even about Garvy, even though these two — Delma and Janelle — had been at the dinner at the resort when I'd asked about him. I must not have seemed as obsessed about locating the guy as I'd felt, since although Janelle asked at one point if I'd found the real estate guy I was looking for, she didn't press it when I said no. It was only a partial lie anyway, since the man I'd found — or who'd found me — wasn't in real estate after all.

That night, after I got home, I chatted briefly with Reed over the phone and said good night to Neal. Then, lying in bed, I obsessed a bit more about Garvy.

Would it be a good idea to tell the PI the little I'd learned today about Tim and his possible move back to this town?

I would tell the authorities first, of course. And I'd make Garvy promise to keep me informed of his every move trying to locate Tim and the dogs, since I'd let him know something that might lead to finding them.

But how could I be sure he'd do so?

Could I trust him?

He was already undercover and he'd shown he was quite capable of keeping secrets if he considered it in his best interests.

On the other hand, I'd no idea whether the authorities would keep the best interests of the dogs in mind even if they happened to also be looking for Tim to question him. And it would definitely not work to tell Loretta I had some information she might need but that I'd only share it if she made promises — either to tell me what the cops found or to make sure the dogs were immediately turned over to Mountaintop Rescue.

I doubted I could get any information from the delivery company or find Tim's location myself.

What was I going to do?

By the morning, I'd gone back and forth a zillion times about how to handle things.

I hadn't really gotten anywhere by attempting to befriend Chief Loretta and ask for her help. Had she even tried to find Tim Smith, or contacted any law enforcement agencies down the mountain to attempt to rescue the dogs I'd seen, or at least check to see if Tim was one of the thieves? The news I'd heard on the LA TV stations, which we could access up here, hadn't mentioned alleged connections to any other location.

I didn't trust the two detectives who'd given me a hard time in the spring and were now riding Janelle. Of course, they wanted to solve their murder case. They did appear to be animal lovers — maybe. But I didn't especially like them, let alone trust them.

The only thing I was certain of was that, if I told Garvy anything, I would most likely trust him even less than the detectives.

So, attempting to figure out the lesser of the many evils, I decided I'd at least start with the local police chief.

I thought about asking Billi to come with me again but decided against it. Her presence the last time had made it clear to the police chief that we were friends, with similar intentions regarding the saving of dogs. If the police chief stonewalled me, she would have to assume I'd let Billi know it.

So, right on time that morning — which wasn't too hard, considering how little I'd slept — I headed for my shops and began the day's baking.

Janelle was the first of my assistants to arrive, and she thanked me profusely again for paying for dinner last night — and for remaining on her side regarding Ada's murder. I'd kept her somewhat informed that I was checking into things, but I didn't tell her all.

I definitely didn't mention my intention to go see the police chief that morning. If all went well, or at least better than I anticipated, I could fill her in later.

I took on the Icing side and Janelle baked on the Barkery side, and we opened both stores at exactly seven a.m.

Dinah came in around then, too, so we were fully staffed. That meant I was able, when nine o'clock rolled around, to walk outside and call the police department. I asked for Chief Jonas and got one of her minions I'd met before, Sergeant Himura.

I explained again who I was and my interest in the situation involving the death of Ada Arnist and her alleged involvement in dog thefts beforehand. I let him know I'd gotten some information that might lead to the location of a suspect they might not yet have spoken with — and also, hopefully, the location of the missing dogs.

"Is there anything different from what you suggested the last time you were here, Ms. Kennersly?" The man sounded jaded and uninterested and generally difficult, and I didn't want to have to deal with him any more.

"Yes," I said curtly. "When can I come in to talk to Chief Jonas?"

"She has a full schedule today."

"And tomorrow and the next day, I'm sure. But what I have to tell her won't take long." *And I don't want to tell it to a twerp like you,* I thought. "Maybe it would be better if I brought City Councilwoman Matlock again." Would threats get through to this guy?

"Why don't you just come in now?" He sounded resigned. "I'll fit you in as soon as I can."

■ ■ ■ ■

"I assume you know better than to be bothering me with some other suspicion of yours about Ms. Arnist's homicide," Chief Loretta said dryly. She had told the officer on reception duty to let me know, before I came to her office, that she would give me exactly five minutes. When I entered and sat down on the same chair I had before, facing her over her pristine, empty wooden desk, she'd spoken first without allowing me to at least start the conversation. "So what are you here about? Something about those supposedly missing dogs?"

As before, she sat in her plush, gold-colored chair, looking pompous with her erect posture, although this time she wasn't wearing the jacket over her white, many-buttoned shirt with its service bars over the left pocket. Her frown lines were etched even deeper into her face than I recalled, probably because of her irritation about my being here again.

"That's right," I said. "Those *actually* missing dogs. You know I'm a dog lover, and even though I've watched the news for any information about the LA police investigating the dognappings, I haven't seen anything except reports that the dogs remain missing. Fortunately, that may mean there've been no new thefts, but the dogs haven't been returned home either, unless the news simply isn't covering it. I think it's the kind of situation most media would really jump on if there was any break in the case, or whatever."

"Exactly. Or whatever." The chief's dark eyes were leveled on mine and she seemed to wait for me to continue talking, like a lion crouching to leap on its prey. "And before you ask, yes, we've been in touch with several law enforcement agencies in the affected areas to get their information about the thefts and let them know that, since one of the stolen animals showed up at our shelter here, we're keeping our eyes open in case more are around this area, too."

That was good, at least. But just keeping their eyes open? Not jumping in to investigate?

"That's why I'm here," I said. "In case your eyes are open, I wanted to let you know some information I've uncovered."

She glared at my sarcasm but said nothing, apparently waiting for me to continue.

I made myself relax, since I wanted to appear earnest but not critical — no matter what I was thinking. Then I began. "I'd like to give you a bit of an update, since I'm getting even more concerned about the wellbeing of the missing animals. I already told you about the rundown-looking place I located that had a lot of dogs in the yard, where I was hoping to talk to Tim Smith." No need to get into whether that was actually his name. "I went back there the other day to check it out. You might already have looked into it, too." I paused to let her jump in and say of course she had, but she remained silent — although she appeared to nod just a little. "Like before, I saw no indication that it was Tim Smith's home. And this time, I neither heard nor saw any dogs there."

"Yeah? Well, neither did we when I sent a couple of my officers there to check it out."

So she had paid attention. That was a good thing.

But the fact that she'd seen no indication that what I'd said was true wasn't so good.

"They *were* there before," I assured her. "And they've been moved. When I was there this time I saw a neighbor walking her dog past the house and stopped to chat with her. That's why I'm here."

"She gave you information about Tim and the dogs?"

"Kind of." I explained that she'd told me

the house was in foreclosure but someone with a lot of dogs had moved in, then out, fairly quickly. "I can't be certain it was Tim, or that the dogs there were the stolen ones, but what I can do is give you the information the neighbor gave me that could lead to a forwarding address."

I'd apparently gotten Loretta's interest at last. She leaned forward, her dark eyes glimmering in anticipation. "And that address is . . . ?"

"For you to use your authority to find out," I told her. "A delivery driver had stopped at the house to drop off a package of food, but, when no one was there, he apparently called his office and asked about a forwarding address over the phone — the lady heard that part, but not where — and then he drove off. She only heard that it was in Knobcone Heights. I'd imagine the delivery company has the new address."

"And you didn't follow up to obtain it?" Ah, the sarcasm was back.

"If I could have, I would have," I assured her with a smile. "But since I couldn't, I figured I'd give you the information so you could check it out officially."

"Good call." She paused. "I don't have time right now, but I'll get Sergeant Himura to meet with you and take your statement."

"Fine." The sergeant hadn't been especially friendly before, but I felt fairly certain he'd be at least civil once under orders from his superior officer to get information from me.

Chief Loretta rose, so I did the same. I was surprised when she said, "And thanks for coming and following up on this."

"You're welcome. Anything to help find and rescue those dogs." I turned to walk toward the door, then pivoted back to look at Loretta. "By the way, how's Jellybean?"

The police chief had stopped scowling but her expression had remained serious, until now. Her facial features softened considerably as she smiled. "She's fine. I'll stop by your shop one of these days to pick up some healthy treats for her."

"I'll give you some free samples of the healthiest," I said. Then, with a wave, I walked out her door.

Twenty-Six

I waited in the station's fortunately roomy reception area for about five minutes, watching civilians like me line up at the desk to talk to someone, or move away from the growing line to wait, until my good pal Sergeant Himura came in. He showed me through a door and down a lengthy hallway into a small conference room, then waved me toward a seat at a rectangular metallic table. I complied.

He took another seat facing me, his expression even blanker than when he'd first taken my report. My prior wish that I wouldn't have to deal with him again had clearly not come true.

On the other hand, he acted all business, not nasty, even if he wasn't especially welcoming.

"I understand you have some new information that might lead to the whereabouts of an alleged friend of the decedent Ada

Arnist, as well as to some allegedly stolen dogs."

"Yes. We discussed some of this before."

"Right. So tell me what this new information is." I was surprised he didn't use the word "alleged" before information.

I related to him, briefly, what I'd told Loretta about going to the now-empty house and talking with the nice neighbor. "I'd imagine you can get a warrant or whatever to require the delivery company to provide you with the forwarding address, right?"

"Possibly. In any case, thank you for bringing this to our attention."

Did the guy ever smile? He stood and immediately gestured toward the door.

Once again I complied, as much because I didn't want to stay in his presence as because I wanted to obey his silent order.

I wished, though, that there was some way to get him to contact me once he got the forwarding address, even if he couldn't pass the specific information along to me. Or else to let me know if he wasn't able to obtain it, which I doubted.

But I couldn't even feel sure there would be the promised follow-up. The police chief and sergeant might just be placating the concerned citizen who was sticking her nose into not one but two crimes that were, from their viewpoint, none of her business.

As we reached the door to the hallway, I said to the cop, "No, thank you for your help. And all those poor people whose beloved dogs were stolen will undoubtedly line up to thank you even more, if you're able to find this guy and he actually does have all the missing pets." I didn't mention that this police force might get additional kudos in the event the dog thief also happened to be Ada Arnist's murderer, and they captured him and found some evidence against him, too.

As I walked out of the station and toward my stores, I started pondering how I could, in fact, obtain the information I wanted about whether the police actually did follow up or not. And, if they did, what they learned.

Sergeant Himura, it was true, wasn't a good pal. But someone who was truly a good pal might be able to get all the details I wanted — and also make sure that there was, in fact, some follow-up.

While I walked, I called her: Councilwoman Billi Matlock.

But Billi didn't answer her phone right away. She might have been conducting a class at her day spa, or showing people around Mountaintop Rescue — or, better yet, handling an adoption of a needy pet.

She could also be in the middle of a City Council meeting of some sort.

Or she could be busy with none of the above.

I soon reached my shops and hurried into the Barkery to let Biscuit know I was back and take her for a walk.

Janelle was the assistant present in the Barkery. I considered telling her what I'd been up to, since it could wind up helping her if anything came of it. But she was busy waiting on customers, so this wasn't a good time. Besides, I'd said things before that might have raised her hopes without merit.

I'd stay quiet this time.

I went into the kitchen since we were getting a little low on some of our favorite dog treats, including our dog cookies with spaniel faces that had long ears — really cute, if I did say so myself. And tasty, even for humans who tried them.

Besides, baking right now would give me time to think.

I was glad I had a call pending with Billi. Would her assistance and input be enough?

I'd have to see.

Billi called me back at lunchtime. She was at her Robust Retreat giving classes that day and was finally on a break.

I was in Icing when I heard my phone ring. Fortunately, Janelle hadn't left for lunch yet, although Dinah had. I was able to slip into the kitchen and close the door of my tiny office behind me.

I'd already said hi to Billi and asked her to wait for a minute so we could talk. "All good," I finally said. "Are you wearing your councilwoman's hat? I've got some stuff I want to run by you."

"Hmmm. Official and important, I gather."

"You gather correctly." Holding my phone tightly against my ear, I leaned forward, placing my elbows on my tiny desk. My longish hair spilled forward a bit, and I brushed its blond waves back out of my eyes. I wanted to be able to see as well as concentrate.

But I didn't really have to concentrate yet. "Can it wait for tonight, for us to discuss it over dinner?" Billi asked. "I was thinking about trying out a new veggie pasta sauce recipe anyway, and that way we can have some quiet time, which I gather would be a good thing if you've locked yourself in your office."

"That's fine," I said. "Is Biscuit invited?"

"Of course. Come on by at six thirty after

you've closed your shops."

I had a shift at the clinic that afternoon, a good thing to distract me from my impossible desire to stomp back to the police station and ask the sergeant or chief if they'd followed up and finally gotten a local address. And, hopefully, saved the dogs. And arrested Tim Whatever-his-name-was for Ada's murder, so that no one would bother Janelle about it again.

But I heard nothing about any of that, and it was all unlikely. So, after I left Biscuit with busy Faye and her assistants in doggy daycare, I changed my clothes and was immediately found by Reed, who commandeered my presence in one of the examination rooms. He did manage to look me in the eye and give a quick nod and smile, but I knew he was preoccupied with the medical emergency we were about to deal with.

It was an older cat, who'd apparently lost her grip and fallen out of a tree. Fortunately, although she'd gotten some very deep and potentially dangerous scratches, x-rays didn't show any broken bones or damaged organs. I shaved around her wounds and helped to stitch her up. The good part was when her owner, as senior a human as she was a cat, was invited back into the room to see her.

"She'll need to stay here for a day or two," Reed told the lady, "but it looks as if she'll be fine."

Tears rolled down the woman's cheeks, and she hugged first Reed, then me. I held the kitty gingerly as I walked her down the hall to our hospital holding area, letting her owner follow to see the crate where she'd remain for observation and to stay and talk to her for a few minutes. An extra bit of soothing love never hurt.

I worked with Arvie on a couple much more minor cases the rest of my shift, from a large and not very well-trained wolfhound who needed shots to a Chihuahua requiring flea treatment.

As I eventually was getting ready to leave, I changed back into my normal clothes and strolled the hall for just a minute, looking for Reed. I found Yolanda first, and my fellow vet tech, fortunately, was in a good mood that day.

"That kitty, is she okay now?" Yolanda asked, raising her brows in concern.

"She should be just fine with some rest and TLC," I said.

Yolanda popped into a different exam room just as Reed exited another. "Good job with our cat patient," I told him.

"You, too. In fact, I owe you," Reed said.

"It was my job," I replied. "And my pleasure." I grinned at him and basked in his responding smile.

"Well, join me for dinner anyway. We maybe should work out a standing dinner date, every night? Every other night?"

Did this mean we were getting even more serious? Or was it just because we enjoyed talking as we ate and, sometimes, what happened afterward?

In any event, I had to decline this time. "Sorry," I said, meaning it despite my eagerness to get together with someone else that night. "I like the idea, but I'm having dinner with Billi tonight." I considered inviting Reed to join us, but that wouldn't be a great idea since I had something specific to discuss with the City Councilwoman. "Rain check?"

"Or non-rain kind of check this time. Either way, let's plan on it tomorrow."

I agreed, and considered getting close enough to exchange a little cheek kiss, but then recognized how unprofessional that would be here.

"See you tomorrow," I said, heading toward the door to doggy daycare.

Biscuit and I set off on our walk back to

the stores. My little dog pranced happily and stopped to sniff every few feet, which was often her norm. I'd been told she'd played a lot with a couple of other dogs her size that afternoon, so all in all this had been a good day for her.

For me, too, I thought, recalling the now-healing cat.

As we waited to cross the street from the town square to the block where my shops were, my phone rang. I removed it from my pocket. Garvy.

If my discussion with Billi tonight turned out to be unproductive, Garvy still remained my last resort. But for now, I didn't need to tell him anything.

"Hi," I said.

"Hi. Are you at your stores?"

"No, but almost. I just ended a shift at the vet clinic."

"Anything new and exciting there today?"

If I was guessing correctly, he just wanted to touch base with me. Was he flirting, or did he have some other agenda?

Since I'd learned he was a PI, I suspected he didn't do much without having a rationale for it.

Although maybe just being friendly was enough of a rationale.

"Absolutely," I said, answering his question. I told him proudly about how a vet and I had saved an injured cat's life.

I could almost hear him yawning, but he let me continue until I reached the Barkery's front door. Then, while peering inside and smiling at the number of customers we had, I said, "How about you? Have you had a good day today? Found any dogs or clues?" *And will you really keep me informed?*

"Still working on it," he said. "Anyway, I've got plans tonight but I want to catch up with you. Maybe tomorrow?"

"I've got plans both nights," I said, glad I did. "We can talk next week." Then I said goodbye, and Biscuit and I went inside.

It was early afternoon by now. Go remained leashed to Biscuit's enclosure, and Janelle still staffed the Barkery but she looked stressed.

Had the cops used the opportunity to harass her yet again while I was out? Not that I was her protector. No, her attorney Ted took care of that. But the authorities knew I'd give them as hard a time as possible if I happened to be around.

Janelle was waiting on a customer with a golden retriever as I came in. The owner was a local schoolteacher who'd been in here often, and I greeted her warmly and caught Janelle's eye. She nodded, so I knew she'd already given them a sample treat.

I let Biscuit greet the golden, and Go, and then gently urged her behind the fence of her large crate. I watched while Janelle finished helping the customer, deciding not to interrupt to ask if she wanted me to take over. That might lead to more stress.

As soon as the teacher and her dog departed with their large bag of treats, I approached Janelle. "Everything okay?" I asked in a low voice.

She shook her head vehemently. "No. Those detectives? They called and want me to come to the station *again* tomorrow. I didn't gather they have anything new to discuss, so I figure they just want to harass me, maybe scare me enough into confessing something. But before you ask, yes, I'm bringing my lawyer with me every time."

"And I'll be with her as much as I can, too." That was Delma, who had just entered from Icing. She had a half-eaten large sugar cookie in her hand. Apparently she hadn't brought Shobie along. "This just isn't right, the way they're treating Janelle." Her scowl distorted her entire face, making her curved lips reach nearly to that snub nose that seemed to dominate all.

"They should put their efforts more into figuring out where all those other dogs went." Janelle dashed over and gave her Go a huge hug. "If they found them, maybe they'd also know who killed Ada — maybe that Tim guy, who was at least her friend if not her boyfriend."

"You're absolutely right." Delma nodded and regarded Janelle with a staunch smile on her face now. "They should get Tim. Arrest him for murder. Since he's on the run, that's got to be a sign of his guilt. And maybe once they find him at least some of the missing dogs could be brought home to the people who love them."

Should I tell them what little I now knew: that I'd at least given the cops a possible way to track down Tim, and thereby maybe also locate the rest of the stolen dogs?

And that I was hoping, by talking to Billi at dinner tonight, that if the police weren't doing anything, the City Council or even the media might be able to shame them into it?

But again, I didn't want to impart hope to Janelle before I knew that the authorities were actually doing something with the information I'd given them.

"I agree," was all I said.

The Barkery bells over the door chimed behind me and I turned. More customers!

And no more time for this discussion now.

I only hoped that, within the next day or so, there'd be some major action along the lines we'd been talking about.

The dogs would be found.

And Janelle would be safe.

Twenty-Seven

Delma remained at the Barkery for the rest of Janelle's work day. I couldn't help smiling at her each time I caught her eye.

She was definitely one wonderful friend to Janelle, although I wished she wouldn't keep bringing up the whole murder situation each time the shop was empty of customers. Or at least she did when I happened to be in there with them.

But her take on it was that things would work out and the killer, Tim, would be found, and so would the dogs. Janelle would be fine. It had to be that way. Period.

I could only hope she was right.

I spent a lot of time in Icing, too, working with Vicky and with Dinah, who'd taken charge again after she'd returned from lunch. My human bakery had a lot more customers that afternoon than my dog one. I could never seem to gauge which shop would be busier. I just had to ensure that they all had enough product.

Having fewer customers in the Barkery also reminded me that I'd talked briefly to Billi before about maybe scheduling a pet adoption day at my dog treat store. It would potentially bring in more customers on the day of the event, get the word out about my shop even more, and, most importantly, hopefully result in more adoptions of pets from Mountaintop Rescue.

Maybe even find Sweetie, my favorite dog there, a home at last. Yes, I'd asked Billi again about the little golden dog that so resembled Biscuit, and she was still there.

Tempting . . . but I wouldn't do anything that would take my attention away from my own beloved dog.

It was finally nearing closing time. Things started to slow down in Icing, so I made my way back into the Barkery to see how many customers we had.

Still not many. But one of the people there I knew didn't currently have a pet, even though he was allegedly looking for one. Or many, as was the case — in his undercover PI role.

Garvy Grant.

I was puzzled by his presence, since I thought we'd planned to get together next week, and I approached him, knowing my gaze must look quizzical. I hoped he was here to tell me he'd found the missing dogs at last.

Even though I hadn't given him the tiny clue that I'd learned about Tim's whereabouts.

"Hi," I said, putting more of a question than enthusiasm into my tone. "Can I help you find something here?"

"I just thought I'd pick up some treats to take to Mountaintop Rescue tomorrow."

I didn't tell him I was about to have dinner with its manager and could — and would — ask her about any purebred dogs who happened to be there now, including English bulldogs.

"That would be very nice," I said instead. "I make sure that a lot of our leftovers are brought there while still fairly fresh, to be given out to the residents."

"Very nice," he echoed, and smiled, his green eyes looking straight at me in a way that made me feel uncomfortable, as if he could see inside my mind and realized I knew something I wasn't telling him.

Janelle was behind the counter at that point, getting our cash register total for the day. Delma had been with the two dogs but I saw, around Garvy's shoulder, that she was approaching us.

"Hi," she said. "Do you have a dog?" Before he could answer, she said, "I've met you before — oh, yes, at the Knobcone Resort, I think."

Garvy had turned to look at her. His expression had morphed from incisive to blank, as if he didn't recognize Delma at all. I wondered if they'd seen each other on that fateful night at the bar.

Not that it mattered.

"Maybe so," Garvy said. "And no, I don't have a dog, but I'm looking for one." Something about his tone suggested irony that Delma wouldn't understand, but I did.

I had no intention of smiling at him about it or otherwise acknowledging it.

"Well, I'm sure we all hope you find the right one," Delma said.

Or ones, as the case may be, I thought.

Although I considered hinting to Garvy that the cops might be aiding him in his quest, I didn't get the opportunity, which was probably a good thing. He left almost immediately after that conversation, and I gave Janelle the go-ahead to leave soon thereafter. She unhooked Go from the enclosure and they and Delma exited through the shop's front door.

I locked it after them, then finished the day's initial accounting, checked the refrigerated case in the Barkery for items to put aside for the vet clinic or Mountaintop Resort, and then got ready to leave as well.

To go to dinner.

Dinner that night at Billi's house was delightful. As a member of the Matlock family, she lived in the neighborhood where Neal had taken us on the hikes I'd participated in. Her place was a gorgeous stone mansion near the top of Pine Lane.

Before letting her know we were arriving, I drove onto Vistaview Place past the Arnist house. I saw no activity there beyond the closed gates, no indication as to whether Ada's parents were still in town or not. I heard no dogs. Still, could this be the forwarding address for Tim's dog food?

I had no idea.

I turned and headed back to the hillside street and stopped at the curb in front of Billi's. I called her on my phone and said hi, and the huge wrought iron gate opened immediately.

I pulled onto the blacktop driveway and parked.

The house looked like a European castle, both inside and out. All it needed was a moat. The front door was large, ornately carved wood, with round towers of worn stone on either side. The door opened almost eerily as Biscuit and I approached, but I nearly started laughing when Billi's dogs — Fanny, a beagle mix, and Flip, a black Lab — raced through it right toward us.

What followed was a love session of woofs and sniffs and wagging tails. They'd both met Biscuit before. They occasionally all got together at Mountaintop Rescue since Billi brought her dogs there sometimes, although she most often left them at her day spa. All were buddies.

Billi stood in the doorway. I was used to seeing her in her workout clothes or shelter apparel, but sometimes got an occasional glimpse of her all dressed up for a City Council session. Today, though, she was dressed not like a wealthy local citizen at home but like anyone else, in jeans, athletic shoes, and a loose-fitting gray T-shirt.

I looked even dressier than she did in my black slacks, snug black knit shirt, and dressy black loafers.

"Come on in." She motioned for me to enter. Biscuit scooted ahead of me and so did her canine companions.

Billi was the only Matlock in Knobcone Heights these days, so she lived here alone. She had been married once, or so she'd told me when we'd first bonded over our love of dogs. That had ended in what sounded like a nasty divorce, and she'd been alone since.

Although recently she had hinted that she might be seeing someone . . . I still wondered who, and how serious it was, but figured she'd tell me when she was ready, at least if it continued.

She showed me past the entry to the living room and down a high-ceilinged hallway into the dining room. There, the long table of thick wood was already set for two people at the end closest to the kitchen door.

"It may be too late," I said, "but is there anything I can do to help?"

There wasn't. She was just happy to have me be her guinea pig of sorts for her new veggie spaghetti sauce. She'd cooked penne pasta to serve it on. She also brought out some cabernet from a California vineyard around Napa.

Even so, I accompanied her into her kitchen, where I made sure the dogs had water in the metal bowl near the refrigerator. Plus, she'd put out some high quality kibble in another bowl, and I assured her it was okay if Biscuit partook of it.

In addition, I handed her a large paper bag. It contained some of the doggy treats we'd baked that day at the Barkery, as well as a small box of red velvet cupcakes and a bag of chocolate chip cookies for her from Icing.

And then, after she placed pasta on two plates and ladled out generous helpings of a delicious-smelling tomato sauce — obviously containing onions, green peppers, mushrooms, and more — I carried them in and set them at the table.

As soon as we sat down, I took a forkful of her creation and grinned. "Mmmm," I said. "Delicious."

"Glad you like it." She took a bite of her own. "Yeah, not bad if I do say so myself."

"Which you did," I reminded her with a smile that she returned.

We continued eating for a few minutes while talking only about our respective careers and how they were going and how much we enjoyed them. That was one thing we had in common. We both liked who we were and how we'd gotten here.

After a while, though, I decided it was time to address what I really wanted to talk to her about.

"Care to put on your City Councilwoman hat for a while?" I asked.

"I wondered when you were going to get serious," was her reply. She donned an equally serious expression and used well-manicured fingers to push her dark, highlighted hair away from her face. "So tell me what's going on."

I gave her a quick rundown on everything, including my discovery that real estate agent Garvy Grant was actually PI Grant Garvy. "I know that you can keep things like that confidential," I warned her, and she promised to do so.

Then I got into his ruse of trying to find a replacement for his supposedly deceased bulldog, and how he had actually been hired by some of the people in LA whose dogs, like Janelle's, had been stolen — including a bulldog, the kind he ostensibly was seeking. His investigation had led him to Knobcone Heights, similar to Janelle's quest. He had sought Ada as part of his attempt to find the missing pets, and now he was after the guy known as Tim Smith, aka Tim Thorine.

"Could he have killed Ada after finding her?" Billi issued the question that had run through my mind.

"He claims he didn't — said he wouldn't have done that, certainly not without finding the missing dogs first. And his continued failure to find them, or Tim, gives some credence to that."

"Maybe," Billi said.

"Maybe," I echoed.

I then hurried through the rest of the scenario: meeting Tim at the vet clinic; tracking down the address he had given and not finding him or the dogs; discovering a house on the same street, where dogs in fact were located; discovering they weren't there the next time, but talking to a neighbor who provided a lead about a possible forwarding address given to a dog food delivery company.

"I told Chief Jonas about the delivery company today. But I don't know if she'll follow up on it."

"She will," Billi said grimly. "I'll make sure just the right amount of information leaks to the media to ensure that it'll look really bad for the local police department if they don't follow up."

"My hero!" I said to her.

"Of course," she responded.

Twenty-Eight

Billi didn't seem as much like a hero to me as our meal progressed, though. She seemed human — and, under the circumstances, that worked okay for me.

We had just finished our pasta. "Would you like any more?" she asked. "There's plenty."

"It's tempting, but no, I'm really full."

"Coffee, then?"

"That sounds good."

I went into the kitchen with her while she made us each a cup with her expensive brewing machine, the dogs following close behind us. She handed me mine first. "Milk? Sugar?"

"Milk, please," I said, and instead of getting it for me, she gestured toward her fridge. She had a quart of regular milk inside, among fruit juice bottles and yogurt cups. I extracted the milk and poured a lot into my cup, filling it nearly to the top. I took a sip so it wouldn't spill.

When Billi reached out her hand I gave her the milk carton, and she added a lot less to her cup than I had.

We soon returned to her dining room and sat back down at the table. That was when she looked straight into my face with her intense brown eyes. "So how are things going between Reed and you?"

I laughed. "What, no subtlety about asking? Never mind. My answer is that things are going fine, whatever thcy are. We are developing some kind of relationship. We eat meals together a lot. We . . . well, we sometimes get closer than a dinner table. But what does that mean for the future? Heck if I know."

"You want to know why I asked?"

I sent her a puzzled look. "Other than curiosity about a friend?"

"Yeah."

"Then, yeah."

"I've been communicating with your buddy Jack Loroco a lot lately, even when he's not visiting here. I like the guy, but I haven't encouraged him — although I'd like to."

"You? And Jack Loroco? What, do you want him to contribute VimPets products to Mountaintop Rescue?" I didn't recall introducing them, but it didn't surprise me that they'd met, especially if Jack had visited the town's wonderful pet shelter.

"That, and maybe more. But I know he expressed interest in you before, and I'll tell him to get lost if you want me to."

I sat still for a moment, looking at the pale milk swirls in my coffee. I liked Jack. I'd considered getting to know him better. But I liked Reed a lot more, and, honestly, I thought we might be heading toward a real relationship.

Besides, I considered Billi a really good friend. I didn't want to stand in her way if the two of them had bonded more than Jack and I had.

"Go for it!" I told her.

She grinned, stood, and drew me up to hug me. "I was hoping you'd say that."

I wondered whether Jack Loroco would be considered good enough for someone of Billi's family background and stature in the community. But he seemed nice. He had a good job and was dedicated to it. And all that was her concern, not mine.

"I just hope, whatever happens, that you're happy," I said.

"Yep. You, too."

I then asked if she happened to have any purebred or designer dogs at Mountaintop

Rescue whom I hadn't yet met.

"You know I'd tell you if I did. Or if I heard of any at another shelter, especially if they happened to magically appear right on the doorstep."

"I figured," I said, and then we both changed the subject, talking about the fun things our own pups had been doing recently. I also told Billi about Chef Manfred Indor's contribution a few days back to our saleable dog products. "He's also emailed me a few new recipes and said he'll send more soon if I want them."

"I thought you liked to come up with your own."

"I like to have new ones available, too. And I don't have as much time now to experiment. Fortunately, my new assistant Frida is helping with that, too."

We also talked more about holding an adoption event at my Barkery to help find pets at Mountaintop Rescue new homes. It would require a lot of planning and help, but we were both committed to the idea. Soon.

When we were done eating, Billi suggested that we take the dogs for a quick walk around her neighborhood. "It's getting dark out but the area's pretty well lighted."

We walked out her door, across the driveway, and through the gate after she punched a few buttons to open it. Then we walked along the sidewalk and down the hill a few houses, since her house was near the top. After we returned to her place, it was time for Biscuit and me to head home.

"Thanks for dinner," I told her.

"You're welcome. And I'll keep you posted about my efforts to get the media on our cops."

When Biscuit and I returned home that night, Neal was just pulling up in his car.

"Hot date with Janelle?" I asked him with a smile.

"I wish," he said, but his reddened complexion told me I was right on.

It turned out that Billi didn't need to keep me posted after all — when I turned on the local TV news the next morning, a commentator was talking about how "sources" had informed them that the Knobcone Heights Police Department was hot on the trail of some dogs that had been stolen from Los Angeles. I wondered if Billi had called or emailed them last night or early in the morning.

Even more important, I wondered whether having a reporter or two at their doorstep would finally nudge the cops to follow up on my little clue.

And if they did, whether it would lead to anything helpful — like the location of Tim. Or, more important, the dogs.

The situation was a hot topic at my shops that day. Even on the Icing side, people wanted to know what was really going on. There had been reports now and then from down the mountain about the theft of some dogs, but were they really in Knobcone Heights now? If so, where? Who had brought them here, and how?

All excellent questions, and whenever I heard anyone talking about the situation in either of my shops, I made a point of saying something, too. I didn't reveal I had any knowledge at all, not even the scant amount I knew. But I did say how upset I was to hear that there had apparently been so many thefts.

Janelle was in the Barkery that day, and I encouraged her to talk about how it was a major reason she had traveled up here, having heard rumors — ones she shouldn't elaborate on — that the dogs might be here.

And her own happy conclusion of finding her Go.

Both stores were pleasantly busy that Sunday. Even so, when I had a minute between customers, I checked the news via my cell phone to see if there had been any breaks in the case.

Apparently not, but the ongoing investigation was mentioned often.

Later, when it was nearing closing time, I called Reed. There was a place in town where gossip was often rampant, and of course he and I had a dinner date. "I'm not very hungry," I told him. "I can survive on a drink at the bar and some appetizers there, if that's okay with you."

"Fine by me. And since a lot of people have been talking about the news of lost dogs, I suspect you'll want to see if any of them turn up there — or if folks chat about them."

"Exactly." I smiled at my phone. "Oh, and by the way, I'm hoping that Janelle and Neal can join us for a while. Is that okay with you?"

"It's fine," he said, earning him an even broader smile from me, despite the fact that he couldn't see it.

And though it's hard to believe, I had even more reason to smile as the day drew to a close. Billi called as I was removing older items from Icing's glass display case and putting them in bags and boxes for the charities.

"Guess what," she said.

My heart started racing as I pondered the most likely reason for her call. "Are you at Mountaintop Rescue?" I ventured, since the likelihood was different if she was at her spa or City Hall.

"I sure am. And so are the cutest little Yorkipoo and, yes, a white English bulldog, both apparently dropped off in our alley. Too bad they're possible dognapping victims and I can't let that guy Garvy adopt the bulldog."

Should I tell Garvy about him? Maybe. I'd have to ponder that.

"Did you check them for microchips?" I asked.

"Of course," Billi said. "They're both chipped, but just like with Go, even though our scanner works fine on other dogs, neither chip is readable this time."

Not surprising. "Have you called your friend the chief?"

By then, Frida, who was in Icing with me cleaning up for the day, had joined me behind the counter in one of the special aprons I kept in the kitchen. Her expression was both quizzical and hopeful, and her brown ponytail swayed as she moved her head from side to side.

"Are there some new dogs at the shelter?"

she inquired softly.

My turn to move my head — in an emphatic nod.

She engaged in a happy fist pump.

"Yes, I've called her," Billi said, responding to my question. "She said she'd check her contacts in the LA area tonight to learn if my descriptions match any of the missing dogs, and if so, she'll send some of her officers over tomorrow to interview me. She wants me to hold them for now just in case."

"Will they notify the people whose dogs with those descriptions were stolen?"

"Sounds like it won't be right away, but eventually."

I leaned against the display case, wanting a whole lot more information — some that Billi might not have. "Did Chief Jonas mention anything about looking for the rest of the dogs, or the thief?"

"I asked her. She just gave the usual non-answer of not being able to talk about an ongoing investigation, which implied that they're looking, but it might just be a hedge so as not to admit they aren't."

"I figured."

We soon said our goodbyes. I didn't bother telling her to keep me posted, since I knew she would. She knew the same about me.

I dared to hope that the authorities were in fact trying to find Tim and the stolen dogs. Maybe knowing he was being sought was the reason he — apparently he, at least — had dropped off a couple more dogs at the shelter. But I believed there were still a lot of missing pups.

Like with the two dogs Tim had brought in for veterinary care after their fight, the microchips in the dogs who'd appeared today were useless — and Billi had mentioned that one was an English bulldog. Could it be the same dog we'd treated at the clinic, who was called Butch?

I wanted so badly for all the stolen dogs to be found and returned to their owners.

And for Tim to be found as well. He remained my primary suspect in the killing of his accomplice, Ada.

Maybe, if they located him, the police would discover that, too.

Reed and Hugo picked Biscuit and me up at our house that evening. I'd talked to Neal and let him know we were coming to the resort. He'd said that Janelle and Go would be there, too, and he hoped to at least have a drink with us.

And yes, apparently the news reports on how Knobcone Heights was indirectly involved with the dog heists was a major topic of conversation at the resort. In fact, when we got to the bar, Neal's boss Elise was there, too, talking with a bunch of people about dogs.

Reed and I managed to push some tables together inside, and no one chased us out to the patio with our dogs. That was a good thing, since I wanted to eavesdrop on as many people as possible.

I ordered a beer, and so did Reed. I also asked for a water bowl for the dogs, and that was no problem either.

We had purposely walked past the reception desk on our way in, and I'd waved at Neal. He'd joined us soon after and also ordered a beer.

"What's the story about the dogs?" he asked me. "I mean, beyond what the news has been crowing about — that our town is a haven for dognappers but the police don't have answers yet. Is that right?"

"Possibly," I said, even though "probably" was more correct. I hadn't kept my brother fully informed about what I'd learned, nor Reed, either. But before I could get into it, we were joined by Janelle and Go, and Delma and Shobie were with her, too.

Janelle, wearing an attractive black dress for the occasion, appeared exhausted. Neal stood, shared a brief kiss with her, and pulled a chair out for her. My brother, the gentleman.

"What's wrong?" I asked as she sat down.

Her expression, as she looked at me, didn't seem at all surprised at my question. "I've got yet another session with the cops scheduled for tomorrow." She shook her head, and her wavy brown hair skimmed her shoulders. "And before you ask, yes, your lawyer friend Ted will be with me, as usual."

"I don't think you told me what happened the last time you were there," I said.

"Nothing different."

"Just harassment," Neal grumbled. My brother was wearing his standard uniform for working at the resort: a nice button-down shirt, in a blue shade tonight that went well with his eyes, and black trousers. He also wore an irritated expression.

"That's for sure," Delma chimed in. She was all decked out in a flowing red blouse with a poufy scarf around her shoulders that just touched the ends of her black cap of hair, and a long black skirt. "I think you hit the nail on the head when you started suspecting the guy who's probably got the dogs, and who helped that Ada steal them, as the person who killed her." She looked at me. "I heard the news mention the dogs, but not the connection to the murder."

I wondered if I should suggest that Billi add that to what she'd told her media contacts but decided it wasn't necessary and might just complicate things more. People around here were mostly interested in the dog story, or at least some people were. If they happened to see a whole pack of dogs somewhere, they'd undoubtedly report it. But they might be a lot more reluctant if they thought they were endangering themselves by outing the location of an alleged murderer.

"Well, the police know of it," I said, then asked the group to keep what I was about to say to themselves. They all agreed, and I told them my latest small twist: the supposed forwarding address given to the dog food delivery company after Tim and the dogs had moved away from their last probable location.

"And the cops aren't following up by subpoenaing the delivery company or whatever?" Delma exclaimed. Fortunately the crowd noise was loud enough, with all the tables occupied around us, that I doubted anyone heard.

"I don't know what they're doing," I said, much more softly.

"If anything," Neal added.

"Well, someone should do something to find him," Delma said. She'd gotten the message and her voice was lower, but still loud enough to hear.

I realized she was right. I also realized that I didn't have the skills or contacts or professionalism to do it myself.

I might never hear if Chief Loretta Jonas was doing anything with the information I'd provided her.

But I knew someone who could check — and do something about it if she hadn't. Much as I didn't relish the idea, I needed to contact PI Garvy, tell him what was going on, and let him follow up.

At least I knew he'd do it, since it was part of his current investigation.

TWENTY-NINE

I felt exhausted on Monday morning as I prepared baked goods for that day for both shops. I assumed it was mostly because of staying out so late at the resort last night, but as my mind drifted while mixing and kneading several different doughs I realized that all the excitement and concern over Janelle and the lost dogs was taking its toll on me.

Well, maybe my decision to tell Garvy what I knew would result in quickly finding Tim, finally resolving Ada's murder, and locating the remainder of the missing dogs. I hoped taking care of all that would erase a lot of stress from my life, too.

And so, at the relatively decent time of nine o'clock, I called Garvy. I couldn't wait around until we got our dinner date arranged. "Can you meet me at Cuppa-Joe's today?" I asked him. "I want to bring you up to speed on some things I've found out."

"You mean what's being alluded to on that local TV channel? KnobTV, isn't it?"

"Something like that." That was what the announcers called it, at least.

"Yeah, I want to hear any insights you have on that. How does ten o'clock sound?"

He was obviously eager, too, since ten o'clock was just an hour away. I changed the time, though, to late afternoon, when it would be more convenient for me. Would I tell him everything, including about the appearance late yesterday of the bulldog at Mountaintop Rescue? Sure. He'd find out about it anyway if he stopped in to visit and check out the current residents.

I was glad that the TV news reports weren't entirely complete. They'd described some of the dognappings in LA and the possible link to someone here in Knobcone Heights. But they hadn't yet mentioned the drop-offs at the shelter. That appeared to be by design, at least according to Billi's theory. The cops seemed to want to make the thief sweat without connecting the news reports directly to Mountaintop Rescue or Billi . . . yet.

Janelle came in with Go, and I asked her to help out in the Barkery again until she had to leave to meet with the cops. Frida along with Dinah, who'd swapped hours with Vicky, were taking care of Icing. We'd had customers in both shops from the minute we'd opened, and I was glad I had three assistants there that day.

I remembered when I'd first opened my stores and sometimes had my two part-timers alternating, even on days when I had shifts at the veterinary clinic. My shops had not only survived but prospered, but the way I was able to handle things now was a whole lot better.

I flitted around, helping on both sides with talking to and serving customers, who were plentiful throughout the day. When the afternoon was nearly over I checked in with each of the assistants to make sure all was well from their perspectives, then leashed my pup and patted Go goodbye, and Biscuit and I headed to Cuppa-Joe's.

I purposely headed there a few minutes early. When I got to the coffee shop, I didn't hesitate to avoid the sprawling building and go through the gate to the main patio, my favorite. I didn't see Kit, but I asked the young girl I did see to let the Joes know I was here. She took my order for coffee with room for milk, too.

I sat down at one of the few empty tables but didn't have to wait long before both Joe and Irma sped through the coffee shop door onto the patio. They glanced around, saw me immediately, and came over.

I stood to hug them both. Irma was dressed nattily, in a silky tangerine blouse tucked into slender brown slacks. Her hair was perfectly styled, as always, framing her nearly wrinkle-free face.

That was in contrast to her dear husband. But Joe still looked great, even though he was showing his age.

He grinned at me now, stepping back after our hug. "So good to see you, Carrie."

"Are you here alone?" Irma didn't wait for my answer before dragging an additional chair to my table and sitting down. Joe took the other one as I, too, settled on one of them.

Biscuit went from Irma to Joe for the pats and hugs she knew she'd get. Each fussed over my dog as if they hadn't seen her in ages. It had been only a few days, though.

"I've got someone joining me," I said in response to Irma's question. "I came a little early to say hi, though, so I could warn you that it's the same guy I met with last time I was here. We're talking some business." No need for them to know what that business was, at least not for now. "I'm still not sure where things are going with Reed, but he's the man I'm closest to now, not the one I'm meeting here. I just want you to know that."

"Got it," Irma said. "And I'm glad to hear things are going okay with Reed."

The server brought my coffee, as well as cups for the Joes, but when I saw Garvy and waved for him to come over, they both stood. "We'll leave you to your meeting," Joe said.

"Have a good one," said Irma, and they both walked away.

"Hi," Garvy said. "I hope I didn't interrupt something."

"Not at all," I said. "We're close friends, so they came over to chat while I waited for you. Have a seat."

He chose the one that had been occupied by Irma, across the table from me. Today Garvy was dressed in his PI garb, a nice blue shirt tucked into trousers. This was going to be an official conversation, which was exactly how I'd planned it.

The server came over, and Garvy ordered a large coffee with no room for cream. He also asked for a chocolate scone. "Sorry," he said. "I didn't have time to get to your Icing shop for a sweet this morning."

"No problem," I said, "as long as you give me a small piece."

"Of course." He cocked his head slightly as he looked at me. "So what's going on?"

His green eyes stared encouragingly. "As much as I enjoy getting together with you, I got the impression you wanted to talk to me about something."

"You're right." I glanced around to make sure each table near us had more than one person there and that they appeared to be conversing. I didn't want any eavesdropping.

"We're good," Garvy said. But he did put his elbows down on the metal table and leaned toward me, noticeably enough that Biscuit rose again and planted herself on the cement patio between us, sitting and looking from one of us to the other.

I smiled and reached down to pat her, then moved back. That had put me a little too close to Garvy.

"So tell me what's going on," Garvy prompted. "The TV news suggested the local PD was on alert that some dogs stolen in the LA area could be around here and said they were checking it out. It's true, of course, but how did the media get that information — or do you know?"

"I do," I said. "The thing is, I fed a little bit of information I came by to the police but wasn't sure they were following through. I asked a resource I have to throw it out to the media, hopefully to prod the cops to act on it. I've no idea if they are, but I figured it wouldn't hurt to let you know, too, in case it'll help you find the dogs."

"Good girl," he said, much too warmly. Fortunately, the server of the day came out just then with our coffee and Garvy's scone.

"Okay, here's the thing," I said when she was gone. "This is a follow-up to some information I found before, but I'd thought it would be better and more efficient to tell the police than a private investigator. I've no idea whether the police are checking things out effectively or still ignoring it."

He continued to watch me, taking a sip of coffee, but the warmth seemed to fade a bit from his gaze. I realized I was giving too much background without saying anything helpful.

"Here it is. When we spoke last week, I had some information about Tim Smith — or Thorine — that I didn't relate to you, but I followed up on it myself." I then told him about extracting the address Tim had given the clinic, and the whole situation of finding a bunch of dogs nearby. "When I gave that information to the police, I hoped they'd act right away and rescue the dogs, but they didn't. Next time I went by there, no dogs were around. I talked to a neighbor, though." I told him about the potential forwarding address that the dog food delivery company had been given — an address in Knobcone Heights. "I was stymied, but then figured the authorities could get a subpoena or something to get the address. But I've heard rumors that the address was simply a P.O. box at a private company, and it didn't lead to Tim. Not directly, anyway." Billi had told me this in a phone call last night.

Garvy seemed all business as he pulled a small notepad and pen out of his side pocket. "Give me all the information about the address where the dogs were, and which delivery company the neighbor mentioned."

"Then you can follow up as well as the police?"

"Maybe, but I won't tell you my methods." His grin was wry, lighting up his face again, and I suspected that whatever he did wouldn't be within the constraints of what private detectives were allowed to do.

At this point, I didn't care. All I said was, "I'll tell you everything I know as long as you promise to keep me informed every step of the way — and actually do so."

"All right. I promise."

"Fine," I said. I told him the details. I also realized, promise or not, that he'd do whatever he wanted as far as keeping me informed, even just about his progress.

I considered again whether to tell him about the dogs that had been dropped off at Mountaintop Rescue and decided it wouldn't hurt, especially since he'd probably stop by there himself again one of these days if he hadn't already. My plan, in any event, was to go there right after he and I were done here to see the dogs and talk to Billi and her staff about their arrival — when and how and if anyone had seen anything.

When I informed Garvy about the appearance of a couple of the dogs he was probably after, including the English bulldog, he looked even more excited. But he seemed to be very antsy after this part of our conversation. Oh, he still acted fun and even charming, giving me nearly half of his scone and talking about the pleasure he hoped to have in saving about a dozen still-missing dogs.

"Look," he finally said, gazing right into my eyes. "I apologize, but my mind's focused on following up on this. I want to jump into using my resources right away. I hope you understand."

"Sure," I said.

He insisted on picking up the check, which I particularly didn't mind this time.

He was, after all, being paid to find those dogs we'd discussed, and now, with luck, he'd actually find them and get paid by all the frantic owners waiting for his success.

And also, if he was successful, he'd find Tim and hopefully tell me so — and I could let the cops know and, if necessary, set them on Garvy to get the information. I would again ask Billi to have her media friends urge that the dog thief be investigated further in the murder of his associate.

Would it work? Who knew? But it'd be better than the way things stood now.

When the server came by for the payment, Garvy stood, and so did Biscuit and I. "Thanks," I said. "And don't forget to let me know if that turns out to be helpful."

"I will." He leaned forward unexpectedly and planted a quick kiss on my lips — not sexy, but too friendly. "Talk to you soon." And then he slipped around the crowd and through the door to the sidewalk outside.

I glanced around. Fortunately, I didn't see the Joes on the patio anywhere. Instead of going inside to say goodbye, I found the server who'd waited on us today and asked her to convey my farewell to my friends.

Then Biscuit and I left, too.

On the sidewalk, I hesitated, looking both

ways up and down the not-very-busy street for Garvy. No sign of him. Good.

I started around the corner onto Pacific Street toward Hill Street, where Mountaintop Rescue was.

I wanted to see those new residents.

I took my time, though — partly because Biscuit wanted to sniff a lot and do what she needed to. That worked out fine since I used the lull to check my smart phone for the latest newscasts by KnobTV on the missing dog situation.

Interestingly, they hinted that there would soon be some more news about at least a few of the dogs, and the commentator implied that an arrest of whoever had stolen them — and now might be abusing them — could be imminent.

But the hints fortunately did not mention Mountaintop Rescue, or say that dogs had been dumped near a shelter a couple of times under similar circumstances, then brought inside to be kept safe.

Did Tim care?

Presumably so, since he apparently hadn't abandoned all the dogs — yet.

But with each news story, would he get flustered enough to leave more dogs at the shelter? Or would he be so worried that he would simply leave?

He had to be located. Fast. Preferably by the cops, but even Garvy would be better than having the dog thief get away, since who knew what he would do with his prisoners?

Biscuit soon did what she needed to, and I took care of it. Then we hurried the rest of the way to Mountaintop Rescue.

Billi wasn't there, but the receptionist Mimi was staffing the front office. "Hi," she said. She looked young and eager, full of smiles and wearing a white T-shirt decorated with black silhouettes of dogs of every shape. "Billi told me you might be by to see the dogs that were dropped off yesterday. And guess what! Two more dogs showed up this afternoon, too, just a little while ago. Apparently no one saw how they got here either day."

Good news and bad news. Good for these dogs, as it turned out, because now they were here, and they were okay.

But, unsurprisingly, no one had seen who'd dropped them off. I figured I knew who, though: Tim.

"What about the dogs who were abandoned here yesterday?" I asked. "Were they left in the same location as today's dogs?"

"We think so. At least, they were found at the back of the shelter, near the rear gate.

Around the same time of day, too."

Would there be more — or not? Soon — or not?

I had to know. I had to get more involved.

Nothing might come of it but some wasted time and energy.

But it wouldn't hurt to try.

I visited Sweetie first, determining that, despite how well she was being cared for, I'd make sure she found a new home soon.

I then enjoyed meeting all four of the new residents, even as my mind percolated around the idea the latest drop-off had planted there.

THIRTY

This really was absurd, I thought the next afternoon. And a real waste of time.

Even if Tim had dropped some dogs off here twice, in just a few days, that didn't mean he ever would do it again. Or that he'd do it around the same hour as before, near four o'clock. Or, even *if* he was going to do it at the same time and in the same place again, that he'd do it today.

More likely, with the recent news reports suggestive of possible police interest, he would simply run away. With dogs? Without them?

In either event, thinking that he'd drop any dogs off today in the late afternoon at Mountaintop Rescue was a stretch.

Even so, I'd called Billi earlier and suggested that she give Chief Loretta the information about the two drop-offs directly, so Loretta could have an undercover cop or two hang out in their unmarked cars in this area to wait and observe, just in case. And maybe assign them to try it every day until it actually occurred, or for a week, whichever happened first.

Unless they got actual evidence that Tim had fled.

When Billi got back to me, though, she was really doubtful the chief would divert resources this way even for one day, despite the fact the suggestion was phrased that she might find a possible killer this way, not just a dognapper.

And now that I was here in that capacity — undercover, more or less, just hanging out in my car near the back of Mountaintop Rescue — I'd seen no indication that anyone else was around doing something similar.

But what the heck? Maybe it was a stupid maneuver, but here I was. I'd stick it out, at least for today. And if nothing happened, would I try again in a day or so? That would depend on my state of mind, and if there were any other options I thought of for tracking Tim.

I really wanted those dogs rescued safely.

I'd left Frida and Vicky in charge of the shops for the afternoon. They both had enough experience to keep things going well till my return.

I didn't tell my assistants where I was going, but I did make it clear that it was important, and, although I should be back to close up the shops, they should do so on time if I wasn't there. If that was the case, I requested that one of them take Biscuit for a quick walk, then return her to her nice, roomy crate to wait for me. And give her a couple of treats, of course. But one way or another, I'd be back there tonight, and it shouldn't be very late.

So now I just sat here. Despite my instructions to my helpers, I didn't really anticipate staying for much more than an hour. Well, maybe two. That should give me time to return to my shops and close them myself. Plus, I'd brought a bag of treats from the Barkery to bring into Mountaintop Rescue before I left, but I hadn't taken them inside yet because I didn't want Billi or Mimi or anyone else there to know what I was doing.

Being foolish, most likely.

My smart phone was in its charger beside me, but since the car engine wasn't turned on, I doubted it was getting any juice. I had a notepad with me, though, and was occasionally jotting down some ideas for additional treats.

Mostly, though, I just watched the alley at the rear of Mountaintop Rescue. The four parking spaces behind the wooden fence were filled. The chain-link gate was closed and undoubtedly locked from the inside. There really wasn't anything to see.

And not much to keep me awake, especially considering how tired I was that day . . .

I must have nodded off, but I was awakened by the sound of a car door slamming shut. I jumped in my seat, glad that I'd slumped a little. If anyone happened to notice my probably illegally parked car across the alley from the shelter, they were unlikely to see that someone sat in the driver's seat.

I carefully raised my head barely enough to look out — just in time to see Tim Smith or whatever his name was jump back into a silver SUV, the same car I'd seen him in before.

Yay! My instinct, foolish as it had seemed — or had it been desperation? — had been correct!

Tim wasn't looking my direction, which was a good thing. I sprang up in the seat so I could check out the area behind the shelter.

Sure enough, a couple of dogs were on the ground there. The bad thing was that they weren't leashed, so they might run away. But a bowl of food was in front of them, so at least they were preoccupied — for now.

First thing? I pulled my phone from the console and pressed in the Mountaintop Rescue phone number. Billi answered.

"Don't ask any questions," I ordered, "but have whoever's closest to your rear alley come outside and pick up the latest dogs who were just dropped off. Got it?"

"Yes, but —"

"Good. I'll explain later." Like, possibly way later, when all this was done.

By then, Tim had driven to the end of the block along the alley. That was good. I didn't want him to notice me, so I couldn't speed after him. Instead, I waited to see which way he turned — praying he wouldn't go so fast that I wouldn't see him when I could turn the corner, too.

He went right. Trusting that Billi would do as I'd said and have someone take in the loose dogs, I started to follow, using my phone again. This time I called the Knobcone Heights Police Department — not 911, since even though I considered this a kind of emergency, they probably wouldn't. Chief Jonas was busy. Could she call me back? So were Detectives Bridget Morana and Wayne Crunoll. I left a voicemail for

Detective Morana, since she was in charge of both of them.

"I'm following Tim Smith," I said. "He just dropped some dogs off outside Mountaintop Rescue, and I'm hoping to see where he keeps the rest. I'll call you again when we reach whatever his destination is, and you can catch up with us then and maybe even question him about a certain murder."

I smiled grimly to myself, imagining what the detective's reaction would be. Would she ignore my message? Think of some imaginary crime I was committing by this action so she could arrest me and forget about Tim Smith being a much more likely murder suspect than Janelle?

By that point, I'd reached the corner where Tim had turned and made the same turn myself. The streets were as busy as they usually were in Knobcone Heights but I could see he was heading west along Hill Street, in the direction of the resort and lake.

Would the cops ignore me? Maybe not, but could I count on them?

I'd already made the decision to let Garvy Grant in on some stuff that I'd learned that the police might be following up on — or not. If nothing else, Garvy could provide some kind of belt-and-suspenders help here. With his assignment regarding the stolen dogs, I could at least assume he wouldn't ignore this possibility of finding them.

I called him, and he answered immediately. "Hi, Carrie," he said. "I don't have anything new to report yet, but I'm following up on what we —"

"I'm the one with something new to report," I told him. "Where are you?"

"In Blue Jay, learning what I can about those two houses you mentioned."

"Well, I'm in Knobcone Heights and I'm currently in my car following Tim in his."

"What! Where are you? Where is he going?"

"I don't know, but he just left some dogs at the shelter and he's heading toward the lake now."

"Okay, continue to follow him but check in with me every few minutes. I'll catch up with you as soon as I can. Don't do anything foolish like confronting him if he stops, though."

"I won't." Or at least I didn't intend to.

But I wasn't really sure how to play this. Instead of turning toward the resort as we reached that area, Tim turned left, as if he intended to drive around the lake. Was he heading to Ada's family's house on the other side? I hadn't seen much of her parents lately and had no idea whether they were still around. Had he moved in there after leaving the place in Blue Jay — with or without the Arnists being home?

I couldn't drive too close to him. I wanted to continue to appear like any other driver in town who had a destination in mind — one they knew about, not an amorphous idea about wherever the guy in front of me ended up.

I considered pulling over. Stopping. I'd already reported to the police, as I should. If they failed to act on it, that at least would give Janelle's lawyer Ted an argument of some kind of police ineptitude and failure to follow up on possible evidence if they did decide to arrest her for Ada's murder, wouldn't it?

But clearing Janelle wasn't my job, even if I wanted things to work out well for her.

The thing was, I also wanted things to work out well for the dogs. Would Tim keep dropping them off a couple at a time at the shelter — and, if so, would someone there always notice and bring them safely inside? Or were those I'd seen today the last of them — or the last he'd kept alive?

That wasn't my responsibility either, but I'd never forgive myself if there was some way I could have saved canine lives but stopped trying too soon.

I didn't need to get too close to Tim or do anything foolish. But I did need to know a lot more about the dog situation.

Fortunately, other cars were going the same direction so I doubted Tim would realize I was after him. At least I hoped not.

He reached the end of the straight road on this side of the lake and although this wasn't the same trail we'd hiked with Neal, the streets here paralleled the foot paths. He turned the corner that circled the end of the lake, as did most of the cars in front of me.

There was a stop sign at that part of the main street, too, so it took a short while for me to turn after him. But then I didn't see him ahead of me on the street.

The road here, curving around the end of the lake at water level, was surrounded by woodlands, unlike the straight parts of the road on the sides of the lake, where there was development. In the spot where the resort was located, the street was on top of a hill, with sloped pavement at both ends. I continued forward on the curving flatland, assuming I would see Tim's car along the far side.

But once I'd finished the turn and was

again on a straight road, I no longer saw him.

Where had he gone?

I pulled off onto one of the streets that went up the mountainside on this side of the lake so I could turn around and go back. What should I do now? I sat there for a few minutes pondering, knowing that if I didn't hurry — somewhere — Tim might get away.

The question was, where should I go?

He'd probably already gotten away. Had he figured out he was being followed?

Could I still follow him somehow?

I'd passed a two-lane, semi-paved street where the main road curved at the end of the lake — the only other street I'd seen there. It had appeared to lead even farther into the woods. My mind started to focus on it, assuming he'd pulled off there. But had he?

Not having any other ideas, I decided to give it a try, so that was where I headed. *Good thing it'll stay light out for a while,* I thought as I curved back into the woods, since the overhanging trees were thick and blocked the sun. On the other hand, the automatic lights on my car went on and I considered shutting them off, so as to be less obvious on this route. I didn't, though. I turned onto the small road. Since there was some pavement — albeit narrow and cracked — other cars must go this way, too. Sometimes, at least. Hopefully, this particular one wouldn't startle Tim.

I had to go pretty slowly. Soon, I began passing some wooden cabins on both sides. A few looked in good condition and even occupied, probably vacation homes of normal people, not the elites who bought properties around Billi's place or the Arnists'. Others I didn't think looked so good; there were more of those as I continued on the road. Then they became even more sparse, but I still had no idea where Tim had driven. Had I been mistaken?

Maybe I should go back.

But I'd kept my window open in hopes that I'd hear a dog or two to indicate I was on the right path — and just then, I did.

I consequently kept inching forward.

The road curved a little, and as I went around what passed for a corner, I saw a dilapidated chain-link fence with parts of the top curved over. Beyond it was a wooden hut, maybe the most decrepit of the shacks I'd already passed.

There was a driveway of sorts, a good thing, since I could turn around.

But as I got a little closer, two things prevented me from leaving.

First, there were several dogs near the shack inside the fence.

Second, two cars were parked on the far side of the fence, and one looked like Tim's.

So what should I do next?

First, I tried calling Detective Bridget Morana again, but I had to leave a message. I kept my voice low, as if Tim, presumably inside the house, could hear me. "I think I found Tim Smith," I said. "I followed him to a distant cabin in the woods and there are dogs here as well as his car." I described how I'd gotten here.

Would she follow up? Send Detective Crunoll? Ignore me?

Just in case, and also because I'd promised, my next call was to Garvy. Unlike the detective, he answered. I told him basically the same thing I'd left in my message.

"You're inside your car?" he demanded.

"That's right."

I expected him to tell me to stay here and out of sight. Instead, this time, he said, "Be very careful, but I'd suggest you show Tim you're there. Tell him help is on the way so he'd better not harm any of the dogs. Do you have any kind of weapon with you?"

Who, me? A bakery owner and vet tech? "Unfortunately, no," I said.

"Well, from what you've described, there's

no water nearby so he's not likely to try to drown you like Ada. I'm in my car headed toward you, and now I'll know where to go."

Again I anticipated he'd tell me to wait, until his arrival at least. "Good," I said. "Any idea how long?"

"Not really. Go ahead and do as I said — carefully, of course. Non-confrontationally, but let him know he's been found so he can't harm the dogs. Can you handle it?"

Could I? I didn't know.

"You realize, of course, that those dogs' lives may depend on you," Garvy emphasized. "If he's really shaken, he might kill them all and flee."

Damn. Garvy could be right. He might not be, but was I willing to take that chance?

"All right," I said. "I'll do it. But please come as fast as you can." I didn't bother telling him about my call to the cops since that was undoubtedly useless.

"I will. I promise."

We hung up. I checked the charge on my phone and it had a fair percentage of power, so I couldn't give myself the excuse that I needed to stay here charging it in case I had to make some calls.

Besides, dogs' lives could be in the balance. I wasn't sure I'd be able to save them if Tim really did intend to harm them —

but I wasn't sure I couldn't, either.

I would stay cautious, of course. I couldn't help dogs if I was hurt.

Carefully, I undid my seat belt and opened my car door. Barely thinking about it, I picked up the bag of dog treats. I wasn't sure when I'd get close enough to pass them out, but there certainly were a lot of canines here who might be hungry and whom I could treat.

The dog barks ramped up in noise, and those who were outside threw themselves toward the fence. They appeared all to be purebreds or designer dogs: Irish setters and goldens and a springer spaniel and a cocka-poo. Even a couple of Chihuahuas and a Papillon and a German shepherd. And that schnauzer — was it the dog Tim had called Waldo when he'd brought the two injured dogs to the clinic? I wasn't close enough to see if the dog had any wounds.

How many were there? *More than a dozen,* I thought.

"Hi, guys," I said in a low voice. With their acute hearing, they'd be able to hear me talking even if the guy inside couldn't over their barks. "Let's get you home soon, okay?"

But if I'd had any thought of sneaking away without Tim's knowing that someone was present, that opportunity was gone. The dogs' barks had outed me.

The fence drooped around a path up to a door into the cabin, and that's where I headed, dogs following me from inside. When I reached the door, I debated knocking, then decided against it. No, even after my discussion with Garvy, I should go back and wait in my car till he got here. Unless, of course, I had reason to believe a dog was being hurt.

Tim would know someone was here anyway. As far as I could tell, he hadn't looked outside to see who, but if I knocked to announce I'd reached his entry, that might be worse than simply peeking in first.

Although . . . if he'd killed Ada, even though it was by drowning, he could be standing inside there aiming a gun at the door, or who knew what?

Okay. I'd decided. I was going to ignore what Garvy had said, get back in the car, and wait — after calling 911.

Before I moved, though, the door opened. I gasped and felt my heart start racing even more. Was Tim going to come outside and grab me?

"Please come in, Ms. Kennersly," called a voice. Male? Female? I really couldn't tell over the noise.

Definitely too late to run. Instead, I decided to obey and hopefully be able to talk Tim — he was rational, wasn't he? — into not harming the dogs . . . or me.

"Okay," I called, and started forward.

And stopped right away. Yes, there was a human inside aiming a gun at me.

But no, it wasn't Tim Smith.

It was Delma Corning.

Thirty-One

This had to be some kind of mistake. Delma was Janelle's friend, and I was trying to help Janelle.

But what was she doing here with a gun? And, more important, why was she aiming it at me and not at Tim?

Where was Tim?

"Hi, Delma," I said. "So glad you're here, too." I tried to sound relieved and happy, although the opposite was true thanks to the gun. "You found this place, too. I'm really happy you're here to help save the dogs. And maybe also Janelle."

"Yeah, well, part of that's true. But what trumps it all is saving myself — and getting some more money out of the damn situation."

She waved the gun at me, her hand long-fingered and steady. The snub nose on her round, forty-something face no longer looked cutish, but that could also be because of the angry dip of her black brows and the grim set to her mouth. Neal had mentioned seeing her short temper. I'd noticed it before, too, but not as bad as this.

"Come on in and sit down. We'll talk," she said.

I couldn't exactly tell her no. Nor did it make sense to duck and run. I'd never get away without being shot, if that was her intent. And judging by the way she kept that gun pointed at me, I couldn't assume otherwise.

What was really going on?

Yes, I'd considered her a suspect, but not very seriously.

Not till now.

"Sure." I took a few steps forward. There had to be a door open into the yard since I was suddenly surrounded by dogs, and they appeared to be the same ones I'd seen outside. No Boston terrier, though, so Delma's dog Shobie wasn't here. Was he back at the hotel with Janelle and Go?

One of the Irish setters bulldozed his way through the rest and came up to me, nuzzling my hand as if demanding to be petted. Of course I complied. I even bent and started hugging and caressing all of the dogs I could reach, for my comfort as well as theirs.

Poor things. They had to have been the ones who'd been dog-napped, most likely all from loving homes. Now, they probably weren't receiving much individual attention, if any.

I realized I was still carrying the treats I'd brought, in a plastic bag dangling from my arm. I carefully tucked it under my arm so it wouldn't open. The aroma must be attracting the dogs. When I eventually parceled out the biscuits, I would make sure they each got some, not just the dogs who considered themselves alphas and got closest to me.

Assuming I would be able to feed them at all.

I realized then how absurd this was. Though I didn't understand why, my life was in danger, and yet I felt in some ways more worried about how to give out treats fairly. I must be in some kind of shock.

I gave a few more pats to doggy heads in black fur and red and brown and white, then straightened up.

Nothing had changed. Delma still pointed the gun at me.

I wished, instead of the treats, that I'd brought Neal's hiking staff with me. But it might only have given me a false sense of security. Against a gun?

I shook my head in confusion and disgust. "Do you care to explain what's going on? How did you find this place? And where's Tim?"

"I've got you to thank for finding this place. I followed you."

Really? How? I hadn't noticed anyone else. But maybe she'd done as I had and stayed back — and been smarter, turning onto this narrow road into the woods.

And if so, why had she been following me in the first place? Had she been at the shelter, too, hoping to help some of the stolen dogs?

I started to ask her, but she gestured with the gun. "I'll show you where Tim is," she said. I wouldn't have objected anyway, but now I definitely started walking in the direction she designated.

The cabin was every bit as dilapidated inside as it appeared from the outside. If there ever had been any plaster or other covering lining the walls, it wasn't there any longer. All that showed was wood that appeared to be rotting, especially around the windows, just like on the outside. I saw no furniture except for a mattress on the floor beneath one of those windows, with dirty, crumpled sheets on it.

The place, not unexpectedly, smelled like

dogs and their excrement, which also was visible here and there on the equally decrepit wooden floor.

If this had once been someone's beloved getaway cabin, it sure hadn't been maintained. Maybe it was a good place to hide stolen dogs, but it probably wasn't usable for much else.

Delma gestured for me to go through one of two doors in the only wall I saw on the inside, also made of disintegrating wood. In moments, I stood on a half-disappeared linoleum floor — and across what must once have been a kitchen I saw Tim lying on his back. He looked unconscious, but was it worse?

Was he dead?

I hurried over to him and looked down. I saw a little bit of motion as his chest rose and fell. I noticed no blood, so maybe Delma hadn't shot him.

"Good, you found him," I said, rising again to look at her. Dogs had also followed us in here, and that gun was still trained on me. "Let's call the police so they can pick him up and question him. Since he's got to be the one who killed Ada, they'll stop harassing Janelle."

I knew things weren't that simple, though. Sure enough, Delma just laughed, a gritty, almost evil sound.

"No, if they come, they might start questioning me. Sure, they'd leave Janelle alone then — since they'd have that bitch's real killer in custody."

I'd kind of suspected that, from the moment I'd first seen Delma plus gun. What I didn't know was why.

"I see," I said, not really seeing at all. "What happened, Delma? Did Ada attack you first?"

Another laugh. "No, she just refused to answer my question."

I continued staring at her with an expression I hoped looked both quizzical and sympathetic, as if I might think she was a victim in this situation, too.

For all I knew, maybe she was.

"I . . . I'm sorry," I said, hoping to encourage her to continue.

"Well, you will be." When I just continued to look at Delma, she shook her head. "I might as well tell you about it, since it's kind of the reason you're about to die."

I tried unsuccessfully not to flinch. Was there no way to save myself?

At least I had help on the way, but would Garvy get here in time? The cops surely wouldn't, if they even decided to pay attention to what I'd told them.

I wished there was someplace to sit down besides the decaying floor. My knees were weak, and I didn't want to fall.

"Yes, please tell me," I said hoarsely.

"It's like this. Shobie and I went with Janelle a lot to those dog parks, including when dogs went missing. We talked about it a lot, too: who was stealing the animals? There were other people who did like we did and visited a number of dog parks at different times, and we started keeping track of who was where when, of those we saw multiple times. That included Ada Arnist and her friend Tim Smith."

I nodded encouragingly. "That's what I understood from Janelle."

"The dog thefts started, then went on for a while. There were dozens of people who hit all those parks, so figuring out who was stealing wasn't going to be easy. But one thing I noticed was that none of the people whose dogs were taken received any ransom demands."

"But —" I began.

"Yeah, yeah, that's not what got into the news or what Janelle said. I know that. But it wasn't the dognappers who started doing that." Her smile grew big and appeared proud. "It was *moi.*"

"What do you mean?" I demanded, then

took a deep breath. It did no good to come down hard on her verbally for this, even though it had to have made the human victims feel even worse.

"All the dogs being stolen were purebreds or designer dogs. Since none of their owners were being contacted to pay up to get their dogs back, I assumed they were selling them instead to other people at premium prices. Pedigrees? I don't know what they did about that, but I assume they'd figured out some way to counterfeit them. That gave me a really welcome opportunity, since I've been having some money issues, thanks to the paltry pay I get as a teacher."

I saw where this was heading. "So you demanded ransoms despite not being able to deliver the stolen dogs if people paid up."

"You got it. And I got it — a fair amount of money. But — well, my conscience started nagging at me, especially when Janelle's Go disappeared. We talked a lot, and Janelle settled on Ada as the most likely thief because of how often she and Tim showed up at some of the parks where dogs were disappearing. Ada had talked a lot about her family home in the mountains, and then just stopped showing up at the parks. So after Go disappeared, Janelle decided to come here to check out the place, and I joined her. We pressed Ada for an answer, and she denied everything. But lo and behold, Go showed up at that shelter. I wanted the other dogs, too. I would still demand ransom, yes, but then I'd do a good deed by actually delivering the missing dogs this time, saying I found them and getting rewards as well."

"I take it that didn't work out." The longer I kept her talking, the longer I'd stay alive — maybe. I still hoped that help would arrive in the form of Garvy, but I couldn't count on it. My mind frantically sought a way to stop Delma.

"No. Ada wouldn't answer my questions about where she'd put the dogs, of course. Even when we found out where her family lived, we didn't find the dogs there. By that time, Janelle and I had figured that Tim was doing some of the stealing, but Ada was doing most of it and bringing the dogs to town a few at a time. Tim was in charge of hiding them till they could sell them. So the night of Janelle's celebration . . . well, I went back to our hotel and pretended to feel really sick, told Janelle I'd go down to the lobby restroom for a while to throw up. Instead, I went back to the resort, saw that Ada was still there, and followed her when she left. I was really glad when she walked farther down the beach, where it was dark. I grabbed her then, threw her into the water, and planned to hold her head mostly underwater till she told me where the dogs were. She was strong, but not stronger than me, so it was working — but then she stopped breathing altogether. I couldn't bring her back, so I left her. I didn't think the cops would assume it was anything but an accidental drowning, even though I knew I might have left bruises on her. She could have gotten bruised just by falling into the lake or trying to get out."

Bruised around the neck and head? I'd heard about the bruising there on Ada, but I wasn't going to mention it now.

"Anyway," Delma continued, "the cops did look at it as a murder after all. And unfortunately, since Janelle and she had argued that night, it was logical to accuse Janelle."

"You were going to let your friend take the blame for murder?" I was incensed but kept my voice level.

"I liked the idea of blaming it on Tim," Delma countered defensively. "So did you, and I encouraged that. But the whole situation made me truly feel ill — for a while."

I'd wondered about sharing my thoughts — and I was sorry now that I'd said anything. Delma's eyes had been drifting away from me a little as she spoke, but now they centered on me again, almost accusingly.

"Yes. It made sense," I said, not looking at the still-unconscious body of Tim lying on the floor near us.

But Delma glanced at him. "So here's how things are going to go now. You accused Tim, and he's going to prove his guilt by shooting you. Then he'll drive his car into the lake and die, too, out of remorse. There's another small road near here where that can happen, and I've got gloves and all so it'll all work out fine."

I saw a lot of potential flaws in her idea, including her current grip on the gun, but I didn't want to point them out to her. She probably already had some ideas on how to wipe the gun clean and wrap Tim's hand around it and whatever else might be necessary to make her imaginary scenario come true.

So what was I going to do?

By then, all the dogs had lain down on what passed for a floor in this place. They weren't going to be particularly helpful.

Then —

A noise. Had I really heard something? It seemed to come from beyond the door leading into this non-kitchen.

I glanced again at Delma. Had she heard it? She didn't look concerned, so maybe not.

Suddenly, a form stepped through that doorway. Garvy!

"Look out, she's got a gun!" I shouted to him.

I expected him to lift a weapon of his own from a holster or pocket or whatever. After all, I'd called to tell him where I was, where he could find the dogs he'd been hired by a bunch of people down the hill to find. He worked in a form of law enforcement, even if it was private.

He would save me.

But he just looked at me, nodded, and then smiled at Delma.

"Good work," he told her.

Thirty-Two

"What?" I demanded of him. "I thought you wanted me to find the dogs and Tim and let you know where they were."

"I did," Garvy said calmly. "And now we can take the dogs and I'll do my job of getting them back to their owners — and get paid for it."

"But Delma was collecting ransom for them. She said she wants to collect more." I looked from one of them to the other, thoroughly confused.

Or maybe not so confused. The answer, or at least part of it, was fairly clear. Whether or not they'd started out working together, they were doing so now.

"And all's well at last," Garvy said. "I'll give Delma some of what I earn for helping me. We've got the dogs, and no one's going to stand in our way of getting them back home so I can successfully conclude my case." He looked down onto the floor where

Tim lay.

Had Delma drugged him? Why else was Tim staying unconscious so long?

"I certainly won't stand in your way either," I assured him. "I've wanted to make sure these dogs get home safely from the moment I heard about the dognapping situation."

"Oh, but this got a bit complicated," Delma said. She was smiling broadly at me now — and her gun hand hadn't wavered. "I didn't really intend to kill Ada, but it happened, even though Garvy tried to help get her to talk. Oh, did I neglect to mention he joined me there at the lake and even helped to hold Ada for a while?" Her grin widened even more, if that was possible. "Didn't want to mention him before in case you happened to get away, though it was unlikely then and definitely not going to happen now. Anyway, when Garvy and I discussed it afterward, we figured that most of our goals could be achieved in common, so we decided to hide what had really happened to Ada. But the thing is, you know about it now. So what I've told you, about Tim killing you and then committing suicide, well, it's still about to happen. But if you were wondering how I could handle all that myself — now I don't have to." She turned her head to level a smile at Garvy for just an instant, then looked back to me, a more serious expression back on her face.

What was I going to do?

Some of the dogs, who'd settled down for a while, had roused when Garvy had entered and were now wandering around the floor, sniffing at him or the other humans, including me. And Tim.

Garvy hadn't pulled out a weapon, but he didn't need to with Delma's still aimed at me. I'd considered him a potential suspect, too, but I'd never considered there'd be two killers working together.

I suddenly became even more aware of the foul smells around us. Was this going to be my last contact with dogs? With people?

I glanced around, trying not to completely panic. And then I got an idea.

Would it work? Probably not. But I had to do something. And if nothing else, it might make Delma's shot miss me, or, if it hit me, it wouldn't be fatal. Sometimes people survived gunshot wounds.

Would I?

Out of the corner of my eye, I thought I saw Tim move. Was he awakening? Even if he was, that didn't mean he'd be able to help, or even want to.

I had to try this myself.

I pasted a mournful expression on my face — not hard to do under the circumstances. I turned my head toward Garvy. "I thought we were becoming friends," I said. "Even the possibility of something more." Fortunately, I didn't gag on that. "I promise I'll keep quiet." But not that I wouldn't move; I started to shift very carefully. "Can't you give me a chance?"

"That's pathetic," Delma said, and I could have kissed her since her speaking also provided a bit of a diversion.

Suddenly, I pulled the plastic bag from beneath my arm, reached into it, and threw as many treats as I could hold toward her, yelling, "Treats, dogs!"

I only hoped that, if she did get off some shots, they didn't hit the dogs who now leapt and swarmed around her trying to get some of those biscuits.

That's when I saw that Tim actually was awake. Groggy, maybe, but he rolled himself toward where Garvy was and grabbed at his legs.

Garvy fell. Delma screamed and I dropped to the floor, watching her and her gun hand, waiting for her to shoot — but glad that she now appeared to be aiming up at the roof.

And then — then I really smiled at the next thing I heard from outside the kitchen door. "Drop your weapons. Police!"

It was Saturday evening now, four days after the excitement at that hidden cabin in the woods.

I sat at the Knobcone Resort bar, surrounded by friends who were celebrating my survival as well as the saving of all those dogs.

I hadn't counted the number of tables that had been pushed together beneath the dim light, since I hadn't counted the number of people who were here to celebrate my survival — and the imminent homecomings of all the dogs we'd found in the decrepit old house. There were quite a few of them, even though this group didn't include the ones who'd already been resold. I was glad to hear that the police, with information from Tim, were still looking into those cases.

I sat closest to Reed. He'd spent a lot of time with me since the showdown at the cabin, and called often when we weren't together.

I really liked this guy.

Hugo and Biscuit were at our feet here in the bar, as well as Billi's Fanny and Flip. So were Go and Shobie, since Janelle was taking care of the miserable Delma's innocent dog for now. She would try to find her a great new home — most likely with Billi's help.

Sweetie, the adorable pup from Mountaintop Rescue who looked so much like Biscuit, was there, too. I'd introduced her to the Joes, who already loved Biscuit, and they'd fallen in love and were adopting her. They, too, had come here to help me celebrate.

"You won't ever do that again, will you, Ms. Kennersly?"

That was Detective Wayne Crunoll, who sat across the table from me. He and Detective Bridget Morana had shown up at the cabin at just the right time, despite how I thought they'd planned to ignore my plea to at least come check out a potential murder suspect even if they didn't care what happened to the dogs. Their boss was here as well, but Chief Loretta was a few tables down from me, sitting and chatting with my friend and City Councilman Les Ethman. He was here with his bulldog Sam and his other family members, Neal's boss Elise and her husband Walt Hainner.

"What — try to save dogs?" I replied to Wayne. "Or a friend who was almost unjustly accused of murder? Heavens, no."

I knew Wayne caught the utter sarcasm in my voice but all he did was smile, though grimly.

Despite the sarcasm, I truly never wanted to go through anything like that again. I'd do my utmost to help dogs in difficult situations, of course. But I'd already been involved in solving two murders. That was way more than enough.

"Let me be the first to toast our hero Carrie." That was Jack Loroco, who sat at one of the nearer tables — with Billi. He'd been utterly charming to me since they'd arrived here at the bar together. But I saw the way the two of them looked at one another and knew that they were an item, at least for now. That was fine with me. I liked Jack and his idea about buying some of my recipes for his company — maybe. But my one-time thought about us developing a potential relationship had been a non-starter.

"Hear, hear," shouted Dinah. My chief assistant had been thrilled to hear not only that I was okay, but how complicated things had gotten as I'd tried to save the dogs and catch a murder suspect. She had taken a lot of notes for her writing.

"Then here's to our Carrie, and to Icing on the Cake and Barkery and Biscuits. Oh, and to her dog Biscuit, of course." Jack had lifted his mug of beer into the air, and everyone else lifted their own drinks. "May you always be well and successful, and never again get involved with a murder."

As people began to clink their glasses, I raised my own wine glass and said, "I'll drink to that."

"So will I," Neal said vehemently from across the table.

"Me too," Janelle said from beside him. She had been grateful for my attempts to help her before, and now she was filled with so much gratitude that nearly everything she said to me contained a thank-you.

But I was thanking her, too. After taking a sip of her wine, she stood and started taking photos. She was not only memorializing this event for me, but would use it to provide more publicity online for my shops, as she had already been doing with other pictures of me, my treats, and my patrons.

I was glad to see that, down the end of the table to my right, Chef Manfred Indor was present, along with George Sackson and Frida. No doubt they were discussing food — and, hopefully, more treats for both shops. Vicky, who wasn't quite as into food as Frida, sat with them nevertheless.

My friend and one-time attorney Ted Culbert had slipped in just a short while ago. He, too, raised a beer mug to toast me.

When the toasting was over, at least for now, I looked at Wayne Crunoll. He and

Bridget and Loretta were all dressed casually, clearly off duty — a good thing, since they were all drinking. I assumed they'd be sure not to drive away drunk.

"What can you tell us about your investigation into Ada Arnist's murder and finding the dogs?" I asked him. Unsurprisingly, neither Ada's parents nor Tim had come here to celebrate. I still didn't know if the senior Arnists were in town, and Tim, who had indeed been drugged by Delma, was under arrest — though only for dog theft, selling about half a dozen stolen dogs, forging their pedigrees, and using something, maybe a strong magnet, to damage the radio frequencies emitted by their microchips. These were paltry charges compared with murder.

Still, there could be some nice stiff penalties for all of that. I hoped.

Even so, I'd learned that Tim was in fact a dog lover. He had kept moving around, dumping dogs at Mountaintop Rescue. He'd wanted to flee but couldn't fit them all into his car at one time, and he hadn't wanted to abandon them.

At least Tim had some redeeming qualities — including helping to save my life.

"I can't say much, since the investigation is ongoing," Wayne said, then glanced at

Bridget.

She smiled, something I liked to see on the serious detective. "No, we can't talk about a current investigation," she said, "but here's a little off-the-record speculation." She glanced at Janelle. "No photos, please." And then she looked toward Dinah, whom she apparently knew was an aspiring writer. "And don't write anything about this."

"All I write is fiction," Dinah assured her, "so anything I'd say would be all made up anyway."

The speculation and off-the-record discussion indicated that both Delma and Grant Garvy — his real name — were under arrest for the murder of Ada Arnist. Delma had allegedly been the one to toss Ada into the water to get her to talk, then hold her there. Grant, also wanting information about the location of the missing dogs, had joined them and also held Ada under — apparently after claiming he would save her from Delma if she'd only talk. Purportedly, Ada had started talking a bit about Tim Thorine, aka Tim Smith, and where he might have gone with the dogs, but even with that they hadn't gotten her out of the water, at least not in time to save her life — if they'd even wanted to.

We talked about all that for a while. Billi

had been called in to have the now-found dogs brought to Mountaintop Rescue for a while, and the place was crowded but they had somehow made room. Some of the dogs were still there, waiting until their owners could come get them. Owners of a few of them hadn't yet been identified, but the media had been alerted, so the likelihood was that they, too, would be claimed soon. Information about all the dogs had been gathered, and law enforcement agencies near where the owners lived had been put on notice.

Having the dogs housed temporarily at the shelter would mean a delay in our first planned adoption event at the Barkery, but it would come. And thanks to Jack, the dogs who got adopted through it would not only go home with some of our treats, but with a supply of VimPets products, too.

And Janelle would help publicize it, whenever it happened.

The important thing, of course, was that the stolen dogs had been saved — even the couple that Tim had dumped outside Mountaintop Rescue on the fateful day when I'd located the rest.

To my surprise, Gwen, the server, also joined us for a while, sitting near Neal and Janelle. They all seemed to be acting like friends, although I still wasn't completely sure if Gwen had dumped Neal or vice versa.

The party went on for another hour or so. Unlike at Janelle's celebration, no one argued or exchanged harsh words — a good thing, since it suggested that tonight was unlikely to result in anything like murder, or someone becoming a suspect in one.

When it was over, Neal took me aside and said he was going to Janelle's hotel with her for a while — although she would soon be looking for an inexpensive apartment in town. She planned to stay for a good long while, and he seemed entirely happy about it.

That meant Biscuit and I would also be alone, at least at first, at our home. I invited Reed and Hugo to join us there.

That way, the celebration could continue for a while.

And I would be able to raise a toast once more to the excellent conclusion of my non-investigation, as well as to the hope that I would never have to conduct one again.

Plus, I'd have really good company doing it.

Barkery and Biscuits Dog Treat Recipes

I've tried these with my dogs, and both loved them! Of course, be careful to use only ingredients that agree with your own pups. And definitely make sure you use carob, NOT chocolate, in the Dog Carob Cookies.

Dog Carob Cookies

Thanks to, and with comments from, Susan Frank!

1 1/2 cups oat flour (I use oat, but regular should be fine)
1 1/2 cups brown rice flour
1 cup carob chips
1 egg
1 teaspoon vanilla (I use a dash more)
1/2 cup water

Heat oven to 350°F. Put all ingredients

together and mix well. Roll them into balls (like meatballs) and place on cookie sheet. (I use parchment paper as I hate cleaning a cookie pan.) They don't spread while cooking, so press them down with your hand. I sometimes use a funny cookie cutter after I've pressed them down, but I think that's more for me than the dogs. Bake them about 18 minutes; the edges will get brown. Cooling them on a wire rack so air gets under them will also make them crispier.

Susan also suggested leaving them in the oven a little longer after turning off the heat, which is my preference to make the cookies crisper.

Dog Apple Cinnamon Buns

Thanks to Lisa Kelley!

2 cups whole wheat flour
1 teaspoon baking powder
1/8 teaspoon salt
1/2 cup skim milk (water works fine)
1/4 cup canola oil
1 large egg
2 1/2 Tablespoons honey
1 1/2 teaspoons cinnamon
1/3 cup chopped dried apple (or crushed into small pieces, but not into powder)

Frosting (optional):

1/4 cup light cream cheese
1–2 Tablespoons skim milk (water works fine)

Preheat oven to 350°F. In a large bowl, combine flour, baking powder, and salt. In a small bowl, stir together skim milk, oil, and egg. Add to the dry ingredients and stir, just until you have a soft dough.

On a lightly floured surface, roll the dough into a rectangle that measures roughly 8×14 inches. Drizzle dough with honey, sprinkle with cinnamon and dried apple pieces.

Starting with the long edge, roll up jelly-roll style and pinch the edge to seal. Using a sharp serrated knife, slice half an inch thick and place slices cut-side down on a cookie sheet that has been sprayed with nonstick spray.

Bake for about 15 minutes, until springy to the touch. Wait until they have cooled completely before you drizzle them with cream cheese.

Makes about 2 dozen mini buns. Store extra in a tightly covered container or freeze. If they are frosted, store the container in the fridge.

Icing on the Cake People Treat Recipe

LA Lime Pie

Thanks to Fred Johnston!

1 14-oz. can sweetened condensed milk
4 egg yolks
1/2 cup, or a little more, lime juice, preferably fresh
1 9-inch graham cracker pie crust

Combine the condensed milk, egg yolks, and lime juice, and blend until smooth. Pour that filling into the pie crust and bake at 350°F for 8–10 minutes. Let it stand for 10 minutes before refrigerating.

You can put whipped cream on it, if you'd like, before serving.

Also, you can garnish it with lime slices.

ACKNOWLEDGMENTS

Once again, many thanks to my amazing agent Paige Wheeler. Thanks also to my fantastic Midnight Ink editor Terri Bischoff, production editor Sandy Sullivan, and publicist Katie Mickschl.

I once more thank the wonderful people who helped me improve *To Catch a Treat* by reading and commenting on the manuscript. You know who you are!

This time, I get to thank a couple of wonderful online friends and street team members who provided the dog treat recipes at the back of the book: Lisa Kelley and Susan Frank. I additionally thank my own dogs, Lexie and Mystie, who got to try the treats — and loved them. And I also thank my husband Fred, not only for providing the recipe for LA Lime Pie as the people treat, but also for baking those pies, mostly for visits to friends and special occasions . . . and for growing the limes for them!

ABOUT THE AUTHOR

Linda O. Johnston (Los Angeles, CA) has published forty-one romance and mystery novels, including the Pet Rescue Mystery series and the Pet-Sitter Mystery series for Berkley Prime Crime. With Midnight Ink, she's published *Lost Under a Ladder* and *Knock on Wood* in the Superstition Mystery series, along with the first Barkery & Biscuits Mystery, *Bite the Biscuit.*

ABOUT THE AUTHOR

The employees of Thorndike Press hope you have enjoyed this Large Print book. All our Thorndike, Wheeler, and Kennebec Large Print titles are designed for easy reading, and all our books are made to last. Other Thorndike Press Large Print books are available at your library, through selected bookstores, or directly from us.

For information about titles, please call:
(800) 223-1244

or visit our Web site at:
http://gale.cengage.com/thorndike

To share your comments, please write:
Publisher
Thorndike Press
10 Water St., Suite 310
Waterville, ME 04901